FIRE: Demons, Dragons, & Djinns

Edited by

Rhonda Parrish

FIRE: Demons, Dragons, & Djinns

Edited by

Rhonda Parrish

TYCHE BOOKS LTD.

Fire: Demons, Dragons, & Djinns
Edited by Rhonda Parrish

Published by Tyche Books Ltd.
Calgary, Alberta, Canada
www.TycheBooks.com

Cover Art by Ashley Walters
Cover Layout by Lucia Starkey
Interior Layout by Ryah Deines
Editorial by Rhonda Parrish

First Tyche Books Ltd Edition 2018
Print ISBN: 978-1-928025-91-7
Ebook ISBN: 978-1-928025-92-4

This book was funded in part by a grant from the Alberta Media Fund.

Dedicated to Jo.
Always to Jo.

Contents

Introduction

By Rhonda Parrish

THE ABILITY FOR people to control fire was a major step forward in human evolution, but when fire eludes or escapes our control it is also one of the most destructive forces on earth. Associated with passion, power, transformation, and purification, fire is a ferocious element with an unquenchable appetite. Fire is dramatic. It is bold. Powerful. Beautiful. Terrifying. It can consume everything in its path or push back the darkness so you can see the terrors which loom all around you. It can purify or purge. Brand or bless. I wanted this anthology to explore the many facets of this beautifully furious element and the creatures associated with it.

When it comes to fiery beasties, we've got phoenixes, superheroes, aitvaras, demigods, hellhounds, sentient fire, ifrits and, of course, demons, dragons, and djinns. And when it comes to tone, style, and theme, these stories run the gamut as well. Even the settings are manifold—the Arctic circle, fantasy lands, Alberta highways, Hollywood, crematoriums, London during the Blitz . . .

There are some really interesting intersections too, perhaps as a result of the wishlist I posted on my blog during the submissions window. In it, I asked for some very specific kinds of stories that I'd like to see . . . but here's the thing. I do a wishlist for pretty much every anthology I edit, and usually I see a handful of stories in the submissions that clearly reflect what I asked for in it. This time was different. I don't know why, but for some reason instead of three or four submissions that included settings, characters, or topics I asked for in the wishlist, there was like thirty or forty of them. It was beautiful. Magical. And also a nightmare. Because then I was tasked with having to cut amazing stories that were *exactly what I'd asked for*. That was extremely difficult, but I was aiming for as much diversity as possible in this anthology so, for example, I could only include one story about fiery shapeshifters who live on Mars and work as haberdashers even if I got three that were amazing. I didn't get any stories of that specific description, but you know what I'm saying . . .

Even with that idea front of mind as I was crafting the Table of Contents, I still ended up with some similarities. For example, two of the stories potentially take place on the exact same night in the exact same city. Two others involve superheroes. Another pair of stories are both set in the tundra. Belonging was a recurring theme, as was acceptance, purification, and the problems of genie wishes.

Still, overall, I think I achieved my goal of including as many different fiery creatures and characteristics of fire as I could possibly pack into an anthology. And best of all? Not only do they work together as a collection, but each story is also pretty special all by itself. Of course, that might be my bias showing . . . but I don't think so.

Rhonda Parrish
Edmonton
2/7/2018

She Alone

Blake Jessop

1.

IN THE VAST, vaulted halls of the sunken city, great walkways form concentric paths through a sea of magma. The Empress' palace is far beneath the waves, but the grand dome rises so high that it could be a dark summer sky. The empire the heroes have leapt hither and thither through time to destroy is a monument to hubris, to the infinite reach for power, forever exceeding the grasp of the souls who seek it.

"Crack the seals," Jinn says, "I'll keep them away from you."

"Alone?" the Soldier cries.

For an answer the little creature smiles and rockets skyward. Rising, there is nothing to her but the abstract beauty of a violent sunset. It's her descents that are meteoric. The Guardians crane their necks, then yelp and scatter.

Jinn is an Ifrit, a fire spirit from the misty past, born of pure magic. The talons and cogs that make the Guardians so fearsome represent the extinction of her race. The Guardians are weapons made to build an empire, banish doubt, bring order. To do a lot of things she doesn't believe in. The rivalry is personal; they would have used Jinn's soul to power one of these monsters if she'd let them, so she turns the air they breathe into a spiralling inferno. Chaos and anger swirl in her heart. She shares them freely.

While she does, the Soldier swings the Titan Arm into the mechanism. Like the Frog, the knight who refused to be kissed, he is not the same man he was when the tale began. How he came to wear the arm of an ancient golem is a part of the story that varies more than most. They all agree he opened the door, though, so he sinks the infinite weight of the Titan's fingers into the lock.

He glances back just in time to see a Guardian charge down the walkway toward him. There is nothing he can do with the arm buried in metal. The beast is going to plough into him at a terrifying sprint and use its great teeth on the parts of him that aren't invincible magical artefacts.

Jinn saves him, again. She streaks into the monster sideways, a comet tail dragging behind her. The impact would kill anything merely human. It barely slows her down. The Empress was right to fear her kind. The Guardian ploughs up a rising wave of magma then disappears beneath it, drowning in fire.

Jinn arcs back as the Soldier finally frees his arm. They hear the grinding of titanic gears as the way forward opens.

"Too close," he says.

Jinn dimples and bares her entire array of fangs, joyously panting smoke, when an arm erupts from the lava and grabs her by one tapered ankle. The Guardian is a skeleton now, everything living burned away. It drags her under the surface in a final vicious plunge.

Her mouth opens wide, as if to say something before she vanishes; their passage marked by nothing but ripples. The Soldier pushes fingers through his steaming hair. This habitual gesture would once have required his left hand, but he only made that mistake once.

He calls her name. Heat shimmers and little bubbles pop. He raises the ancient hand to reach in for her, wondering if it can stand the heat but stops when he hears a slap.

Jinn clambers out of the fiery lake, first one palm, then the other. She drags herself back onto the walkway as magma pours off her, a maiden emerging from the pool. She tries to rise back into the air and finds herself too heavy. Laughing, she shakes herself and wrings molten stone from the burning mane of her hair. The Soldier realizes the Ifrit didn't have anything to confess in that final moment; she just needed to hold her breath.

Far away, the Prince, his one true love, and the Frog fling the great doors open and fight their way into legend. The Robot, the only one of the band of heroes culled from the future, slams the gates closed. The Soldier and the Ifrit still need to join the Prince; the story isn't finished yet.

There are many ways down to the Mammon Machine. Many paths to the end. They find a funicular and descend toward the heart of the palace. The lift is redundant for her, but it's a chance to rest.

"There's something we haven't said," Jinn sighs, "the Titan's arm, your eye, your heart—they're all powered the same way the guardians are. I was born magical. If we win—if we destroy the machine—we won't just change history; we'll erase magic from this world entirely. Neither of us will live."

"I'll follow you," the Soldier says, "either way." They descend in silence.

"Do you still wish I'd been born human?" the Ifrit says after a while. They would both be dead already if she had been.

The Soldier replies. No one knows what he said. Jinn laughs, the doors open, and they head into battle to die.

2.

I LOVE THE legends. I love the tale of the Prince and his bride and the Robot and all their friends. This is not a fashionable position; my parents are very traditional and it drives them nuts. What did they expect? If our holy books had a Frog cleaving titans to pieces with his legendary Sadamune blade, I'd have paid more attention.

In their defence, they've always made a point of disapproving quietly. It's the same for my work; when I first took an apprenticeship as a steam engineer my parents forbade it. How could their daughter labour in the heat, and immodestly clad at that? I broke a lot of delicate things and stormed out, never to return. It worked out well. We're all closer now, though it still surprises me that I could be their child. They're so mild; grateful just to be free of the endless wars of the Southern Continent and safe in the North. I'm short and round like my mother, however, and I inherited some of the green in my father's eyes, so at least my parentage isn't in doubt.

It's a hard walk up to the famous bluff—the sheer cliffs give a wonderful view, and the tree is the oldest on the entire coast—and takes a while if you're only five feet tall, counting your hair. I make do.

Grit goes with being an engineer; climbing to fit brass pipes makes every part of you strong, and knowing the city will get very cold if you stop makes you tough, if the occasional scalding hasn't already. I have to give myself both time and a fine ploughman's lunch to make the ascent before sunset, but make it I do. Every autumn, on the same day. I have the timing down to an art.

I'll never get used to how fast the northern summer fades away. You sweat during the climb and shiver when you stop. I hate being cold, but cresting the ridge and catching sight of the bare tree with sunlight glinting through its skeletal branches is pure delight. This is the place where the time-travelling Prince and his friends made a pact to save the world from the Empress who tried to steal all of history for her own.

It's a good story and parts of it are probably true. Not the Frog who refused to be kissed, obviously. There isn't really any magic in the world, but there have always been people trying to control it. Anyway, wouldn't the first woman to detonate gunpowder have been a sorceress? If I could take a peasant from the year 600 and show him what I do for a living four hundred years later, he'd think I was some sort of fire goddess.

So I ignore the chill and forget my blisters. Coming here is as close as I get to faith. Have you ever grieved without having lost anything, or at least nothing you knew you had? Explain that and you'll explain this. I have no homeland, and being here gives me a sense of place.

Unfortunately, I won't be alone. Someone is standing in my usual spot, precarious, right up on the point.

Tall and fair, he hears me with a start. He's thin, and his left arm scarcely fills its sleeve. It's been replaced with struts and cogs, which makes him a veteran. It hasn't been so long since the North fought its own war to banish those who would rule without mercy or concern for others. I'd rather be by myself, if you can be alone in a place with so many spirits, but this year I'm out of luck.

We assess each other awkwardly.

"Hello," he says, "what's your name?"

Not much of a conversationalist.

"Kassia Kamina," I say.

He looks at me with momentary incomprehension. I have to explain where I was born often, even though a single glance at my amber skin ought to do it for me. While I explain, I realise that this man may not be well. He has a queer look, and he's struggling to say something. Or not say it.

"Is that so?" He shakes his head with a kind of desperate negation, "I thought your name might be Jinn."

That stops me. I stare at him and the wind quiets. Time fails to pass.

"Only my friends call me that," I say.

It's the best my mates can do pronouncing *Djinn*, which is what Southerners call desert spirits. I adore the nickname. I think it's supposed to be mildly insulting—Djinn are capricious and wild—but giving you a pet name is how Northerners show they like you. I try not to feel either wild or capricious, but the idea that this man knows me is disconcerting.

"I'm sorry," he says. He runs a distracted hand through his hair. I was right; this is a man on the edge. He stares at me with such intensity that I start thinking the smart move would be to turn around and take off.

Instead I stand my ground and stare back into his solitary blue eye. A hard patch covers the left one. He looks too young; most veterans are late in their middle age. He has a chilly gaze, but my eyes are little explosions of brown and green. Besides, I have two.

I win, and he's the one who looks away. When I see his profile I try to imagine him with both eyes. I begin to see a resemblance, though I can hardly remember to whom. He looks like someone who's about to slip and fall. A long time ago, I saw that look on the faces of other refugees. I've seen it on my father's face. Never in the mirror, though.

"I'm sorry. I came here to meet someone. I was about ready to give it up."

This actually makes me feel better about him. I have a soft spot for that kind of story.

"That's romantic," I say, and step past him toward the bluff. Blades of cold light slice through the clouds. The name was just a coincidence.

I stand in the same spot he did. He could push me off, I guess, but I don't think he will. He's just a little lost. That's something I *have* seen in the mirror. "I'm sorry she didn't come."

"So am I," he says, "but I didn't really think she would. You look like you've been here before."

"I've stood here every fall since I was old enough to ride the trains alone. I love old books, and this is a famous spot. The Prince and his one true love were reunited here, and the heroes made their pact under this tree. I start dreaming about them the instant the leaves turn. When I was young, I thought I'd meet my one true love here, too."

"You want to meet a prince?" His tone is half-mocking.

"Not exactly," I say. I might be blushing. How did we start with this? "The Prince isn't my favourite character. I like the Frog, he makes me laugh, but my favourite is the Soldier who wears the Titan's Arm and opens the door. I'd rather meet him."

The veteran looks like a brass pipe hit with a hammer.

"It can't be," he says.

"What?"

"I said I came here to meet someone. I think it's you."

"We've never met," I may sound angry. I usually can't tell.

"We have. Not in this life, not even in this world, but we have." His certainty is vast.

"Make sense," I say, "or I'll leave you here to wait for whoever you think I am."

"If I do, you'll think I'm insane," he says.

"Fine," I already knew that much, "jump off a cliff."

"Wait," he says, "please, wait. You said you had dreams about this bluff, about who you'd meet. Tell me the best one."

I really, really ought to leave him alone with his hungry ghosts, but I've never been good at turning away. I sigh.

"I don't dream about them, I dream I am one of them. I'm the Ifrit. I can fly. I'm small and fast and I burn. I'm with the Soldier. I know the legend says they all faced the Empress together, but we're alone. We're riding an elevator in the sunken city, which is silly because I can fly, and I've just saved his life, and I say, 'do you still wish I'd been born human?' and he says—"

"'Yes,' which makes you angry," the veteran interrupts, "so you ask him 'why?'"

Wonder starts a war with anger in my heart.

"And he says—"

"'Because as it is I can't touch you, and I already love you every other way there is.'"

The broken soldier really does reach out to touch me, then, and I raise a hand to stop him. Normally he'd get slapped for that, but he's right. It's not in the legend. No one knows what they said; it's just what I dream they did. My heart thumps. We both need to pull away from the edge.

"Come and sit by the tree," I tell him, because this is simply too strange to let go of, "and tell me how the story ends."

3.

THE DESTRUCTION OF the Mammon Machine is a cataclysm that should have been impossible. The Empress had power and will and all the time in the world. All the heroes had was each other; the Prince's courage, the icy intelligence of his one true love. The Sadamune and the Robot's guns. The Soldier's arm and the Ifrit's fire. None of them could have taken even the first step on their own but together, they topple an empire.

When the Prince strikes the final blow and takes his lover's hand, every kink and fray in time draws itself inexorably straight, and they are thrown through the maelstrom one last time. They have changed history, written magic and immortality out of it, drawn truth and equality in.

The Soldier's magical heart no longer beats, as inert as if it never had.

Jinn cannot escape the vortex of time no matter how hard she flies. The Ifrit fades, flakes away as she tries to hold onto the Titan Arm, her grasping fingers burning parallel grooves into its palm. The tears that fleck into space as Jinn loses her grip are molten pearls. She is sucked into the eye wall a half second before him. Every heartbeat is composed of two parts; push and pull, life and absence. The emptiness that pulls them apart is the end of magic itself.

4.

I SHIVER. IT'S cold up here, and the end of the story you read in most libraries is a lot nicer than that. The heroes all go back to their own times, except for the Prince and his one true love, of course, who stay and get married.

"I can't imagine myself doing that."

"If you'd seen how the world ended you could," the veteran says. "You did."

"I'm sure I'd remember that," I say, although I've had nightmares that contradict me. "Besides, there's no apocalypse in the legend."

"Of course not. The world didn't end. The Empress never got a chance to get bored with it."

That makes an illogical kind of sense.

"Well, at least in your version they still win," I say.

"We did. Though dying for what you love is hardly the difficult part."

5.

SPAT FROM THE void, the Soldier opens his eyes with a start and says the Ifrit's name. He is staring at a wall covered in names. There are flowers leaning against the base, and the monument stretches far in either direction. Citizens are walking along it, heads covered against the drizzle, fingers tracing for names as though they were despondent children drawing in sand. The rain is so fine it's almost mist, but the peak of his uniform cap keeps his face a little dry.

He coughs, almost retches. Alive. Resurfacing in a world he helped create but has never seen, thrown back out of the well of time. A wave of residual anguish washes over him. He looks down at his hands. The right is calloused and strong, the hand he remembers. His left arm is loose in a drab regimental sleeve, the hand a skeletal claw supported by a crosshatching of fine wires and tiny cogs. It has three fingers and one thumb. When he flexes it there is a tiny creaking, the squeal of metal bathed in rain.

His heart would beat hard now, if he had one. The thought invades his mind and he reaches the living hand to his chest.

Finds a hum under the brass buttons. *Be still. Think.* He breathes while his heart hisses along with the wind. Finally, he reaches up slowly to touch his left eye. Finds nothing but a hard patch. *So that is beyond this new world,* he thinks, and finds his good eye hazy with tears.

One of the memorial's attendants, black-clad and carrying an umbrella stops by his side, glances at his uniform.

"Are you well, Captain?" he asks. A train clatters and exhales steam in the distance.

"Alone," he says, "that's all."

6.

I SIT UNDER the tree and listen. The veteran is an unconsciously talented narrator. He tells the story better than anyone I've ever heard, and the tale of waking up in a new world gives an ethereal sense of shifting currents in time. The grass trembles less than his voice, and when the Mammon Machine shudders so do I.

"Honestly, it never occurred to me that I'd survive," he finishes, and the strangeness sets back in. "No soldier ever imagines what comes after war. I came here to stand on the edge and wait for you. I knew you wouldn't come. I was sure that magic died with you. With us. We fell into the vortex less than a heartbeat apart and you beat me here by twenty years."

"You really believe this happened." I try to make this a question, fail.

"I do, and this is the second time you've shaken my faith," he almost laughs, "another one of your habits. Don't look at me like it's so strange. Do you know why you come here? What exactly do you have faith in?"

The question curls my lips. Surprising bitterness.

"There is one God, one prophet, one world," I say. The profession ends there, but I can't stop myself; "one, or so they say. One sky and one earth and one life and one history. One of so many things I'm not sure I believe."

He smiles. Really, this time.

"There you are," he says, and I'm not sure if he means her or me.

7.

JINN FINDS HERSELF, every morning, in the position of the sultan who must decide whether to kill the story-teller. As days pass on the long road to the Empress' palace, she decides not to burn the Soldier.

It's not an easy choice; the scales dip and rise, almost even. On one side he was, until recently, a servant of the same dark forces that nearly exterminated her entire species. On the other, he did his part to free her from her crystal cage, or at least failed to stop her. Balance. This isn't really Jinn's kind of dilemma, but it is better than being drained of her soul and turned into a lapel pin. She loves the rest of her companions, and the Frog's accent makes her laugh. They accept what she is without fear. Around the campfires she starts for them, familiarity opens her heart, and she tries not to set anything important ablaze by accident.

Their friendship makes hiding from men in the age of technology a game, and watching the world end a call to arms. Jinn finds reason to believe in something, even if she isn't sure what. She ignores the petty details of what they'll destroy. What it is they haven't said. The Empress and her machine are worse than the cage. Worthy of risk. Worthy of sacrifice. Worthy of her. There's a difference between abandon and losing control.

I EXHALE AND there's a hint of frost in the dying afternoon air. When I was young, I would pretend I was a dragon breathing smoke.

"The way you tell it, it's not a love story anymore."

"I think it is," he says, "listen."

THE HEROES TRAVEL to the distant past, even further back than the misty middle age of spirits that Jinn calls home. The Doctor, Jinn's former captor, seems to have survived their first encounter. Just as well; he built the Mammon Machine, and might know how to break it. The Empress should never have let him out of her sight.

The men and women who inhabit the golden age that gave birth to sorcery understand magic the same way Jinn understands heat. Their art and science are indistinguishable, and even their ruins are cities in the sky.

Among them, perhaps for the first time in her life, Jinn feels at home. Courtiers blush and fawn over her hair rather than run to their huts to pray. They reveal the Doctor's plan with the unconscious simplicity shared only by children and artists. He wants to reactivate the Titan of legend, give himself a new body that no one will ever be able to harm again.

When Jinn and the Prince and their friends discover him in the Titan's mausoleum, it is already too late to stop the ancient golem's resurrection.

8.

"YOU'RE LEAVING SOMETHING out. We don't live in a fairy tale and people don't abandon everything they love to go running after the Evil Empress. No one sacrifices themselves for someone they just met. Why would you follow her? Why did she even let you?"

The soldier seems taken aback. Like he's surprised that anything isn't that simple. That he can't just say it and make me believe him.

"Well," he says, "you know how the Soldier got his arm."

"From the dead Titan. They found it in the city in the sky. The evil Doctor who made the Empress her machine got there before them and tried to take control of it. During the battle, the Soldier was hurt and the Prince saved him with ancient magic."

"Is that all the legend says?" He scowls.

"You've never read it?" Anger builds in me like steam.

"I'm not the reading type. Besides, they got it wrong."

"So the Prince and the Frog didn't cleave the Titan to pieces, then?"

"They did, but you're right—something has been left out."

9.

THE DOCTOR BRINGS all of his cruel knowledge to bear in preparing for them. He knows the Titan is only *almost* invincible. He has to kill the Ifrit, who could heat its armour to the point of softness, electrocute the Frog, whose sword could break it, and confuse the Prince, the only one with the courage to try. He plans to accomplish all of this in a single stroke. Trust is his enemies' primary weapon, and their only weakness.

"Ah Captain, we meet again," the Doctor's voice booms from his seat in the Titan's breast. He has knelt to speak to them, left the plates of the golem's chest open so they can hear him. "You have done well bringing them to me."

Jinn's fists clench into fireballs. Faith is not something she has ever pondered, but she finds hers shaken by the Doctor's taunt. She vibrates with something that's either rage or mind consuming anxiety. Maybe they're the same thing.

They all glare at the Soldier. He can't still be one of them, can he? Did he manoeuvre them here to end the quest, not complete it? It is the second time Jinn has tested what tiny patience she has watching him decide.

"I sometimes wish you'd been born human," the Soldier says, almost grateful.

He shoots the Doctor in the same spot as the first time, low, and the trap goes off in his face. The Doctor hasn't exposed himself just to talk. He has armed the Titan with some of the same nets the Soldier himself once used. Their electricity will serve equally to neutralize the Ifrit and the Frog. The Soldier glances back at Jinn. He owes her a life.

Everything changes. The salvo of crackling gossamer disintegrates the arm the Soldier raises to shield himself, one eye and, as it wraps itself about him, his heart.

Jinn experiences a sensation of profound cold. The siphonings don't compare. Not even being torn through time leaves the same chill. As the incoherent madman closes himself into his new body, the Prince and his companions charge.

They dispatch the Titan together. As clever as ever, the Prince's one true love reasons cold will serve just as well as heat. Her icy magic paralyzes the Titan while the Frog leaps from pillar to pillar and the Robot throws the Prince high into the air. They come down at angles, flashing blades carving a deep cross into the armour over the Titan's breast. The hulk thrashes and staggers.

The Ifrit flies a wide arc, gathering momentum and incandescent fury. Her friends have marked the spot for her. The Titan's heart. There are few limits to what she can do, but this might be one.

Jinn strikes the Titan like a meteorite, blasting herself

through the weakness with a sound like cosmic hammers striking steel. For an infinitesimal instant there's stillness, then the Titan blows apart at the joints in a concussive holocaust.

Impact. Rebirth. Save him or fail. Live or don't. Ascend, or fall, or both. The Ifrit corkscrews wildly from the Titan's sundered spine.

Jinn skids to a halt on cold stone. Her eyes open and she coughs up little clots of molten spit. She regains the air, and as her agony fades, exultation remains. It may never leave. Her friends look up as one to watch the Titan fall.

Afterwards, while the Ifrit flits about in anxious spirals, the denizens of the golden age save the Soldier. They are the Empress' citizens, theoretically; prototypes of the idle elite who will enjoy leisurely immortality as her subjects, dreaming away centuries under a corrupt aegis. They delay death the way fate delays trains.

They return his sight, give him a magical heart, and take one of the Titan's arms to replace the one he lost. They do this not in gratitude, but because every dream is too precious to waste.

10.

"So the golden age was true." This fills me with hope. I love what I do and who I am, but it always feels like a lot of work. I enjoy the idea that there was some point when it was all easy, that there was a garden before the flood. I also like the Ifrit blowing everything up; the story is better that way.

"Entirely true. They stopped time to save me. They gave me a ten-thousand-year-old arm that was as tall as my body, and I swung it as though it weighed nothing."

"How much did it weigh?"

"Everything, as far as I can tell."

I'm getting sucked in. The legend has sharp hooks. I feel angry for so easily abandoning objectivity, then angrier still for being mad at something that makes me happy. Does that make any sense?

"We didn't all fight because we believed in the Prince and his quest. I see the Ifrit and the Soldier as a pair, like the Frog and the Robot. I think he did what he did for her."

He's having trouble talking about this like it's just a story.

"Jinn inspired that much loyalty in him?" It feels odd to say her name the same way I say mine.

"She did," he says. "You did. From the very first time we met."

"Would you stop saying 'you?'" I say, though I'm not sure I want him to. Not sure it would be accurate if he did.

11.

JINN HATES BEING confined. Born flying, it is impossible for her to imagine just how much she'll loathe being dragged to earth until someone locks her in a cage.

Captivity is the history of spirits like Jinn, of her gender, of her species. Endless flight from those who wouldn't let them live in peace. Less is written about what happens when you give them a chance, even the shadow of a chance, to break free.

The Soldier rounds the corner to a crowd of grim faces. The atonal disharmony of annihilation booms at his back. Everything behind him is burning; men, an empire's certainty, his own faith. The cacophony sets every one of his fellows on edge.

"The Ice Wolf escaped," he roars, "get the flamethrowers!"

Something far worse than noise pursues him. Jinn carves her way through the factory with pyroclastic finality. She turns her prison into a fountain of ash.

The Empress' men hear the monster come. As it arcs into sight they bathe it in fire. Its eyes are dark embers lost in the flames, and for a moment they think they're winning. Only when the liquid blaze starts to spin and weave does fear quicken their hearts. Not for long. The Ifrit burns them until their cries echo even in the smoke.

Jinn's rage has the straightforward trajectory of sparks falling into oil. The conflagration scarcely satiates her soul-deep craving for the immediate and total immolation of everything that has ever hurt her. The sweet release of it cools her aspect just enough to grant the Soldier provisional permission to live. He lied for her, after all. It's something.

They escape on the ore carts the wretched facility once used to supply its chambers with prey. Spring wind rushes past and makes Jinn's hair flicker and spark.

"Well, you avenged your brothers and sisters. What about me? You've burned everyone else."

"Not everyone," Jinn says, and her breath shimmers the air, "not yet."

She calculates, balancing the complexity of what she is owed against what she has given, against what has been taken away. Before she arrives at an answer, the cart finally creaks to a stop.

Behind them, in the distance, a column of smoke billows skyward like the plume of a volcano. On the platform is a handsome young prince, a beautiful girl in pure white, and a giant talking frog dressed as a knight.

With infinite caprice, and perhaps to delay decision, Jinn abandons her newly won freedom and takes on a hopeless quest instead. Mutely, the Soldier takes his place at her back.

12.

ON IMPULSE I take both of his hands and turn a professional eye on the left. The workmanship is excellent, but it isn't magic. Nothing is. "It seems a shame to have lost all that."

He talks to hide how uncomfortable he is.

"Perhaps, but everything said about the Empress' thirst for power is true. What she wanted to do with magic makes me glad we destroyed the machine. This world feels like an empty cage most of the time, but immortality doesn't bring corruption, it is corruption."

I run my fingers along the intricate gears. What does it mean to believe in magic? Not my kind of question, but try it anyway. That world either is or it isn't. Will or won't be. Was or wasn't, though I'm leaning toward was. Soaring toward it. One day someone will use a machine to fly, and I know how they'll feel. What do you think the difference between knowing and believing is?

"You're saying that you are him. Not that you're like him. And that I am her. Literally."

"Yes."

Now we're at the heart of it. It's time to choose, though I don't think I get any more choice than the sun does when it rises. You can't believe in just part of someone. Love is everything or nothing at all. We're as powerless before it as paper before flame. The question, I have come to think, is not what will convince me that the legend is true, that I am part of it, but whatever convinced me that I wasn't.

That decided, I laugh at him.

The sun has nearly set, and this would be a good place to stop. There is more to the story, though, and we both know it. I know how it begins, but I want to hear him say it.

13.

THE IFRIT TRIES to remember her name. She awakens each day as a test subject, a sacrifice, a prisoner in time. She has come to understand what it means to be fuelled by hate. The scientists and academicians of this late age certainly don't know how to feed her, but that isn't the point of the facility. It is not a zoo. None of them are going to make it out of this colossal lattice of metal and stone alive. Magic is weakening in the Empress' iron epoch, and she bends time itself to get her hands on what remains.

Today the screaming is canine. Skoll and Jinn never got along as young ones, both temperamentally and elementally unsuited, but the Ice Wolf is still her kin. There ought to be some grand realization in the howling but Jinn can't hear it. The idea of dying without figuring it out makes her angry.

Worse, she will apparently soon be stripped of even the mournful dignity of a burnt offering; she's part of a tour. The Doctor, the lab-coated monster of her nightmares, mounts the stairs with two other men. A soldier with cold blue eyes and his adjutant. She would know those eyes at the end of the world, but he doesn't recognize her immediately.

The Imperial academician is in an expository mood.

"Well, Captain. I have shown you every aspect of this facility but it has been merely an introduction, a prelude to your admission into the highest realms of the empire. You alone captured one of these magical creatures single handedly; your reputation precedes you!"

The Soldier looks seasick, dazed. Summoned by the Empress herself, he had expected something else. Well, this exactly, if he's being honest with himself, just not *like this*. He is a man without doubt, but touring the facility, doubt coalesced around him like the condensation that coats the infinite brass pipes. He faces the consequences of his victories, the aftermath of glory.

The gravity of what he's done bores into him when the Doctor shows him a siphoning. A giant beast, like a dog with a coat of crystalline frost for fur, is suspended in one of a hundred crystal tubes, barely twitching as current flows through it.

"This one is close to finished," the Doctor says.

The Soldier likes dogs. The Ice Wolf twitches as vials fill with something luminous. Mounting the stairs to the next demonstration, the Doctor's speech flows with the confidence of a young river.

"Everything we are is born here. These animals provide the power that fuels our citadel, our Guardians, our empire. Even the charges in your pistol would be impossible without their by-products. Magic is a resource we cannot neglect; it is far better than water or wood or electricity! It is wasted in them, as are so many things in nature, and we must use it to the maximum. It is our manifest destiny!"

They mount steel stairs to Jinn's platform. Inestimable lengths of tubing carry spurts of beautiful liquid all around them. At the top is another crystal prison, too large for the little creature that inhabits it. The tower of the soldier's faith is leaning, but doesn't fall until he hears the Ifrit speak.

"You," she says.

The Soldier's face is a mask.

"This one in particular is an Ifrit, or *Creatura Flammidemia*, if you want to be perfectly accurate."

They scrutinize her. Her skin has the glow and texture of brazier coals. Instead of hair, she has a luxurious mane of slow burning fire. Her shape is small and broad-hipped. Clearly female to the Doctor, uncomfortably so to the soldiers. She is floating an inch above the brushed metal base of the cage. She rises a little as they approach.

"Look, Captain. It remembers you. Interesting. Did you know that when they die, they leave behind gems? Living essence. It is my greatest discovery; there are many uses for it." The Doctor laughs fatly, "Including the creation of the Badge of Order. No matter what your military rank, there is no greater promotion than this. Destroy this thing and join us. We need a man of your courage and loyalty."

"You drain the life out of them," the Soldier says, "and then turn them into decorations?" His face is ashen. The Doctor finally notices. Even now, Jinn feels a faint trill of irritation. There is no limit to how much time a human will waste. As if there was an infinite supply.

"Captain, the extraction of magic from these creatures causes no harm. Their cries are the squeaking of springs, the clicking of clockwork. The concept of soul is a pretension of the flesh. It perishes. The empire we build with these stones will last forever. Courage, love, hope, honour; all these things die," he taps the glass and the Ifrit flinches, "don't they?"

Jinn knows she ought to grovel, so she roars. The Doctor flinches in his turn, then angrily depresses a lever. Energy courses from a bulb at the top of the chamber. Jinn stretches and writhes. The crystal gives her screams polytonal resonance. After a moment the surge stops and the doctor taps again.

"Courage, love, hope, and honour all die," he says again, "don't they?"

"Yes," Jinn says, and her voice would be less beautiful without pain, "but hope dies last."

Everything slows, like time won't pass. The look she gives the Soldier is not anger or hate, which are easy for a man to dismiss. It's scorn.

"Your badge will be red, I suspect," the Doctor fingers his own with great complacency. "Fitting."

"It is," the Soldier says. "Thank you for this demonstration, Academician. I learned a great deal."

It is only when the Doctor sees the agony of spirit in the Soldier's eyes that he truly begins to worry. "What's wrong? This is a singular honour."

"Wrong? We are creating an empire founded on death, not immortality. These things aren't killing our country, you are."

I WAS WRONG. I don't want to hear it. It makes me feel sick.

"Stop. I know the rest," I say.

"You don't. It isn't in the legend. It can't be."

"I do. It wasn't the Empress who travelled back to the dark ages in search of magic. She didn't put me in that cage. You did."

"You remember," the Soldier says.

"I believe. It's the same thing. Were you ever able to tell her why?"

"There are no reasons, other than that I was following my orders."

The sun has set.

"Did I forgive you?" I say. He looks surprised, as though he expected me to ask something else, as if there was anything else.

"I don't know," he says, "but all the evil I did, I did in some way because of you. All the good, because of you."

THE IFRIT KNEW the Soldier at once, more deeply than he can conceive. Up on the bluff, he used the glowing nets to catch her and so many of her brothers and sisters. She listened to his troops call him a man without fear. Jinn might have found some satisfaction in watching him fall apart, but there's too much pain to care.

What she has sensed is a chance. This miserable human can make right what he's done. She watches him. He closes his eyes to her captivity and walks away.

Jinn has long since accepted that there is no way out. Has listened to her fellows cry in the night. Has taken her turns under the siphon. She hasn't any tears left and wouldn't shed them for him if she did. She tried using them to burn her way out. It didn't work. She hammers her tiny fists against the concave crystal.

"Coward!"

The soldier puts a hand on the rail to steady himself.

"Turn away then, fool!" The Doctor screams, "turn away if you don't have the stomach!"

When the Soldier answers, the tone of his voice makes Jinn look up. She sees total loss in his posture, and understands what she has taken from him. Only faith, not courage. Good.

"It's funny you should put it that way," he says.

The Doctor has scarcely voiced the obvious question when the Soldier's coat billows outward like a sail catching the wind. A crashing report careens between the brass tubes. He has fired his pistol without turning, close to his body. The Doctor collapses as if the strings supporting him have been cut.

The Soldier operates his weapon with the fluidity of an automaton. He breaks the gun open as he turns, and his steps follow the path of the red-hot casing that jumps from the breech.

"Captain?" his adjutant asks, dumbstruck, half reaching for his own weapon.

"There is no reason to follow orders if you cannot trust in their justice," he says, and levels the weapon again, "I'm sorry."

As the second shot fades, the Soldier turns back to the Doctor to find him gone. He looks at the pistol in his hand. Brass, ironwood, ornate locks and levers. He can't bring himself to look at her.

The Soldier turns his gaze from Jinn the way children shy from the sun. He touches the controls of the infernal machine.

"If I let you out of there," he says, "are you going to kill me?"

"Yes," Jinn says, "I'm going to burn every single one of you."

"Fine," the Soldier smiles in spite of himself, "but I can help you escape. Wait until then."

14.

THE DAY IS an afterglow. Faint smells catch the wind and carry the city. They were alien, once, but now they just remind me I'm hungry. I rise and pull him up with me.

"Walk with me down the hill. We'll eat."

In a book, it would be the soldier who takes the girl's hand. Instead I drag him down the hill and away from the bluff. The reunion is the last chapter of the story. We keep walking, finding our way carefully so as not to slip in the fading light.

I have scales to balance, but he can help me find home; I can wait until then. Actually, if I'm being honest with myself, I've already decided how the legend ends, but that's only my second favourite part. I like beginnings, and the feeling that you never know where the path will end.

15.

HIGH ON THE bluff, cold wind courses between cutting edges of light.

"You're a slave," the Ifrit says, and her voice is laden with rage and the faintest note of melancholy.

"You're an animal, and your time is up," the Soldier re-joins.

"We'll see whose time has passed, child of man," Jinn says, and her smile belittles the sunset, "we shall soon see."

Strange Attractor

Kevin Cockle

LAURA DRISCOLL DIDN'T spook easy.

She heard the noise in the back and knew it wasn't her imagination this time. Something was loose in the container-hold of the semi—loose and moving around. "No questions asked" was one thing, but it was still her job to make sure the cargo arrived in good order. She had a reputation to uphold: that made decision-making easy. Check it out, lock it down. No excuses.

Blue eyes the colour of anti-freeze worried in the rear-view mirror.

Thin white-blonde brows frowned.

"All right," Laura said to her reflection.

Laura pulled the semi over to the narrow shoulder of the highway, put her blinkers on, reached into the glove compartment, and checked her Sig Sauer 9 mm, taking the safety off. She was alone on the road over three hundred days a year and though she'd never fired the weapon outside a range, she'd shown it once or twice. Early on in her career, while she was still driving-truck for Corona Western, she'd had the odd run-in, and cause to show force. Once she'd bought her own rig and became an established owner-operator however, the testing of her boundaries had stopped. Guys knew how hard the life was, and if she could pull it off, then her youth, slight build, and elfin face couldn't be held against her.

The gun was for people outside the life. People who didn't know her accomplishments, didn't know to respect her. Roads were full of people who didn't respect much of anything these days.

A waning moon shone cold over the deserted stretch of highway north of Peace River. Normally, Laura would have put pylons out, but they were in the back, and that was where the noise was. Stepping down out of the cab, her boots made a solid, reassuring sound against asphalt. She held the gun in both hands, pointing the barrel down and away from the truck as she walked with measured strides to the back of the container, feeling the autumn breeze frigid upon her cheekbones.

What distinguished Laura from the competition was her engine-craft—learned from her foster dad like other kids would learn sports or yard-work—and her phenomenal driving-endurance. She'd never told anyone, but it had slowly become legend, that Laura Driscoll never slept. She'd passed every drug-test she'd ever taken too, so it wasn't pharmaceuticals that had led to her record turn-around times. She just didn't need sleep, not like regular folks did, and that, along with her maintenance expertise, had been her leg up. You free up all the time you waste sleeping in your life, and you can get to a place at twenty-nine that most folks don't reach until their forties.

Laura reached up to shoot a bolt and brought her hand back on reflex. The door to the container was warm. Not boiling hot or anything, but startling, given the conditions of the night. And then, as she stared at the door, she heard a loud *whump* against a side panel. She took a step back, licked suddenly dry lips.

There it was all right. Proof positive. Truck wasn't moving, so something inside had to be.

It did occur to her that there were other ways of handling the situation. She knew Constable Swartzman was maybe an hour away—she could use the radio to call the shop, and she had his personal cell as well. But that could backfire, given how lucrative the load was, and how off-book the shipping had been. She'd picked up the freight at the terminal in the Port of Los Angeles from a business-lady identifying herself as Ms. Burke. Ms. Burke had been fairly specific about the bonus structure, schedule, and the need for discretion. That was fine with Laura: wouldn't be the first time she'd run something into or out of the oilsands that may or may not have been strictly legal. She was looking at a second truck, hiring a driver, partnering-up in a small warehouse to store parts and inventory. She wasn't in the business of asking questions that might get in the way of her goals.

"Girl like you can make people do things," her dad had once counselled. She'd been thirteen then, starting to get phone calls from boys. She and her pop had spent that rainy Saturday in the covered work-shed, re-engining a restored Fiero with a V8 for one of his friends. They were taking a break, sitting on lawnchairs in the open doorway to watch the water come pelting down. "You know that. You can count on that, I suppose—your call. But my job is to make sure you can do for yourself, whatever you decide." He'd often talk about raising Laura as his "job". He saw it as a duty to his dead wife, the woman who had taken Laura in as an infant orphan from Child Services, raising her to the age of five before the plagues swept north and made their claim. Not that Ed Driscoll hadn't loved Laura in the way any natural father would have. But the duty to Willa was always there too.

What would you do now, Dad? Laura asked the ghost of her father's memory. Stroke had paralyzed him when she was fourteen, and she'd spent a year taking care of him before the end. Left school, got herself legally emancipated. Took care of it all—every last problem—because she could.

She knew exactly what her old man would do.

Holding the gun in her right hand, she stepped forward, worked the eerily warm bolts to the container door with her left, and flung the door wide. She stepped back and raised the gun with elbows locked, taking grim pride in the lack of arm-shake despite the Sig's heft.

A gust of warm air hit her face, blowing strands of blonde back from her hairline. The air was moist, salty, tropical. She recognized it from her Cozumel runs. Definitely not Canadian air.

The container was dark, largely empty. As her eyes adjusted, she could see the single crate she'd been carrying, sitting basically where it had been secured. In the far corner she saw the murky outline of the dolly and other pieces of equipment, also secured. She cursed herself for forgetting the flashlight in the cab, but the door was open now and some kind of line had seemingly been crossed. In the distance, she could hear a guitar riff on the radio, couldn't place the song.

With her left hand, she tugged the step-extender down, and lunged her way up into the darkness. The smell of the ocean was unmistakable, along with hints of rotten seaweed.

She moved slowly towards the crate—a wooden box about a metre-square—and saw that the lid was off. That was weird, as she could have sworn they'd used packing-nails on it, but it was also a relief. It was an explanation. Something rational in a situation that had been threatening to slither away from her.

She didn't fully relax until she'd got close enough to look in behind the crate. There was enough shelter there to hide someone, if someone had been there, but someone wasn't. The box had been tied down, and the lid had come off in transit—that much made sense. The sound she'd heard when she'd stopped the truck and gotten out of the cab still remained peskily mysterious, but it was starting to seem like an anomaly, something that might safely be ignored.

She peered down into the box, frowning in the gloom. Packing straw obscured the details, but the thing appeared to be a stone statue or figurine of some kind. She could make out a misshapen, inhuman skull, slanting into a body of sluggish, repellant proportions. She was about to reach in and feel for better resolution, when a man's voice spoke from outside, on the highway: "Miss?"

Laura whirled, raising the gun and advancing two steps. It was her instinct to advance, despite a small, reasonable impulse she had to retreat farther into the darkness of the container.

A man stood on the highway, his outline dimly visible in the taillights and moonlight. A wolf emerged from the grass behind him and curled in around his leg. Another wolf stood in the middle of the road, staring back the way the truck had come.

The man's eyes glowed like red embers in a face otherwise obscured by darkness. "Miss," he repeated, his accent striking Laura as being vaguely Irish, or Scottish. "Would you mind lowering your weapon?"

"I would," Laura said. Her voice was steady, but her heart was slapping about in her chest. The wolf nearest the man had moved towards the extendible-steps: she could hear it sniffing at the metal.

"Away wi'ya," the man said to the wolves, and they immediately responded, bounding back off the highway towards the treeline. Then to Laura, he said: "Show of good faith?"

"Who are you?" Laura demanded. At this range, she could peg his chest no problem.

"Oh," the man smiled, his teeth shining in the darkness like moonlight off a machete. "I think you have a sense of that."

Laura faltered for the first time. He'd said in words what she'd been suppressing since the first noise had gotten her attention.

"I'll be in the cab," the man said. Long black hair blew in the wind. He put hands in the pockets of a black great-coat and began walking around the truck, out of Laura's line of sight.

Laura swallowed, listening to footsteps, hearing the door on the passenger-side open, feeling the weight of the man legging up into the cab.

Laura took one last look around, then jumped down from the container and shut the doors. Movement in the corner of her eye caught her attention and she glanced into the tree line. Multiple pairs of eyes reflected moonlight from the darkness: wolves gathering in the gloom, waiting. She'd heard a report that wolves had been making a come-back in these parts, along with cougars and other wildlife. *So you guys're probably natural at least*, she thought as she headed to the front of the truck.

She took a deep breath before opening her door, trying to envision the mechanics of getting into the driver's seat while maintaining readiness with her gun. When she was ready, she proceeded, bounding with fluid grace from one action to the next. She didn't always move like her pops—that deliberate country-boy gait. When she was scared and acting on instinct, she moved like something else.

She'd switched the gun to her left hand, holding it across her body as she sat. She left the door open, both for the ease of exit, as well as for the fact that closing it would leave her vulnerable for a moment.

The man was playing with her radio, sorting through the stations. Up close, his hair was long and black and very coarse; his eyes did actually glow with a light of their own and his face—while human-esque—was longer and more chiselled than normal, possessing jutting cheekbones and severe angles at the brow and jaw. He settled on a pop song—Britney, Ariana, Taylor maybe—Laura didn't know much about music. The creature smiled a sharp-toothed smile, turning to lean his back against the door.

"I'm solid enough now that you'll do damage, if you fire that thing," he said. "Good thing you've got ice-water in your veins, hey? Makes me feel safe."

"You're not real," Laura said.

"Yeah, well, reality's shifting, kiddo. Has been for a while now."

"Why am I seeing this? You."

"We're family, lass. It was time."

Laura had nothing to say. In her heart, outside of her words, she felt something true clicking into place. But just because it was true didn't mean it was easy. "What do you mean, you're . . . like my father?"

"Not exactly. It's not family in the human sense. After all, you're making me as much as I made you. I could maybe say you're my mother, but that wouldn't be exactly right either. Part of me is in you though. You're in between, kiddo. Makes you special. Useful."

Laura narrowed her eyes, thinking things through. "What am I carrying?"

"Hey, I thought we agreed no questions asked?" The man had been replaced by Ms. Burke, sitting there in her power skirt-suit and heels, snooty rectangular glasses, and pixie-cut hair. The transformation was so sudden, Laura almost fired her gun on reflex.

The man was back, smiling his smile. "But if you're going to ask, I guess that's the right question, all right."

"What is it?"

"Something old that's new again. Something very, very old, whose time has come."

"You paid me in real money."

"Aye. The electronic age—ain't it a miracle? Makes things a lot easier. Just one part of the reason things're happening now, and not before."

"Can't be good, what you're up to."

"Can't be good, can't be bad, can't be stopped. You signed a contract, honey. Whatever you think of me, I know you'll honour that."

Laura crimped her lips. He had her there.

"Look," the creature said, changing gears. Laura thought of down-shifting as his face took on a less ironic, more contemplative aspect. "We've a few hours together. You've got a delivery to make. I'm not going to hurt you—quite the opposite actually. Why don't we get a move on? Get to know one another? What do you say?"

Laura stared at the man for a moment, taking him in. It was a look she didn't use often, because she knew it made people uncomfortable, but she gave it to him full bore. She couldn't know it herself, but the look was like the look of wolves: dispassionate, alien, predatory. She found that people didn't like to lie to her under that gaze; found they tended to fidget, and give away more than they intended. The man in her cab didn't fidget, didn't seem uncomfortable, and he clearly knew what she was up to. He returned her stare with a knowing look, letting her take in whatever she needed to take in.

Laura got the sense that he could hurt her if it came down to it, but that he'd had the drop on her before, and could've made his move then. She got the sense that he was getting more and more real the more she talked to him. Maybe without her, he'd be all air, and shadow. Maybe he needed her, and while that didn't mean she could trust him, it meant that their relationship was grounded in something. Something she could understand.

She made up her mind the way she always did: suddenly, and decisively. She closed her door, then reached across to the glove compartment, putting the gun away right in front of him.

The man watched her and nodded in acknowledgement of the new bargain struck.

Because this is where the action is, honey—the energy. The oilsands. The blood of Tiamat—the great cosmic dragon herself—in the very soil. Here's where we come through.

It's been a long time coming. Since Greek fire, and the petro-sorcery that protected Byzantine ships from their own conflagrations. The energy of the dragon echoing in the roar of the combustion engine. Panzers rushing across steppe. Nagasaki searing. All of it a symphony, for those who can hear.

Ask me, Standard Oil splitting into the seven sister companies was a little on the nose, what with Tiamat's own body forming the heavens and earth and all. But that's part of her charm—the irony. E pluribus unum—out of many, one. The calculus: differentiation and integration. I mean, really—how could anyone miss the signs?

BRITNEY SPEARS? HER songs are our anthems, baby. Where you hear "Toxic", I hear a triumphal Roman fanfare. I see torches in the night; I smell the pyres.

THEY'D ARRIVED AT daybreak, the sun turning low-lying clouds into thick clots of blood thanks to the late-season forest fires farther north. She'd been given GPS coordinates, not an address: the place was only accessible at all because of an old trunk road built by some oil company, some years ago, for some reason.

To the naked, human eye, it looked like a junkyard. Maybe an abandoned work-site. There were the remains of a corrugated metal shed and some wooden outbuildings. There were the skeletons of old pick-ups, and cable-spools; old railway ties and tractor gears. Everything was rusted and breaking down under the elements. To the human eye, a junkyard: to the eye that could see, a cemetery. Hallowed ground.

"You gonna help me with this?" Laura had asked, working the dolly in underneath the crate; backing the load gingerly out of the container.

The man had grinned, shrugged. His face had changed over the course of the trip—becoming less elongated and angular. Becoming more human. He'd watched her as she lowered the heavy stone idol down the ramp, offering helpful supervision.

She might not have been as strong as some men, but she never pulled muscles, or needed a chiropractor and could work all day long. Worked out in her favour, over the long haul.

RAIN PELTED DOWN, which was odd for September up here. You'd get snow or drizzle this time of year, but this was a good heavy rain; the big raindrops of May arriving in fall. Still cold, but not as cold as it should be. Almost tropical at times: the wind would shift, carrying with it the inexplicable scent of papaya and rot.

"You could stay," the man said. He really had changed by this time. He'd aged maybe—the long, lupine lines of his face had contracted into something that was merely "seasoned" rather than grotesque. His hair was greying at the edges, and he'd grown a salt-and-pepper stubble-beard. His eyes still glowed in shadow, but in full light, they looked normal. Deep-set and penetrating, but normal. Human.

She looked out at the rain—listened to the noise of it, like someone throwing handfuls of stones at the metal. She knew what he was offering.

The more real he seemed, the more dreamlike she felt her own perceptions becoming. They'd set the idol up deep within the shed, placing it on a concrete block foundation. There was already a stone altar in place, brought out of Asia via the ivory-smuggling trails of East Africa, apparently. It was like pieces of a cosmic puzzle, each put in place by some unwitting pawn hired by a mirage, paid in crypto-currency. And it was humid in the shed, like the botanical house at the zoo that housed all the exotic plants. The air was heavy, and time seemed strange: wherever Laura looked, it felt like the first time she'd seen that part of the shed.

"You don't have to," the man continued, "but you could."

"I know," Laura said. "It's tempting."

"But what? You don't know if it's real yet?"

"No. I know it's real."

"What then?"

She turned her gaze from the rain. "You're going to be hurting people."

"I'll be hurting them anyway. It's just what's going to happen. A great and terrible burning."

"Yeah, well. I don't think that's for me."

"Kind of compartmentalizing, aren't you?"

"Yeah, I am. I know I haven't given you your money back. Call me a hypocrite."

"We all draw our own lines. That's probably something you got from Ed."

"Yep."

"It's surprising to us, you know. How much of a difference that man made to you. In you. How much pull he had."

"He's my dad. I mean . . . whatever I am, that's gotta be part of it."

"Sure."

They both turned their attention back to the rain for a while. It would burst and back off, but to Laura's ears, it seemed as though it might be letting up.

"Listen," he said when he mistook her restlessness for a readiness to leave. "You can always come back here, if you have to. We don't want you to feel like you have to choose. Things get hard out there, things don't go the way you planned . . . you've got a home here."

She looked at him, and nodded, knowing that when she looked at him with real attention, it gave him strength, made him solid. When he looked at her in turn, she didn't know what she got out of it, but it was something.

She could feel herself *becoming* under his gaze.

"You know what you don't get about my dad?"

"I guess by definition the answer there would be 'no'."

"My mom."

"Okay, crypto-girl: go on."

"She was an academic—quantum physicist. Worked as a freelance data-scientist."

"With Ed Driscoll? That's some odd couple."

"On the surface maybe. But Ed had a way about him—he grounded people, centred them. I always imagine her gravitating towards him because of that. The weight of him."

"Fascinating stuff. Mortals!"

"She didn't just adopt me by accident. She predicted me, searched me out. Selecting me collapsed my wave function, located me on purpose. Averaged me in. She saw the signs; she heard the music. She died young, but Dad knew the purpose, did the best he could to anchor me in the world."

The man frowned for the first time, mind racing to fill in the gaps in Laura's story. His mind raced, but she was already at the finish line.

"They saw you coming," Laura said as she withdrew the ancient African knife she'd obtained from another demon on another run, the hieroglyphs on the blade glowing a pale lunar blue. "And I've been waiting."

THEY'LL BE DRAWN to you, honey—they'll need you. They'll need to be seen by you. You're a strange attractor, Lor: embrace it.

MOST FOLKS' ROOT cellars were filled with roots, preserves, storage—and Laura's was too. But there were also boxes of her mother's old books and notes; laptops and thumbdrives and external hard drives. Feynman diagrams incorporating unlikely vertices; equations that may as well have been incantations. And there were the objects accumulating on shelves now—statues and masks and talismans from all parts of the globe that made their way to Alberta by some force not unlike gravity. The new one—the hideous, misshapen, tentacled affair—had been too heavy to do anything other than place in a dark corner and put a blanket over. Laura wondered at the confluence of dark energies radiating out from the accumulated artefacts; thought of fission reactors and critical masses. The seething will of the dragon sullen in the dark. Super novae waiting to explode.

She thought it might be dangerous concentrating the items here, but she also thought it was too late to worry about, or change now.

Demon money was stupid-good, and it accelerated her timetable. She had the down payment for the second truck, and had an option on a third, if a nearby oilfield liquidation went her way. She was building the company her father had told her would be necessary, not just as a source of self-sufficient income, but as a bulwark against extra-dimensional incursion. Her mother had had the math, her father the practical, mundane solutions for occult problems. It had fallen to Laura to execute.

She felt the memory of her foster parents like a physical weight, like a force that made her human. She wasn't in-between as the demon had said. She'd made her choice, and the choosing had made her in return.

Magnesium Bright

Lizbeth Ashton

THE SPRITE WOKE when its metal prison shattered. Shrapnel splintered from the chamber, singing as it skittered across rough tiles. The sprite dragged in a ragged breath as it clawed free; sparks ignited in its vision and prickles of fire danced on its tongue. Fully aware for the first time since it was plucked from its grate, it cast its gaze around. A full moon shone high overhead, illuminating the rooftop and cramped terraces in its ghostly glow while artificial beams of light cut across the darkness—moving, searching. Planes flew through the dark sky and explosions rang out in the distance, the smoke they spewed reaching up to brush the stars.

It could have been fascinating, this snapshot of the outside world—but the sprite's attention was caught by glittering powder spilled from the other end of its prison which crackled and sparked where the sprite touched it. It licked the powder; the soft grains fizzed and sent a rush it had never felt before through its being. The sprite squealed and threw itself into the pile, rolling in the sparkling dust and scattering it in its enthusiasm. It burned a brilliant white, and the sprite was enraptured.

The whole street was engulfed in noise; a cacophony of sirens, shouts, and screams bounced between the brick walls. People spilled out of houses and through alleyways and the sprite watched them, recognising families from their linked hands and tight huddles and feeling a sour pang for the family it had lost.

It had been snatched from its hearth, shut in a jar, and transported to the metal prison with stale air and no fuel. The dim light it could generate itself was only a meagre comfort and it had railed against the suffocating darkness. It realised it had to conserve energy or die before a chance for escape, so let the dark enclose it.

It had thought of its family and home in that darkness.

It had been born in a grate, an errant spark from a piece of kindling imbued with spirit. It learnt happiness and joy through its peaceful existence, always ready to dry wet socks and caress chilled faces. The family it watched through the flames offered a steady supply of fuel and cultivated the perfect atmosphere for it. The sprite liked to play with the small child, spit at it when it made gurgling enquiries and clap when it ran around. It devoured paper offered to it with a blush by the daughter, touched she would trust it with her secrets. It helped the mother rearrange the coals, metal poker and fiery fingers working in tandem to keep the blaze alive and the room warm. That was its world, those people its family, and the sprite had thrived.

But the people in the street were not its family, and its family had not stopped the man with gloved hands from delivering it to the dark prison.

Now it lay on a scorched timber and breathed into the wood, feeling it groan as it glowed and creaked. Part of the roof had given way, but the sprite gave no mind to the inferno that raged beneath it. Instead, it listened: above everything was the sound of fire, roaring and fierce as it fed on anything it could. It was a sound of beauty, of freedom. Everything was fuel, not just what people decided was suitable; wallpaper, soft furnishings, children's toys, and blackout curtains all burned in the face of it.

A projectile screamed as it fell from the sky. The sprite realised it was another prison when it spilt its magical dust over the road. It searched the wreckage from afar, and joined in a whistle when it heard the newly freed sprite sing of its fortune. It saw the other sprite flicker before a man with a metal hat dumped sand over it, extinguishing it and smothering both the powder and prison for good measure. He shouted orders at the panicked mass of people clustered near him, and directed others wearing similar hats to where the fire raged.

The sprite recoiled, grief clutching its embers, and felt something new rise within—something unrecognised but powerful. It roared, anger swelling its voice. It circled down into the house, riding the air currents through soot-blackened rooms as it collected the flames and called the heat to its embrace. It surged through a window and lashed out with broken glass and burning air at the people who had killed its kin without thought or remorse.

If it was destined to be snuffed out with as little ceremony, it would take its would-be murderers with it.

It spun down the street in a ball of fire, burnt brick and charred corpses left smouldering in its wake. It rose up to look over the rooftops, and saw the sprawl of people was everywhere—but so was the amber glow of fire. The sky was full of smoke, countless fires belching blackness as it consumed a city desperate to stamp it out. Everything was there for the taking, and the wind was on its side. It would feast well tonight.

The sprite cast off the memories of its former life and *danced.*

Permanence

Dusty Thorne

MARCUS HEYES BEGINS his new job as a furnace operator at Phoenix Mortuary much like many people begin the first days of a new job: damp around the collar from a nervous sweat, tidy to a fault, and afraid to be seen as foolish, for he has no predetermined idea what on earth he is in for. Despite spending years studying funeral rites and practices to work at a job like this, he knows the real thing is never quite like what can be gleaned from classrooms, nor from the shiny, lacquered pages of mass-produced instructive pamphlets.

For the purposes of being shown around his new workplace, he is paired with one of the owners, an elderly man with more wrinkles on his head than hair follicles. Mr. Jamie Light does not seem young enough to still be working hard labour, but Marcus knows enough about life to realize he cannot possibly know the circumstances that bring people to where they are. As such, he merely listens and nods politely as Mr. Light shuffles around beside him through the building, the rubber tip on Mr. Light's long, white cane tapping out an unsteady rhythm against the gleaming, blue tiled floor below their feet.

Much to Marcus's relief, the crematorium in the basement of

Phoenix Mortuary is both well lit and utterly pristine. Every visible surface is free from rust, funny smells, or powdery coats of dust. In fact, despite this being a place where the deceased are brought to their final rest, Marcus genuinely believes the entire building is quite possibly even cleaner than the various restaurant kitchens he worked at while still in college.

When he mentions this to Mr. Light, the old man shrugs a brittle shoulder in a slow, deliberate motion, like an iceberg jaggedly slipping from the glacier it has remained attached to for millennia.

"S'pose it is," Mr. Light croaks in a cigarette-tired voice, and when he smiles, Marcus sees that the old man has several missing teeth, all but one of them filled in with golden crowns. "We pride ourselves on keeping the dust we make in its rightful place." With a tremulous, arthritic hand, Mr. Light gestures to the shelving units that are set up in various locations throughout the crematorium, each stacked to the ceiling with either brown or navy blue cardboard boxes. On each box are labels with dates printed on them that begin in modern times and lead back to the early 1960s. "Of course," Mr. Light continues, "there is some grey area."

"Remains of the deceased?" Marcus asks, and then sucks his lips between his teeth when Mr. Light nods. Marcus isn't sure how to judge his own reaction to this confirmation, except to perhaps be a little embarrassed by it. When he'd been a pallbearer at a different funeral parlour during his senior year at college, he'd occasionally have cause to enter that funeral parlour's crematorium, but there is something unique about knowing he is now going to be working in a place where the dead literally line the walls around him.

"Mm-yep." The rubber tip of Mr. Light's white cane squeaks as he hobbles over to the nearest shelf, and then pulls the lid from one of the navy blue, hat-sized boxes. "Generally, we either give 'em to the families, or else scatter the ash in the big pond outside, but if the families want 'em kept here, we honour the request. You wanna see?"

Marcus prides himself on having a relatively strong constitution, but still he treads carefully across the cold, tiled floor as though approaching a wild, skittish animal when he peers into the box. Inside, there is a clear, plastic bag, and inside that bag are a few handfuls of silvery grey, fine dust.

"Not much left of us at the end, huh?" Marcus comments, as Mr. Light closes the box and slides it back onto its shelf.

"Nothing but the memories we manage to get out there in the big world before we go," Mr. Light says. The old man does not sound troubled, only matter-of-fact. Although there is no dust on his hands from the box, still he brushes his palms together several times and then points to where a large, glass-doored furnace is mounted in the wall at the far end of the room. "Let's hope you like fire! Lemme walk you through what you'll be doing here, okay, sonny?"

Marcus smiles. Though the room is a trifle chilly, Mr. Light's kind personality seems to warm it. "Sounds good."

Mr. Light's knobby, wrinkled hand lays gently on his shoulder, guiding him over to the wall. With Marcus not entirely sure which of them is supporting who, together, they walk.

"It's mostly like a normal job," Mr. Light assures, as he reaches under a table holding a large, metal tray and pulls up a long-handled brush, like a fireplace poker, only with bristles at the end. He hesitates for just a moment, frowning at the floor, but then visibly shrugs away a thought he doesn't voice. "Well. With a couple'a noteworthy exceptions, it's pretty normal, but that part's separate from your job description anyway, so you don't gotta worry about that."

THE WORK DOES end up being relatively routine. After funerals on the ground level of Phoenix Mortuary are done, coffins are guided down to the crematorium in the basement on metal lifts. Once there, they are placed inside the large, glass-doored furnace of the crematorium for two hours. Mostly, Marcus does not even have to look into the coffins before burning them, so long as the paperwork checks out.

Marcus mostly works nights, and after some settling in, he eventually averages about three cremations every work shift. Despite the nature of the job, he is surprised to find the work is actually quite relaxing. When he's not using the long-handled, metal brush to clean the inside of the furnace between cremations, or taking what remains in the furnace that did not become ash over to a secondary, crushing machine to complete the cremation process, he mostly tends to the operations and paperwork side of things. When he's not doing any of that, he reads books in the odd, two-tone glow of the firelight streaming through the smoke-stained glass window of the furnace at his back and the stark, white florescent lights above his head.

There are nights that are more upsetting than others, nights when Marcus is brought the small coffins of babies or young children, or the nameless coffins of homeless people who had been designated the state's problem after no known family could be discovered. Other times, Marcus will be reading his book with his back to the furnace when a sudden chill will run through him. During these moments, a reflection in his eyeglass lenses catches a split-second of motion behind him, or he hears a soft, whispery sound.

Generally, something shifts in the furnace soon after, casting flickering shadows and a crunching whiff of dispelling gas within the flames, and then Marcus will remind himself that coffins collapse as they burn, and go back to his book.

However, some nights his spine remains cold, no matter that he always keeps it turned towards the furnace. On those nights, Marcus has to tell himself even more insistently that the mind is capable of playing all sorts of tricks on a person who is alone in a place like this, especially in the middle of the night.

Logically, Marcus knows that nothing can live inside fire, least of all the dead, but this knowledge does not always lessen the cold, nor muffle the strange, echoey sounds of combustion within the smoke, which sometimes sound eerily like something crunching through bones.

MR. LIGHT ALTERNATES working as a funeral director and a furnace operator, but only ever works the day shift, so Marcus usually finds himself entering Phoenix Mortuary as Mr. Light leaves to go home. As Marcus hangs up his coat and clocks in at the crematorium, the two of them exchange pleasantries: Mr. Light asking Marcus about the latest book he's been burying his nose inside of, and Marcus asking about the health of Mr. Light's wife, Esther.

"Still as luminous as the day I met her," Mr. Light will say, with a wide, gold-accented smile. With shaking hands, Mr. Light will slip his arms into his wool coat and then cover his bald head with a bowler's hat. This he'll tip cordially in Marcus's direction before hobbling to the small elevator that will carry him to the exit on the ground floor. "Happy reading tonight, sonny. Don't burn your eyes lookin' at the fire."

Marcus only laughs and replies, "Yeah, as soon as I get everything set up in there, I always keep my back turned, just like you told me."

Mr. Light nods. It's just one of those things they don't teach in books, he'd said with a grim look when he was still training Marcus, adding that no one in their right mind spends a full night looking into a place where bodies are burned, because no one needs the burden of their mind trying to find life inside a corpse.

WHEN IT IS very cold outside, Marcus sometimes has trouble getting the furnace to stay hot enough. When this happens, he has to call up Mr. Light, who sends Esther over because she's the only one who understands how to get the gas working again.

Esther is an older lady, though not as old as Mr. Light. Her face is wrinkled, but her hair is still naturally a vivid, strawberry blonde colour that falls in waves down her back, and she never wears a coat.

"I don't ever get cold," she'd said while laughing, when Marcus asked her about that, and then she'd shooed him out of the building so she could fix the furnace without having to worry about him breathing in gas fumes. "Only when you see smoke rising again from the chimney," she had said with a wink, "are you allowed to come back in."

Marcus had asked her if she was worried about herself, but Esther had only smiled without revealing any teeth and then patted the wall framing the glass door to the furnace at her back, saying, "What's in there wouldn't dare hurt me."

THERE ARE A couple other people who work at the funeral home, like Mrs. Burnsen, an auburn-haired, middle-aged woman who minds the greeting desk in the mornings and boasts to everyone who asks that their cremation services use the most environmentally-friendly process that money can buy, and Kara Eld, who wears her bright red hair in tight braids, is about Marcus's age, and has skin nearly as dark as his.

"I don't know why we hired you," Kara had complained to Marcus after his first solitary shift had ended. She had arrived to replace him for the morning shift in the crematorium, and had found him struggling to properly adjust the temperature controls of the furnace. She had shoved Marcus to the side so she could adjust the furnace controls herself, mumbling to herself the whole time about "cold people" quotas.

"I haven't been told how to fix it yet," he had tried to explain. "I was trying to figure it out."

Her manicured, red nails clenching tightly around her hot coffee, Kara had immediately snapped back, "Did you ever think to just ask it to get hotter?"

Marcus hadn't known how to respond to that, but after a few months Kara had stopped making fun of him and just started calling him their resident "bookworm" instead.

Marcus doesn't mind that so much. After all, it's far from being untrue.

Anyway, she makes amazing coffee, and sometimes she shares it with him, even if it is usually so scalding when she hands it to him that he has to wait for over an hour after he gets home to even begin thinking of drinking it.

"SO WHAT MADE you leave the last funeral home you worked at?" Kara asks Marcus one day, as she steps into the crematorium and drops her tasselled purse down on the nearest empty metal tray table.

Still immersed in his book, Marcus jumps at the metallic bang of her bag hitting the tray and feels an uncomfortable heat flush over his chest, followed by the clammy chill of blood draining from his face. Her question is one he doesn't like being asked. Last time he'd talked about it had been at his initial interview to work here. Even then he had struggled to explain his reasons to Mr. Light, but had been grateful the man had seemed understanding.

"Uh," Marcus stammers, looking for his bookmark. He sees the corner of it on the floor, sticking out from under a nearby shelf of boxed ashes, crouches to pick it up, and slides it into his book. Though he has an uncomfortable relationship with this particular memory, he swallows his discomfort and offers it to Kara anyway. "Well, when I was a pallbearer there, I dropped a coffin down a staircase."

Kara puts a fist on her hip and tilts her head at him, her dark eyes squinting as if to say, "Yeah, and?"

"And the coffin opened, and the body fell out."

Still, Kara remains squinting at him. She doesn't ask if Marcus had gotten fired for this, which surprises him. She only waits for him to continue, so he does.

"I don't know what happened, but she—I mean, the body of the deceased—was . . . she was . . . she had caught fire, like spontaneous combustion or something, and even inside the coffin, there was just . . . more fire, everywhere. It burned my hand, and that's why I dropped the coffin." He holds up his palm, to show Kara the long, thin line of a burn scar on his palm, which is lighter than the surrounding skin.

Kara's eyes flicker to his hand, but she does not look surprised. If anything, her face seems to get even more impassive, more forged from concrete than ever before. "And after that happened," she says, "your reaction was to come work at a job where that happens all the time?"

For just a second, Marcus glances behind him at where a white coffin is burning behind the closed, glass door of the cremation furnace, but then quickly turns away. He shrugs. "It's not so bad, if you know why it's happening."

Kara huffs. She shakes her head back and forth. "It's only bad when you don't know, huh?"

Marcus sucks his lips between his teeth, biting them just enough to feel the sting. Wincing, he slides into his coat in preparation to leave the crematorium, making sure his book is secure in his pocket as he nods. His throat is too tight to speak.

Kara watches him for a long moment, and as Marcus tries to walk past her to leave, he notices the air around her is too warm. She grabs his arm. This makes him pause, and then he looks at her, to which she solidly returns and holds the eye contact.

"Did the girl you dropped get back up?" Kara asks him, very quietly. Her voice vibrates with some kind of inner power that makes the room around them seem too small, but maybe he's just on the verge of a panic attack, and so perceiving things a little oddly.

Marcus swallows deeply, to calm himself. "What do you mean?" he says, faintly. He's been through enough therapy for this to know the answer, even if it doesn't feel true when he thinks it. "The girl I dropped from her coffin was dead."

"Was she?" Kara asks, still holding onto his arm. "Or did the fire bring her back?"

Marcus's stomach twists at the memory of that young girl, caught in a ball of flames on the staircase outside of the funeral home, her limbs twisting as a sound like a bird's shrieking howl tore from her throat.

A phoenix, the thought had jumped, unbidden, to his terrified mind.

"Air currents," his therapists later contradicted him, "or maybe even your own mind, or someone standing near you."

Kara continues to hold her long, hard look at him, and then she says, very softly, "The next time you're here, maybe you should look into the fire."

For just a moment, Marcus does. He sees the flames, and their shadows.

For a moment, they look like wings.

He turns away, mouth dry, and pretends he has not seen what he has seen.

Old Flames

V.F. LeSann

Vatnajökull, Iceland
Research Team Three
February 7th, 2023

WHEN ICELAND WAS formed, Hell should have been taking notes. Fire and brimstone couldn't compete with a mid-winter storm on an endless plain of blue-grey ice that was just barely older than Alastair.

Shielding his data screen from the driving snow with a gloved hand, he peered through his goggles at the numbers. Still wrong. Nothing drastic, just enough discrepancy to be annoying. And with the weather getting worse, he didn't have the luxury of retaking the measurements.

The bitter air was a maelstrom of whirling cloud, turning the rest of the team into grey shapes around him and the icy wind screaming down the glacier had sleet for teeth. It sought out the seams of their jackets and turned Alastair's beard into a heavy lump of ice.

The cold hardly touched him. Demons ran hot. He could tolerate the storm to recalibrate the numbers, but the rest of the team certainly couldn't last in this bitter winter chill, and there was the need to keep up appearances, so he let his discomfort metamorphose into a shiver.

"What's the matter?" Mike bellowed over the roaring wind. "Getting cold feet, old man?"

Alastair's annoyance over the skewed data boiled into anger. Every team had its asshole, and theirs was Mike. Alastair had established a hands-off policy concerning humans ever since the 1500s, but there was just something about the smirking blond that made him want to drop the guy down a crevasse.

"Speak for yourself," he yelled back, putting the screen away and trudging onwards. "I love this."

He did not, in fact, love it. He missed the research station in Hawaii, where he didn't have to bundle up in a half-dozen layers to keep the heat of his hellfire heart from damaging the environment around him. He missed trekking up to the volcanoes, hiking over miles of sun-baked black rock with a team where everybody's skin was hot to the touch by the end of the day. But mostly, he missed life without Mike.

Mike picked up speed, pulling ahead of Alastair as they followed the rest of the team.

Narrowing his eyes behind his goggles, Alastair lengthened his stride and closed the gap.

"Go at your own pace," Mike hollered over to him. "We don't want you having a heart attack out here." The last part didn't sound particularly convincing.

"This *is* my pace," Alastair shouted back.

"Yeah? Then why weren't you doing it before I . . ."

"Guys, *guys*," Ari yelled from ahead of them, her boss-voice barely audible over the howling wind. She and Gita had both stopped ahead of them. Her cheeks were vibrant pink with cold and her braids were two long icicles, but she shook her head and pointed forward, her disapproval clear.

They made the trek back down together, falling into silence, and Alastair reminded himself what he was doing here. Above all else, he was a scholar. In this life, a scientist, and he would go where he was placed. He hadn't enjoyed Brazil much either, but even in the worst places, he'd been able to scrounge up enough beauty to keep himself going.

There was a terrible purity being inside a winter storm, with no room left in your mind for anything but your next breath and where to place your boots on the booming sheet of ice beneath your feet. And beneath that, against all odds, rivers of magma coursed like veins under the glacier.

The storm ripped him open, hollowed him out, scrubbed his soul clean. And just for a moment, he felt strong and pure, the statue of an old man with a parka and a backpack, carved out of the same blue-grey ice as the glacier, with a molten heart.

THEY REVIEWED WHAT data they'd managed to collect over steaming spoonfuls of fish stew at base, hunched over the small table as the storm battered the walls of the main trailer around them. The wooden bench had one leg slightly shorter than the rest, and each time Mike leaned forward to point at something on Ari's screen, the resulting *clunk* beneath him was another sliver of irritation digging into Alastair's mind.

He'd had a palace once, all jet-black stone and torchlight and tall wrought-iron chairs that would never *clunk*. There'd been a job and he'd been damn good at it, and so they'd given him a palace and thirty-six beautifully competent legions to command. If you were a good environmental scientist, however, you got sent to the most desolate stretch of Iceland in the middle of winter.

Some days he was sorrier than others that Heaven and Hell had closed their gates.

Alastair glared at the back of Mike's head as the bench clunked again. Mike was the kind of man people described as "aging well". Just enough grey around the temples to signify his maturity, but with the body of an Olympic swimmer who probably spent twenty-six hours a day in the pool. Not that Alastair was upset with his own aging looks, he was described as "dapper" and "dashing" on a regular basis, but there was just a certain "Richard Gere in *Pretty Woman*" to Mike that made him want to puke.

Ari sighed and pinched the bridge of her nose, rubbing at the indent her goggles had left there. "Bad news: I think we froze our asses off for nothing today, folks."

Mike made a dumb, baffled face. "Seriously?"

"Seriously," she said, "Al, all your numbers are wonky. Check your equipment calibration tomorrow before you start."

Mike raised an eyebrow at him, leaning back so that the bench lurched under them yet again.

"And Mike," Ari continued, her voice turning sharp, "you didn't even *take* half the readings I asked you to. If you spent half as much time on the job as you do trying to get a rise out of Al, you'd have the Nobel Prize by now."

Mike's blue eyes narrowed, his mouth slanting in offense. "I'm not . . ."

"And I'm on strike," Gita piped up, breaking the sudden tension. When all eyes turned to her, the older woman smiled sweetly. "After the horrible, hurtful thing that Ari called me this morning."

"Ari?" Alastair asked, startled. "What did she . . . ?"

"*Grandmotherly*," Gita intoned. She mimed a dagger hitting her heart.

Ari groaned and looked at the ceiling. "I didn't! I said you *reminded* me of my grandma. Who, by the way, is spry and awesome."

"She'd probably go on strike if you called her that too," Gita said.

"Nobody's on strike!" Ari said. In the resulting silence, the sides of the trailer warped and boomed in the wind, sleet pinging against the waterproofed material like pebbles against a drum. "Except maybe Vatnajökull."

"Old girl's real angry tonight," Gita agreed with a rueful smile. "We've still got a week before we meet up with the other teams. We'll get the data, kid."

Ari nodded, shutting down the datascreen and polishing off the rest of her stew. "Everybody clean up and get some rest. Tomorrow, we get our shit together."

Outside, the wind screamed down the glacier onto the camp, although in agreement, protest, or signifying nothing at all, Alastair didn't know.

ALASTAIR WAS HALFWAY through cleaning up when everything came to a halt. Pulling off his boots and removing the melted icepacks meant to keep his feet from destroying the glacier as he walked on it, he came up with a handful of torn strands of thermal lining. He stared at it in confusion, felt inside again—almost all of the lining had been torn out of both of his boots. No wonder his numbers had been off. With every step he'd taken today, he'd been sinking a few inches into the surface of the glacier.

Getting cold feet, old man?

With a snarl, he hurled one of the boots hard enough at the wall that a map fell down. Grabbing the other one as evidence, he stalked out of his room to find Mike. This was more than just another one of the guy's stupid university frat-boy pranks. It was a full day's efforts wasted, a pair of boots ruined, and the closest Alastair had come to potentially being exposed in a very long time.

He intended to use calm words and an austere tone, to summon up some of his old dignity and authority to show Mike how stupid and juvenile he was being.

When he found the bastard in the communal washroom, Mike was whistling tunelessly, messing with something at the sink.

Dignity went out the window: Alastair hurled the boot at Mike's head. The other man ducked with a yelp and the boot struck the mirror behind him, cracking a corner off of it.

"Whoa, man!" Mike exclaimed, whirling around.

"What the hell's your problem?" Alastair growled, closing the distance between them. "You sonofabitch, this needs to stop. I don't know what you . . ."

There was something green and white in Mike's hand. Something that looked an awful lot like Alastair's toothbrush.

For the first time in over five hundred years, Alastair threw a punch at a human, with the full force of his strength behind it.

And when his hand cracked the side of Mike's face, there wasn't even a moment to celebrate. The mountain of a man barely moved under the hit, but struck back, smacking Alastair's fist aside and sinking a punch into his belly. *Hard*. The toothbrush dropped and Alastair had thrown himself back at Mike before it clattered to the floor. He grabbed at him, trying to drive him back, to bring him down, and Mike struck for his face, grazing his jaw with a fist that burned cold. White heat flared in Mike's eyes, frosting over the blue of them, and to his shock, Alastair felt the hellfire flare of his own in response. His vision shimmered into hues of red and grey as the revelation slammed into him.

The little shit was an angel.

The moment hung in the air like a fog of frost, both men's eyes locked in mirrored shock, realization dawning upon them.

How the hell did I miss that?

Time jolted both men back into the bathroom-ring. The broad

angel was quicker to recover, and squared off first, his blue eyes burning with murderous intent. Alastair couldn't fault him for lack of guts. The air above him shimmered and warped in the ghostly impression of wings.

"You don't want this fight," Alastair warned, the old accent of hellspeak sliding into his words.

Mike grinned, gleaming faintly with power. "Yeah, I do," he said, "and now it makes sense *why*."

He lunged at Alastair, tackling him hard around the middle and driving them both back against the far wall with a crash. The entire trailer shuddered and Alastair scrambled to stay on his feet, striking blindly for Mike's head. It was just an angel, just one lone angel, not even one who he remembered . . . If he could just get a hit in . . .

Mike's fist connected with the side of his head, and his vision exploded into fractured stars. He didn't realize he'd fallen until his back smashed against the floor and Mike threw himself down on top of him, pinning one of his arms with a knee and driving punches into Alastair's face. Alastair clawed at him with his free hands, raking his nails over Mike's face. Thin lines of red blossomed up over white skin, steaming and blistering from Alastair's unholy claws, but Mike didn't stop, landing blow after clumsy blow, his face fixed in a rictus of anger.

"What the hell's going on here?" Ari bellowed from the doorway. "Are you both out of your minds?!"

Mike froze and Alastair threw him off, putting distance between them. There was blood dripping onto his shirt in a sluggish trickle and he was panting, his chest aching fiercely with each breath.

Ari stalked into the washroom, Gita on her heels. "You two are grown-ass adults," she barked, her voice shaking with anger. "I don't care how late in the season it is or what the budget looks like. If you can't act like the scientists they told me you were, I will send you both the fuck out of here! I need a research team, not this . . . this *pissing match*!"

Neither of them said a word and neither of them looked up. Ari made a wordless noise of frustration, slapping her hands against her sides.

"Just . . . just go to bed. Stay out of each other's way. I have to phone HQ. This sort of shit gets reported," she snapped, and left the trailer.

Gita studied them for a long moment, frowning. She pointed to Mike. "Out," she said.

He slunk out past her, with Alastair's blood still coating his knuckles. Alastair stared after him, furious and stunned. He couldn't catch his breath and his hands were shaking. It should've been so easy . . .

"Now you," Gita told him, pointing at the door. "Let it go, Al. He's not worth losing your job over."

Alastair pushed himself to his feet, meeting her eyes in disbelief. He felt like the heat of his anger was still blazing from him, but Gita didn't back down, putting her hands on her hips.

"Not worth it, Al," she repeated slowly. "One of you has to be the bigger man here."

When Alastair slid out of the trailer past her, the frozen night wind didn't even touch him.

NEITHER OF US are men, he hissed in his mind, his thoughts still holding the sizzle of hellspeak.

The lamp hit the wall with a satisfying crash, plunging the room into darkness and doing absolutely nothing to take the edge off his rage.

He'd been a Duke. He'd had *legions*. They'd called him "my lord". An invitation to dine with him was bragging rights for a decade. Alastair stalked, pacing the tiny area, feeling the walls close in around him. His room was too small to hold the size of his anger and disgust.

Lazy, stupid, old fool . . .

He'd gotten slow and soft, and dangerously complacent. To not notice an angel under his nose, locked in close quarters with the creature for weeks now? It was unforgivable, humiliating. There'd been so many signs; the bone-deep repulsion he felt when Mike was around, the instinctive way he'd made note of the guy entering the same room as him.

He caught a glimpse of himself in the little hand mirror by the desk, saw the red gleam of his eyes highlighting the cuts and bruises on his face. The fat lip swelling above his beard. The blood at the side of his nose looked black in this light.

Snarling, he let his form slip, flashing glimpses of charred ebony demon skin in the cuts on his face, and tore the mirror down with a hiss, crushing it under his foot.

He'd *been* a Duke. Alastair sighed, feeling the past-tense of another life crash down on his shoulders. Sitting down, he put his face in his hands.

His therapist, Leonard, had told him dissatisfaction was normal for a man his age. The solution: buy a red sports car and drive down the highway at two hundred kilometres per hour with the top down and a bombshell in the passenger seat. Instead, Alastair had come to Iceland.

He hated it here, the cold and the close quarters and all the care he had to take on the glacier. But this place was *his to lose*, so was his job, and there was no way he was going to let some angelic little upstart take that away from him. He'd worked his way back up to some semblance of a reputation, starting from scratch on the plane of mortals. He'd suffered through humiliating internships, slogged through years of human academia from mentors under a century old . . .

Shutting his eyes and steadying his breath, he mustered his strength and thrust his arm out, plunging it between realms and reaching into Hell.

It was still there, and the comfort of the heat on the other side sang a siren-song to his blood, drawing him in, inviting him to stay. *Foolish old creature, what are you doing living in the ice?*

His fingertips touched the handle of his scourge, locking around it, drawing it back. It was a balancing act, dragging the weapon between realms without toppling over that line himself. He found himself reaching for the ancient pulse of the volcanoes that boiled beneath the glaciers, the molten core of the island, the one part of this place that wasn't alien to him. The fire in a land of ice.

Steadily, with effort, he drew the full length of the scourge into the room with him, and the window to Hell snapped shut once more.

The lashes of the scourge hung like dead snakes, black and limp, absent the hellfire that should have been crackling through them. His age-old weapon looked like something from a discount pirate costume, the onyx handle dull and grimy in his hand. It felt . . . too light.

He raised his arm, wincing at the ache in his bruised shoulder, and cracked the scourge in an arc above him.

Nothing. Not even a spark.

Dismay rose like bile in his throat. He tried pressing his will into the coils, trying to dredge up some of the old power in him, and his knees immediately went so weak that he had to sit down. And yet . . . still nothing.

Exhausted, and bruised in more ways than the physical, Alastair crammed the useless scourge into a spare backpack, and collapsed into bed.

ARI KEPT THEM on tight leashes for the next few days, pairing Alastair with Gita and keeping her eye on Mike. They were never alone together anymore.

It didn't keep them from sizing each other up, circling around each other like prowling lions. Ari had more than a few muttered comments about testosterone and male egos, but all Alastair could think about was the dead weapon tucked away in his room.

He was losing sleep, spending long nights obsessively working with the scourge, trying to coax fire back into the lashes. Kicking himself for letting himself get old and . . . human. Cursing himself for every leisurely cup of tea he'd drank, for every night spent reading novels, for every day wasted watching the sky change colour.

Mike didn't seem to be a prime angelic specimen either; he'd never seen such a sloppy attack from one of the warriors of Heaven. But it had still taken him down. It didn't matter that they were both rusty. Alastair was rustier, and Mike was going to win.

To Ari's dismay, he started turning in work half completed, jotting down sloppy readings with exhaustion-clumsy hands. When he begged off fieldwork for a day (hoping to bring the scourge outside and test it in the open air while the humans were gone), she shook her head, looking sad.

"Strike two, Al," she sighed. "Be here or don't. You don't survive Vatnajökull with a half-assed effort."

Her disappointed words rang in his ears, echoing in his mind. A small part of him thought that he shouldn't care about losing a human job in a place that he didn't like anyway. The much larger part of him was devastated.

He was staring in the broken bathroom mirror that night, dabbing ointment on the cuts that wouldn't quite heal, when his anger finally broke and dissolved into a deep, dark pool of despair, and finally, tears. Subtle streaks of flame streaked down his cheeks, leaving a black trail of coal.

"You're too old for this," he murmured. There were lines on his face that hadn't been there before, and more white in his beard. His bones ached.

"Bullshit," came a voice from the shower stall.

He jumped, wiping his cheeks and charring the cuffs of his nightshirt. But it was only Gita, stepping out with a towel wrapped around her, her feet bare on the icy plastic floor. She frowned at him, grey-streaked curls dripping, and he stared at her despite himself. There was so much fire in her that he often forgot the woman's age. Her skin was a tapestry of wrinkles and stretchmarks, dotted with age spots and old scars; it hung soft and loose on her arms, above her knees, along her throat.

Grandmotherly, he thought. *And steel underneath.*

"Bullshit," she repeated. "You've got as much right to be here as anyone, Al. You've got more degrees than Mike has fingers and, last I heard, you come with one hell of a recommendation from the Dean at Manoa. One of the best she's met, I believe was the wording."

She stepped forward and tapped his forehead with a wet finger. "You're here because you give a shit about the world. And because you're good at your job. Maybe try remembering that for a change, huh?"

HE COULDN'T GET Gita's words out of his head. And when he sat down that night, twisting the lashes of his scourge over his fingers meditatively, he realized that now he was a scientist first, and a demon second. Because he was here as Dr. Alastair Duke, senior environmental researcher, not as Allocer, Great Duke of Hell. And as a scientist, he didn't have to worry about defending himself from the wrath of angels, because he *was doing nothing wrong*.

He was here because he'd been stationed here, and nothing more.

Mike had no more right to this place than he did; neither of them were from this world. And if a demon's only crime was existing, an avenging angel was nothing more than an asshole.

He was a demon and a scientist, and he could be both, he decided. He allowed himself to feel the prickle of fire in his chest and feel calm in his bones. And he breathed.

The scourge flared to life under his hands, casting the room into a riot of crimson, deep shadows writhing in the dancing light.

"Welcome back," he murmured, smiling.

He'd lost one home, his kingdom forged of brimstone and passion. He wasn't prepared to lose another for simply existing.

THE WHOLE ACT of leaving notes felt juvenile, but he wasn't prepared to have his final showdown anywhere near the women. Not because they were women, but because they wouldn't understand, and it wasn't up to them to clean up his body. He didn't want to give Ari anything to report to HQ that was going to put her credibility or reputation at stake, and if she described a middle-aged man combusting into dust and gone without a trace, she'd have more than botched research to worry about.

The note for Gita and Ari was simple. It absolved them from liability, explained his disappearance as a voluntary one, and promised he'd write from Hawaii.

The one for Mike made him giddy the second he'd began to write. It felt so childish, but he'd smirked while scribing the whole thing in sharpie. It was the adult equivalent of "meet me at the bike racks after lunch." Except it was a cave in Iceland, and he'd have to trudge through the storm to get there.

Alastair waited, perched on a rock in a suit. His parka was in his backpack, along with his boots, but that was only to negate any suspicion about his disappearance. He'd actually enjoyed rushing through the storm, gliding over the ice, feeling the prickle of snow on his skin. Brushing back his hair, he smiled, his scourge clutched in his hand.

If he had to make a last stand, he was satisfied with the location at least. The jagged black rocks stuck out like fangs in the mouth of the cave, and the ice that coated the walls and ceiling was the same colours as the waters of Hawaii, frozen turquoise and silver.

It didn't take long for Mike to arrive, similarly snubbing the weather in a t-shirt and jeans. There was a snap of cold that shot through the cave when he skidded in. He'd also brought his parka and boots, but tossed them into a corner of the cave. His features were icy, and his sword drawn.

Alastair grinned, looking at Heaven's weapon, remembering

the pristine blue metal of their blades and the gold inlay at the hilt. Works of art: he'd always admired their artisans for their craftsmanship.

"Now you look like the fiend I knew you were," Mike chuckled, his deep baritone echoing off the ice. He took a step forward, moving from the mouth of the cave into the shadowy darkness.

Alastair scoffed. Maybe it was his posture, or his scourge. Maybe his smile had been more malevolent than he'd intended, or maybe Mike just didn't like Armani. He stood, rolling his neck. He was cool, as though the winter had burrowed into his veins, settling a glacier next to his fiery heart. It was like he finally belonged in this land of fire and ice.

Mike jittered, taking another big step towards him. "Let's do this, hellspawn."

Spreading his hands, Alastair gave the angel a slight bow of his head. "It's what you're good at, after all."

The wind blasted across the mouth of the cave, creating a mournful wail, some ice dropping from the wall into the shadows.

Alastair let his heart burst to life, the complacency of mortal existence giving way to the passion and fervour of the Hells. Cracking his scourge over his head in an arc, the old weapon exploded into roaring flame, suddenly heavy in his hand, like he remembered.

Mike jumped back, his shimmering blue eyes transfixed on the weapon. His sword was drawn but remained lowered, glistening in the reflection of the blazing scourge.

Alastair bowed again. "At your leave, saint."

Shaking his head, Mike tensed his arm, raising his sword high over his head and lunged towards him, bellowing an angelic war cry.

The scourge cracked, throwing white sparks back in his face, and Alastair dodged out of reach of the blade.

"You sonofabitch," Alastair hissed, losing his earlier composure. He stabbed a finger at Mike, insult boiling in his stomach. "You treat me like a feeble old man now? You didn't hesitate in punching my face in before."

Mike blinked, already on his feet with his sword again raised in front of him. He shook his head, charred sections of his blond hair flashing. "What the fuck are you talking about?"

"Light it!" Alastair bellowed, pointing at the sword. "Light your damn blade and fight me like a man!" His eyes were burning now, filled with fury.

Clenching his jaw, Mike lunged again, this time getting hit with the full wall of hellfire and crashing into the dirt.

"We're not men!" Mike spat.

Alastair stared at his opponent's back; Mike was vulnerable as he got to his feet, but there was no glory in fighting a handicapped adversary. He would fight the angel at full strength and die valiantly, or not at all. "Light. The. Sword," he hissed.

The blade was high again, and Mike glared at him, his eyes icy.

"Fight me!" Mike demanded. "Like a demon. Come on!"

"Light the fucking sword! I'm not coming at you without your blade burning, so just light the damned thing!"

"*I can't*!" Mike snarled, his face twisting in a grimace, and he lunged again.

Alastair easily dodged the attack, but did not crack the scourge again. "You what?"

"I can't light it," Mike repeated, not meeting Alastair's eyes, his jaw flexing. "But we can still do this. I have the sword and I'm here to vanquish you! So fight me, fiend."

And for the first time, Alastair truly saw him. Someone, not so unlike himself, spending countless hours shaking his weapon, trying to light it to no avail. Desperation and hopelessness settling in, then determination to see the act through to the end when challenged.

If he hadn't challenged Mike, would the battle have happened at all? Or would the angel have turned tail and left, unable to light his holy weapon, and too ashamed to admit it. Alastair had considered it himself.

The scourge dimmed, turning dark and lax at Alastair's side.

"Come on!" Mike goaded.

"There's not much difference between you and I," Alastair said at last.

The angel scoffed, rolling his eyes.

"We're both making our way in a world that isn't our home. Doing the best we can. I'll say you're doing marginally better than myself, but that could be due to the broadness of your shoulders."

Mike's sword came to rest at his side, the tip zinging over the stone, and he gave Alastair a curious look.

The demon raised an eyebrow. "Do we want to do this?"

Mike nodded, too quickly. “Yeah, of course we do.” The cave was silent a few moments, before he continued. “I . . . think so, anyway.”

“We’re biologically predisposed to be adversaries,” Alastair countered. “There’s a difference. It makes sense why we were at each other’s throats. It felt right.” He lifted his free hand in a shrug. “But do we *have* to?”

A series of expressions flashed over Mike’s face, though the underlying confusion remained. As did the conflict. He was silent for a long moment before he spoke. “No,” he said, “I don’t think so. Not anymore, anyway.”

Alastair nodded, tucking his scourge into his belt. He found himself smiling. “Agreed.” He walked over to his backpack, pulling out his winter clothes. “I like tea.”

“What?”

Alastair shrugged into his parka, dressing for the cold. “We didn’t have tea in Hell. Could never get the hang of it. So now, I like tea.”

Mike laughed. “Football. And butter chicken.” He stuck out his hand. “I’m—”

Putting up his hands, Alastair shook his head. “As far as we need to be concerned I’m Doctor Alastair Duke, and you’re Doctor Michael Archer. And that’s all that matters so long as the armistice exists.” He zipped up his parka thoughtfully. “Or unless the antichrist is born.”

Mike tucked his sword into his sheath and glancing over as he reclaimed his discarded parka and boots. “Is that really a thing? The antichrist, I mean.”

Alastair shrugged, walking towards the mouth of the cave. “We’ve got a betting pool. But that’s about it.”

The winter wind whipped at them but neither found the cold uncomfortable company as they began the trek back to the research station together.

HIGH ABOVE THE cave, braced against the gusting snow, the two women stood in silence and shadow, hidden by the blizzard.

The silhouettes of Alastair and Mike were growing smaller in the distance.

Gita released her grip on Ari’s shoulder. “See? I told you we could wait.”

Shaking her head, Ari compressed the long scimitar blade into its hilt and tucked the weapon into her belt. "You intervened."

"Prove it," she replied with a sly grin. "You just need a little faith."

Ari chuckled, tightened the hood of her parka. "I suppose not having to dispose of two bodies makes today a win?"

"It does indeed," Gita agreed, capering down the hill. "Now, let's go crunch some numbers and play scientist. I like it better when you're the boss."

The Hatchling

K.T. Ivanrest

THE DRAGONS WERE polite and came in through the front gate.

It wasn't unusual behaviour for dragons, of course. Gryphons were the ones to watch out for, sailing like kites over the orchard's hedges, making spectacular dives and loop-de-loops and landing wherever they pleased. And though unicorns had no choice but to walk in, they made every effort to be snobs about it. All in all, Sajar preferred his dragon clients—not that he would have told any of the other creatures that.

Tucking his pruning shears into his apron, he watched his customers ruffle snow from their wings and survey the rows of egg-laden summer trees, as green and vibrant as the grass beneath their claws. No trace of winter's knee-deep drifts could be found within the Cradle's walls, where the trees produced their own ideal growing conditions—useful, though alarming whenever Sajar left the orchard and had to face the temperature difference.

"Good afternoon!"

He wove his way toward them, pausing to give the nearest egg a gentle pat and earning himself a swat from one of the overprotective tree's tendrils in return. The fiery sting, and his accompanying eye-roll, cleared away the last of the lingering melancholy he always felt when working with the eggs. A privilege and a curse, helping others attain what he could never have.

"My lady. My lord. It's a pleasure to see you again." Try as he might, he could not remember their names.

"And you, Master Sajar."

In graceful unison they returned the bow he offered them, curving their necks until the ridges along the backs of their heads aimed skyward, and then the dragoness extended a claw and presented him with two thin, shimmering scales, one the dark grey of a threatening storm, the other tinted like the promise of spring amidst the snow.

"We are hoping to grow our family, if you have trees available."

Grow our family. It was a phrase so common here that he'd almost succeeded in ignoring the guilty twist in his stomach whenever he heard it.

"Of course." He collected the featherlight scales, each larger than his human hand even with his fingers spread wide, and surveyed them for imperfections as he prepared to ask an often uncomfortable question. "Before I draw up a contract for you, might I ask if you have any interest in adopting a child?" He gestured toward the hedge to his right. "There is a dragonet at the orphanage, hatched here recently, who is in need of a home."

Their expressions softened, and the female's wrinkled with curiosity. "For what reason?"

He brushed a calloused finger over her green scale. "Given that you have two children, I'm sure you are aware that this is an imprecise process, no matter how we try to guide it. In this case, her parents were gryphons."

The magic of the summer trees at work—there was no other explanation for how a perfect graft of two gryphon feathers had instead produced a creature more dragon than gryphon. Already she was bigger than her parents and liable to burn down their nest throwing the mildest of tantrums, but Sajar's heart had broken when they'd refused to take her. It always did.

Always a reminder of Kaj.

As if on cue, the gate in the hedge clanged and the object of their conversation came clambering over the ironwork, trilling excitedly, too young to put her euphoria into words or care that the keeper of the orphanage was shouting after her. Clearing the gate, the sunset-red dragonet toppled onto the grass in a tangle of feathered wings and flailing limbs and a little blast of fire from her aquiline nostrils. At last she scrambled to her feet and half bounded, half flew straight at the dragons.

"Oh dear, I'm so sorry!" A rumpled phoenix alighted in front of Sajar, head twitching between him and his customers, her graceful crest swaying with the motion. "We tried to stop her, but . . ."

But no one was listening. Already the dragonet was sprawled on her back, pinned beneath the grey dragon's snout. Her little talons clutched his muzzle as he rolled her back and forth, growling with comic exaggeration; with each rocking motion her broad tail slapped the grass and she yipped in delight.

The familiar combination of relief and envy struck Sajar, and he settled the dragon scales against one of the rocks lining the pathway. At this rate, they wouldn't be needed.

"It's fine, Tsiet. Seems it was for the best, anyway." He hoped his smile didn't look as sad as it felt. Another happy family. Another child grown at the Cradle, off to start a new life while Sajar watched from between the rows of trees, alone as always.

The orphanage keeper flapped her copper wings as though applauding. "Yes. And speaking of adoption . . ."

She peered back toward the hedge, and as Sajar followed her gaze his stomach churned again. A young man hovered on the other side of the gate, a pattern of sunlight and shadow scattered across a body that looked equally patched together. He balanced on two dragon-like legs, clutching at the bars with mismatched hands—one human, the other a claw at the end of a scale-covered forearm. A pair of folded wings rustled behind him, and his eyes were fixed on the dragonet romping around her almost-parents.

Sajar wanted to look away but couldn't, not until Kaj shifted and glanced toward him, and then it was all too easy to turn away and settle his attention safely back on Tsiet. But though he blinked several times, the image of that misshapen silhouette remained, stinging his conscience like a snap from one of his trees.

"He will come of age this spring," Tsiet said, voice quieter though the dragons were making too much noise for anyone to hear.

"I know." Kaj's hatching was so seared into his memory that he might mark time by it forever.

"I'm afraid he won't be able to stay with us any longer, as much as I would like it to be otherwise." She glanced up at him, her golden eyes round, earnest, hopeful. "You've always expressed an interest in his well-being. Might you wish to—"

"No." The word spilled from his mouth on something that was almost fear, even as his heart and mind suggested a different answer. "No, Tsiet, I'm sorry, but . . . I can't." Won't. Shouldn't.

Another feather-fluff, what Sajar had come to think of as a phoenix-shrug. "I understand. Just thought I'd give him one last try at a family."

He winced as the word prodded his thoughts into the past. The day Ensa had left . . . the day the egg had hatched . . . taking little Kaj to Tsiet . . . Clenching his hands, he shook his head. It was better this way. Kaj would be fine.

"I can't," he repeated, but even so his eyes drifted back to the gate, just long enough to see that Kaj was gone.

KAJ WAITED UNTIL the second moon had risen before shuffling through the snow and slipping over the hedge into the warmth of the Cradle, praying that his plan had any chance of success. It was a stupid plan, but it was the only one he had, his only hope of ever having a family, so he was going to do it anyway.

He'd left the gate—it had been foolish to stand there so openly after he'd failed to stop the dragonet from climbing over—and spent the rest of the afternoon watching the new family through a thin spot in the hedge, the place he visited whenever he wanted a look into the orchard, into a life he'd never know. Balls of gold and teal and silver graced the branches, eggs pale like water and others bright as dragonfire, some swirled with colour, others glistening with a single, perfect sheen. Dragons and gryphons, phoenixes and more, all little hatchlings waiting to break into the world and meet their families.

But tonight, rather than looking at the eggs, his dragon eyes instead scanned the pathway as he crept forward. They must be here. He'd seen Master Sajar set them against one of the rocks somewhere nearby . . . Somewhere—

His heart leapt as the moons' light gleamed off his quarry: two dragon scales, one grey and one green, nestled in the grass just ahead.

He stooped and nearly collapsed under the bulk of his wings, which had doubled in size over the last few months. What else his body might have in store for him, he couldn't imagine, but if it had decided whether to be human or dragon before he'd hatched, he wouldn't be falling over every time his wings caught a draft. More importantly, he'd have a family by now for sure, one who wouldn't return him a week later with some excuse for why "it simply isn't going to work."

It never worked, and after fifteen years, there was no more time to wait for the day it would.

He paused only long enough to gather grafting supplies from Master Sajar's workshop before creeping to the far end of the orchard, clutching the scales like armour over his pounding heart. A single row of trees stood apart from all the others and always seemed to be bare. It was far enough from the house that he didn't fear the orchard keeper hearing him, but even so he moved slowly, glanced across the yard again and again, and paused once or twice to check for movement.

Within the curtain of slender branches he loosed a sigh and deposited the tools and scales amidst the roots. The grey disc he put aside, the green he kept before him, a glimmer of light distinguishing it from the thick grass below.

Supplies ready, he rolled up his sleeve until his forearm was bare from elbow to claw and studied his own scales, pale gold against his earth-brown skin, not a third the size of the dragoness's. An imperfect pattern, as though a spray of water had crystallized along his arm without concern for order or elegance. Despite his racing heart and mounting fear, they were only warm to the touch, not that the often-burned fingers of his human hand could much tell the difference anymore.

At last he selected one, large and oval, shimmering as though with eagerness for the task ahead. He closed his eyes and took a breath. Winced a few times for practice and bit his lip.

And then yanked.

SAJAR WAS OUT of bed and halfway to the window before he realized the cry had come from his dream, not the orchard.

It was the same wail he always heard, and by the time he'd kneaded his pillow back into the proper shape, it was already echoing in his mind again. The same wail and the same memory, fifteen years old but still fresh as spring.

Over and over he watched it happen, playing out in the patterned wood grain of the ceiling above his bed: Ensa, striding out the front gate with little Ixi in her arms, the squirming child too young to realize she would never see her father again. Himself, sitting motionless beneath one of the summer trees, listless and lost. Well-intentioned friends had offered meagre comfort, his customers even less—within days their wide-eyed anticipation had ceased to make him smile and their insistence upon visiting the eggs had become bothersome, a flutter of hope he no longer felt.

He rolled onto his side and kneaded the blankets as his mind echoed with Ixi's laughter and faltering attempts at words. He recalled her first time in the orchard, reaching out from the safety of his arms to touch a tiny hand against one of the eggs, giggling and overcome with wonder.

Even then he'd pictured her standing at his side, learning the delicate craft. One day the hands that had touched the egg with such delight would cut careful wedges into the trees, grafting scales and feathers instead of scions. How ready he'd been to share his joy with someone, the beauty of bringing new life into the world. One family helping others grow.

He sat up slowly, drew aside the blankets, and brought his feet to the cool floor, grounding himself in the present, in the stillness, in where he was. Not staggering out from beneath a summer tree and dashing eagerly toward the workshop with a sudden new idea, but in bed in the dark of winter, fifteen years too late to stop himself.

With a heavy sigh he fell back onto the pillow, but still sleep would not return. Instead his memory pivoted around that moment of inspiration, around words he could never take back, vivid and sure.

If I no longer have a family, I'll make another.

"Owwww."

Kaj hunched over his bleeding arm, digging at it as though new pain might distract from the old. "Ow, ow, ow, owwwww."

The rhythm of his words merely called attention to the pang, rocking back and forth accomplished nothing but making him dizzy, and when he unfurled his wings he succeeded only in striking one against the tree trunk. Its gnarled tendrils swayed with displeasure.

He forced himself still, watching the tree through tear-filled eyes while the searing pain slowly faded to a throb, and after a long minute both his heart and the tree had calmed. At last he splayed and wiggled his claw, and the rest of his arm made no protest.

Again he surveyed the orchard master's house for movement or light, but still there was nothing. A strange disappointment pooled in his stomach—that constant desire to be noticed, to cause someone concern. Anyone, even Master Sajar, who looked at Kaj like no one else ever had. The first and only time he'd spoken to the man, there'd been a caution in his eyes that was almost fear, and with it, guilt. Shame. It hadn't occurred to Kaj until that day that he was probably the orchard master's greatest failure, a graft gone so wrong it had produced . . . well, Kaj. It was no wonder, he supposed, that the man didn't want to look at him—not then, not today.

No one else did, either. Once he, too, had gone barrelling outside to meet each new visitor, beating his little wings with excited hope. How certain he'd been that he would find a family. Just a little longer, if he waited, if he was patient.

Patience earned him only apologetic smiles from the dragons, but even those were better than the human families and their broken promises. And though "Next time" had become Tsiet's mantra, repeated after every rebuff, every failed attempt, eventually Kaj had admitted the truth he'd always suspected: no one wanted him.

The thrum of bells echoed in the clouds and he swivelled, but it was only two qilin flying over. Kaj waited until they'd glided from sight and then struggled to his feet, scales in hand, nervousness squeezing at his heart. He'd watched the orchard keeper through the hedge so many times. He knew what to do. And if it went as planned—and it *would*—then in a few months when spring arrived, he'd never be alone again.

If no one wanted him in their family, he'd make his own.

I'LL MAKE ANOTHER . . .

Make another . . .

Sajar cradled his new child in his arms, but he could hardly see its misshapen form through his tears.

He'd spent all afternoon waiting for the egg to hatch. Months since Ensa and Ixi had gone, every day spent diligently tending the tree, talking to the egg, brushing his fingers over its smooth surface, imagining the little creature within—little Kaj, he'd decided.

Never had he imagined this, but now that it had happened he didn't know how anything could have gone more wrong. What a fool he'd been to believe he could grow a human child as though it were a dragonet or fledgling. How completely blind not to have seen the absurdity of his plan.

"I'm so sorry," he whispered, squeezing the child to his chest and dipping his head. It raised a tiny claw and swatted at his nose, but the gesture only brought more tears. "I'm so, so sorry . . ."

The little human-dragon squirmed and whimpered. It had barely made a sound yet, and in the silence between his sobs he heard his tears sizzling away as they dripped onto its skin. The pale scales on its arms and dragon-like legs scorched even through his clothing, but he didn't care. He held it close, wondering how it was possible to feel such love and loathing at the same time. Love for the poor little hatchling, loathing for himself.

You're so selfish, Sajar!

Selfish, arrogant. How could he have thought he had a right to make himself a child? A replacement for Ixi, a comfort created to end his grief and loneliness. A child to end his pain . . . by carrying that pain itself. Who knew how it would grow up, or whether it would even survive. Would its human parts be able to endure the heat of its dragonfire? Would all of its limbs grow at the same rate? Would it even be able to walk?

He'd done this.

You're so selfish, Sajar! Ensa's accusation rang again in his mind, voiced so often it could have come from any of their numerous fights. *All you do is play at being a father!*

The words cut like a shard of egg shell and he lowered the hatchling hastily into the grass, as though Ensa might return at that moment and convict him. She'd been right about him all along, and the longer he stared down at the little child, the more desperately he wanted to look away and the faster his heart pounded.

He couldn't do it. He'd failed Ensa, failed Ixi, failed this little one before it had even hatched. He didn't deserve to be a father, and the child didn't deserve to suffer through his attempts. He would only hurt it more.

I won't let that happen.

Drawing a shaky breath, he lifted his head and gave the tree a long look. He would return to grafting. Help others build lives and start families. Bring children into the world for parents who wanted to give love rather than take it.

And somewhere out there were parents who could give that love to Kaj.

He bent forward, brushing a trembling hand against the hatchling's dark hair before lifting it into his arms and climbing carefully to his feet. "Come on, Kaj," he whispered, giving the child its name even as he prepared to say farewell. "We're going to meet Tsiet, okay? She'll find you a really good family."

Any family was better than Sajar.

THE NIGHT BEFORE his birthday, Kaj waited impatiently at the base of the tree, flicking his now-massive wings with every nervous heartbeat. He'd told himself he would give the egg a few minutes, in case his little sibling knew it was time to go, to come into the world with all the new spring flowers, meet its brother, and run away to something better.

Anything at all, so long as they were together.

But either it didn't know or it was giving him a hard time, because the egg just hung there on the branch, swirling gold and white and perfectly happy to stay uncracked. And perhaps for a good long while, too—it was still so small, not half the size it ought to have been after a whole season of growth.

Fear singed his heart and tingled beneath his skin, though he tried to ignore it. It had to have worked. The fact that the egg was there at all meant he must have done *something* right.

And yet the fear kept burning the longer he stood there in the dark, weeks of increasing urgency and decreasing options all pressing in against him, whispering his doubts, his fate.

Tomorrow, tomorrow . . .

He clenched his claws and swallowed. No more waiting, no more chances. Only his future, empty without this egg. He brushed his hand against the shell, expecting to feel a heartbeat, a pulse of magic, heat, something. But there was nothing, and at last he couldn't endure it another second. If Master Sajar saw him, it was all over, and with every passing moment he sensed the sunrise as though it were coming out from within him.

He reached for the egg, retreated, forced himself forward again. All he needed to do was grab it and pull, and yet it was so final. His one chance for a family, but somehow he felt that as soon as he plucked it from the tree, he would know whether it had worked or not.

And if it hadn't . . .

The sheer panic behind that thought drove him forward, and without thinking he gripped the egg and gave it a firm tug.

Nothing happened. It held to the tree with something far more powerful than the resin Kaj had used to secure the grafted scales. Again he yanked, and then once more, pulling harder and longer as dread made way for frustration.

"Come on, little one," he muttered, adjusting his hold so his claws wouldn't damage the shell. Behind him the tree's drooping branches swayed and snapped, hissing an ominous warning which only made him more desperate to get away. "We need to go."

Still nothing, and now he was more anxious than ever. What if he couldn't remove it? What if he was stuck haunting the orchard until it hatched on its own? Suppose he wasn't there when it happened, and—

No. He *had* to get it free.

Extending a single claw, he settled it carefully against the stem, drew a deep breath, and sliced.

The egg snapped loose and the angry tree erupted in flames.

He yelped and whirled and stumbled against a root, wobbled for a horrible moment, and then fell, dragging the egg down with him, scrambling to raise it high enough to—

A sickening crunch made his heart stop, and through a swirl of panic he saw his future scattered on the ground in front of him, each little fragment shining in the firelight.

"No."

Numb, he crawled forward and ran a trembling finger over the nearest shard. It was smooth and clean. They were all clean, inside and out.

There had never been anything inside the egg at all.

"No!"

He lifted the shard and cradled it against his chest as his lungs sought for air he could no longer find. Around him the branches of the tree thrashed and crackled; a tendril slashed his wings, but he didn't care. He didn't care about anything now. Only this egg full of nothing, just like his future.

"N-no . . . No, please." A well of tears spilled from his eyes, only to sizzle away in the heat of his skin, gone like everything else. "Please, *please*, you have to . . . You can't . . ." With every plea his voice grew higher and thinner, his breathing more ragged. "Please, I . . . I don't want to be alone."

Choking on despair, he screamed, the sound swallowed up by the roaring flames.

SAJAR BOLTED TOWARD the burning tree, clutching a staff and wondering whether he'd need it for the blazing branches or the intruder cowering in a ball amidst the roots. Whoever it was, he was wearing something lumpy on his back. A pack of eggs, maybe, or—

Wings.

Kaj.

He stumbled, caught himself, and sprinted forward as if racing his heartbeat. As he neared he could more clearly make out the young man's body, still unmoving despite the branches whipping at his back. *No.* No, he couldn't be—

"Kaj!" He tore through the flailing vines, swinging the staff to ward them away and ignoring the heat that bit into his shoulder as he stooped. The only thing that mattered was the young man huddled on the ground and surrounded by the shards of a broken egg—but no time to wonder, only enough to dodge another burning whip before he gripped the young man's shoulders and hauled him upright.

"Come on, Kaj, get up."

"Master Sajar?" Kaj's face was soaked with tears, his eyes red and hollow, and as soon as Sajar loosened his hold the boy began to sway. "I . . . the egg . . . I—"

A branch slapped his cheek and Sajar swatted it aside as his eyes began to water. "You can explain later. Up, now."

Kaj clutched a shard of the egg all the way through the

thrashing vines as though it were his last tie to life. He seemed completely unaware that the tree had it in for them or that Sajar was fighting it off one grasping tendril and searing sting at a time. Only when they were free of the branches and their swelter did Kaj emerge from his daze. His widening eyes flew from the tree to Sajar and then to the egg shell, and with every motion his shoulders shook harder and more tears spilled down his face.

Dropping the staff, Sajar pulled him close, relief and lingering terror smothering the last of his pledge to remain distant. Kaj's skin was as hot as the tree, his scales searing through the light fabric of Sajar's shirt, and like so many years ago, it didn't matter.

"Master Sajar." Kaj's voice was weak and plaintive, barely audible above the crackling branches, and though he clung to the shell, he buried his face in Sajar's shoulder nevertheless. "I'm so, so sorry. I never meant . . . He sucked in a breath and dissolved into tears while Sajar drew him closer. "I just wanted a family," he whimpered. "And I can't stay at the orphanage anymore, I'm too old, and so I thought . . . I tried . . ."

Understanding finally caught up with Sajar, a rush of horror that sent him reeling. Kaj hadn't stolen an egg.

"You tried to grow yourself one."

In a heartbeat he was back beneath the tree all those years ago, afraid to be alone and so desperate not to be. Even across time the misery enveloped him, or maybe it was Kaj's pain he felt as the young man trembled in his arms. The same loneliness, the same fear, the same powerful need for the one thing Sajar had denied him.

"I just wanted *someone*," Kaj sobbed. "Anyone. But now I . . . Now I'll never . . ."

Kaj's hands shifted around the shard, and for a moment Sajar hoped he'd slip. Slice its rough edge against Sajar's chest and bleed away all the remorse pooling ever deeper within him. Over his son's shoulder he could see the rest of the fragments, scattered in the grass beneath the swaying, faintly burning branches. He'd collected such pieces once for their beauty and the pride they'd fired in his heart, but now he kept only a single shard. Tomorrow he'd meant to take it down from its shelf, like he did every year, and remember.

Would he even be able to make himself look at it after tonight?

Against his chest Kaj drew a deep, shaky breath and raised his head, the fading firelight shining in his tears. "I'm so sorry, Master Sajar. I should . . . I should go and—"

"No."

He pulled Kaj even closer as everything collapsed around him—his guilt, Kaj's emptiness, and the painful clarity of the truth. All those years watching his son through the hedge, telling himself it was for the best. Telling himself it was for Kaj. Wallowing in his shame with each new egg, each new orphan, each new family. Focusing on how selfish he'd been so that he could continue to justify the most selfish act of all.

How could he have ever believed he was protecting *Kaj*?

You're so selfish, Sajar. The echo of her voice was almost pitying now. *All you do is play at being a father—right up until it actually matters.*

He gave a mournful laugh. "Until it actually matters."

"What?" Kaj sniffled, drawing back.

The tree had spent its energy and sat docile and dark once again, and in the light of the moons Sajar's eyes swept over the young man before him—dark skin dappled with golden scales, wings shadowing him like sentinels, hand and claw together still clutching the shard. His breaths grew short as the urge to look away struck again, and he forced it down and instead stared harder than ever. Tangled hair curling around a face that matched Sajar's; wide-set, dragonish eyes tinted silver in the moons' light; a slender frame shifting back and forth in discomfort, but with an almost rhythmic grace.

Not a visible reminder of his failings, not a painful image of his long-indulged guilt and fear, not an excuse, but a *son*.

Drawing a shallow breath, he raised a trembling hand and brushed it through Kaj's hair. The young man's eyes followed the motion warily, but he didn't move, and Sajar's fingers slid over two lumps near his temples. A moment of alarm, and then he realized Kaj was growing horns.

Growing horns.

Strange though the idea was, it nestled in his chest and became a soft, encouraging warmth. For all the time that had passed, Kaj was still so young. Still growing. There was still time, time for it to matter.

And for everything Sajar could still take from him, there was just as much he could give.

He closed his eyes and imagined seeing Kaj every day, not glimpsed through a hedge but standing right next to him as they tended the trees together. One family helping others grow. He pictured them laughing, talking, fighting, reconciling. Smiling.

What would it be like to look in the mirror in the morning and see himself smiling? What would Kaj look like when he smiled?

As the thought crossed his mind, the expression settled over his face, and determination drove the last of the doubt from his heart. Sliding an arm around Kaj's shoulders, he turned him toward the house. "Come on, let's get you home."

Kaj hung his head and his whole body seemed to wilt. "I don't have a home anymore," he murmured, rustling his wings. "I don't have anywhere to go."

And still Sajar's smile would not fade. "I think there's something I can do about that."

The Djinni and the Accountant

Hal J. Friesen

"NEVER TURN A client away," Mr. Almasi had said to Charlotte on her first day at work. His hand swallowed Charlotte's when he shook it. Charlotte had searched for an accounting job for almost a year—she was determined to move out of the youth shelter and into her own place—so she would have heeded his advice even if his goliath size hadn't frightened her.

The entrance to the Al-Hambra Accounting Firm sank into the middle of a back-alley in an Edmonton industrial area whose tenants had long since moved on. Dust clouds nearby took the shape of trucks, horses, and legless pedestrians. The Firm felt out of place, a leaning townhouse in the middle of a swath of abandoned concrete, a building someone had dropped on their way somewhere else.

Every time Charlotte walked to work from the bus stop, she experienced a disquieting loneliness blended with the sense of many eyes watching her. The loneliness was familiar. The sense of being noticed was not. Every morning Charlotte shrugged off the feeling with a shiver, cleaned her dusty glasses, descended the steps below street level, and entered the crooked door to the office.

Both Mr. Almasi and the dark oak-panelling of the office smelled of old library books. The space was sizeable and the arms on the desk chairs sat just a bit too far apart, the wooden legs just a bit too tall. Although they fit with Mr. Almasi, they didn't fit with much of anything else, and gave the whole room a sense of being off-kilter every time Charlotte walked in.

It was a job though, and Charlotte intended to keep it no matter what. Alicia and the other girls at the youth shelter were happy for her, but Charlotte found herself turning down their offers to socialize. If she wanted to move on, she'd need to distance herself from them anyway. So she lost herself in her work, content in the task of putting everything in its proper place, accounting for every penny of a client's portfolio. For eight hours a day, five days a week, the world made sense to her. Then she'd head back to the shelter, enduring the nights by counting the days until she had enough money to move out on her own—just one more month.

When Mr. Almasi left for vacation Charlotte was ready to prove herself. After working hard all morning she sent Alicia an e-mail turning down an invitation to go to a free concert that night and eyed the clock, debating whether to take her lunch.

The door creaked open, and she turned.

A blue figure floated through.

His body tapered to a glowing ember inches above the ground and his skin was cut from star fire, white wisps drifting across, bobbing in the same way his entire form did. His cheeks were purple, and his eyes glowed brilliant pearls. He had no hair, and if he had ears, they were swathed in flame. The oak-panelling and door smouldered where he had brushed by them, and Charlotte tasted ash. Shadows raced to escape his luminescence, but could find nowhere to hide.

"Whatever this is," she muttered to herself, wringing her hands, "must be a clerical error, a joke—a mistake. No reason to be alarmed, Charlotte. Nope, because it can't possibly be here for me."

Mr. Almasi's hearty voice echoed in her mind: "Never turn a client away."

"Can't do that, can I?" She searched for more pens to put away on the desk, paper clips out of order, and eventually just rubbed her palms on the surface frantically. Out of the corner of her eye she saw the blue figure drawing closer, reeking of burnt espresso.

"He's got the wrong place," she mumbled. "This'll be over in a heartbeat."

"Do you ever talk to someone besides yourself?" the creature said, his voice a crackling wood stove.

Charlotte cleared her throat and straightened. She took one look at the intense fire floating in front of her, then looked abruptly down again. "Do you have an appointment?" She scooted to the notebook and glanced at the entries.

"What?"

"I don't see anything here," Charlotte said, flipping back and forth through the entries. "Did you set something up privately with Mr. Almasi? He does that sometimes."

"I never require an appointment, and especially not for Almasi." He folded massive arms across his chest. His cheeks burned a deeper purple. Had his burning cores for eyes narrowed?

"Unfortunately Mr. Almasi is on vacation," Charlotte said. *Any time now this will be someone else's problem, something for someone more important.* Sweat beaded on her forehead, and her fingertips tingled with heat. She knew what Mr. Almasi would want her to say, though, and remembered how badly she needed to keep this job and get out of the shelter. "Maybe I can help you in his place?"

The creature waved an arm. A tower of papers materialized and slammed onto the desk on top of the appointment notebook. Charlotte jerked back, whispers of wind from the papers still on her hands.

"You think you can manage this? Do you have any notion of the responsibilities, the weary trials of tallying all that I bring into this world? That"—the creature pointed to the stack—"is but from one year. You mortals desire more wishes, but cannot comprehend the paperwork—the import taxes—that burden me for every infernal thing you wish into the world."

Oh my God. He's a djinni.

She swallowed and adjusted her glasses. *Breathe. Import taxes. Breathe.* "We have experience with those types of claims," she said, grateful she could grasp this point of familiarity. "We can help you with that right away, even without an appointment. Mister . . . ?"

"Maimun. Maimun will suffice, child."

Even with the giant paper barrier blocking some of the djinni's intensity, sweat trickled down Charlotte's neck. "My name's Charlotte. I'm not a child." She wasn't sure whether it was the heat, the taste of ash, or the stifling smoke that made her speak the words. She clasped her hands together, feeling even smaller in Mr. Almasi's office chair.

"Charlotte," Maimun said, letting the word hang.

"Thank you," Charlotte said, keeping her mouth moving as much as she could. "As I said, I can help you out with your import taxes right away."

"I should hope so," Maimun said. "Almasi made a vow for prompt service."

"I wish Mr. Almasi would come back and take care of this mess," she muttered.

"What did you say?" Maimun said, tilting his head and leaning in.

"Uh—around here our service is the best," Charlotte said.

She ushered the djinni into a side room, her head feeling lighter with each step she took. With the djinni behind her and out of sight she could almost forget he'd come, until her back tingled and singed from his star fire. She shot glances back to make sure he hadn't set the building ablaze. A black trail snaked across the ceiling behind him along with the scent of campfire, but it hadn't ignited yet.

Deep breaths did nothing to calm her as she took a seat behind a large mahogany table and smoothed out the folds of her dress. Each inhale ushered in a wave of acrid smoke from the djinni, who floated closer to the ground and made the fumes worse. Wherever he went, it seemed he burned but somehow also quenched the fire.

"Let's take a look at your records, then, Maimun," Charlotte said, her hands shaking as she reached for the papers. The smouldering eyes behind the massive stack were finally starting to seem real. She trembled at the sudden shift in the universe, wondering whether she would be a sacrificial lamb for the djinni's greatness. She had never been part of anyone or anything's plan, ever since her mother had given her to child services and disappeared. If she had a father, he didn't want her in his plan, either.

"I am surprised Almasi hired someone so weak," Maimun said, folding his arms again. As they tucked into his armpits, sparks burst from the seams.

Charlotte's hand clutching the first file stopped mid-air. "I'm not weak," she said, holding his fiery gaze for the first time. She may never have been included in anyone's plans, but that didn't imply weakness.

Maimun snorted, and his body surged a brighter blue.

She read through the first file, lifting the pages to block Maimun from her sight. "Early in the year you granted wishes to Mr. And Mrs. Vandermere. The first was for $9,999—"

"That's the most I can give," Maimun said. "You humans always wish for inordinate sums of money, and are so surprised when there are limits. I thought your society understood inflation."

"The second was for a lifetime supply of macarons."

"Most of them spoiled after the first month."

"The third was for every modern tool on the planet."

"They filled his garage and he couldn't do any work after that."

"So they weren't very happy," Charlotte said, scanning the declared amounts of imported goods.

"That's irrelevant to your job," Maimun snapped.

"How do you pay taxes, anyway?" Charlotte asked. "Can't you just magic the money into being?"

Maimun shook his head. "I cannot abuse it this way. I pay with money I've saved and earned along the way, as you or anyone else would."

"People pay you?"

Maimun straightened. "They tip."

Charlotte continued reading, scanning the first few files to get a sense of how long the job would take. Part of her enjoyed making Maimun wait, while another part recognized this approach imprudent to her survival.

The stack of files seemed to thicken with each page she scanned, each file detailed and long.

"Maimun, this is going to take . . . some time," she said. "If you like I can call you when it's ready."

Maimun spread his arms and raised himself, making every surface of the room smoke. "I am not yours to summon," he boomed.

Charlotte choked and coughed on the smoke. "Fine."

She read through the files while Maimun floated and stared. She wondered if she would die from smoke inhalation before she finished the work. Maimun differed so greatly from the images of servitude she had read in fairy tales that she wondered whether he would even let her live.

In the files she learned about a wide assortment of wishes he'd granted in the past year. A little girl had wished for a cat, a pony, and a field to play in. The last of these had resulted in the displacement of a soccer pitch and rearrangement of the local streets that ended in a number of traffic incidents. Someone else had wished for several wives, another for several husbands. Both resulted in large dowries being paid to the bewildered families or former spouses in order to account for their sudden disappearance. The dollar figure couldn't possibly account for the damage done, but it was marked on a receipt nonetheless.

Other wishes involved more abstract concepts, like happiness, satisfaction, and self-confidence. Those resulted in vouchers for therapists, social clubs, walks in nature, and a variety of other solutions specific to the person's individual needs. It was strange to see a $9,999 price tag on a receipt for "Contentment".

Charlotte would have wished out of the shelter if she'd been given the chance, but she suspected Maimun was about as likely to grant her a wish as he was to go swimming. His eyes upon her were unrelenting, and she felt him study her every movement as she worked through the files.

A pegasus, a pegasus that could fly, then a pegasus that could fly that still looked normal. Wishes that showed revisions, continued iterations revealing short-sightedness after the first words spoken. The ability to breathe underwater, breathe underwater and still breathe on land, breathe underwater and still breathe on land and not look like a frog. In many ways it resembled the evolution of a contractual arrangement, where the terms grew more specific but certainty was never granted.

Charlotte was tallying the animal costs of a backyard zoo and the associated rezoning permits when she felt Maimun's heat more intensely on her face. She struggled to keep a professional demeanour under his scalding FBI-lamp. His smoke had taken on a burnt weed smell.

"Charlotte," he said.

She wanted to lose herself in the files and the numbers, find a way to straighten all these loose ends out. Account for everything. "Yes?"

"You are different from other humans," he said. "Have you no desires? Nothing that burns inside, seeking, wanting more? I sense no fire in you."

Charlotte wiped her brow. Fire was the last thing she wanted right now. She felt like she'd spent the last three hours in a boiler-room. But Maimun remained where he floated, his eyes both staring and not staring at her.

"It's never mattered," she said at last.

"So you're wasting my time. Someone who cares so little is unlikely to do a thorough job on my taxes."

Charlotte stood and pushed back her chair, fists curled at her sides. "I care about my job. I care about the things over which I have control." Her head throbbed from the sweltering heat, and she sensed her internal fuse burning. "Have you never wanted free of your wish-granting duties? Have *you* no ambition, djinni?"

"You will call me Maimun." He extended his arms and leaned in until small pyres lit at the edges of the table.

Charlotte had endured far too much to be bullied by a creature she was trying to help. "Maybe I will do as you do, and define you only by what I see in front of me, which is a being of utter servitude. Djinni."

The table ignited, and Charlotte fell back against the wall. She kept her gaze fixed on Maimun. The papers had vanished, and the table now burned an orange fire with blue tips. The scent of burnt plastic filled the air. At any moment, the whole building would light up.

"Do I look like a being of utter servitude?" Maimun thundered.

"Maybe," Charlotte said, struggling for breath, "you should show more compassion to those helping you. Be more understanding, given your experience." The words poured out of her with little thought to self-preservation.

Maimun placed his fists on the table and vaporized holes in it. Charlotte's thighs burned and the tips of her shoes melted around her feet.

"I could destroy you," he said.

"And you would have nobody to help you." Charlotte tried to

fall back on her sense of unimportance, but the thought of burning alive made her insides knot. She prayed it didn't show.

Maimun glared at her. Between them, the desk crumbled and fell apart into a pile of glowing embers.

"You have no strong desires," he said, showing no reaction from having demolished the table. "But you have strength."

Maimun backed off and with a wave of his hand the smoke vanished, though the faint tendrils from the floor beneath him remained. The change felt like a cool breeze. Another wave of his hand and a desk appeared atop the ashes with the pile of papers. Along the edge next to the computer monitor stood a family of troll dolls, each with its neon hair pulled straight up into a point. Sticky notes pasted to the monitor reminded of a woman named Margaret's birthday next week.

"Whose desk is this?"

"Does it matter?"

The trolls gazed vacantly into the distance. "Do *you* like these things?"

Maimun lifted his chest. "They're more accurate than most of your folklore."

"Oh—okay." Charlotte wiped her forehead and brushed sweaty hands on her dress. She scooted closer to the stranger's desk. "I will need more time to get through this, and having you loom over me isn't helping."

"Your care is selective," Maimun said, floating back and forth with his massive arms clasped behind his back. "You guard it so closely I cannot see deeper. Most curious."

If you think I'm going to share it with you, Charlotte thought, *you've got another think coming*. "I care about doing a good job. Isn't that enough?"

"I've never met a human quite like you," Maimun said.

Charlotte frowned. Of all the people who could grant her attention, a pompous, selfish djinni was not on her list. And despite his attention, he didn't seem to be hearing anything she said. "What do you want from me?"

Maimun stopped his float-pacing. "You think it strange I see you as special. Few—or none—have recognized this within you?"

As he spoke the words, water in a well in Charlotte rose until her breath drew short. Of course she wasn't special—her own mother had vanished when she was seven, leaving her to bounce from one foster-parent to another. She was a secondary character in everyone's eyes, an afterthought. She'd been left in grocery stores, forgotten outside of schools, and locked out of houses on countless occasions. Child services barely paid her enough attention to give her file even the lowest priority. She'd eventually run away in search of her mother whom no one acknowledged had ever existed. After years of travelling as a vagrant, stealing library books and scraps of food, Charlotte had ended up in a youth shelter which paid her a sliver of enough attention to let her finish her certification as an accountant.

This job was her key to getting out of the shelter, if she could keep it.

Her lips trembled. Her body remembered the cold nights that penetrated deeper than the weather.

"You're right," she whispered. "Few people notice I exist."

Maimun held her gaze, and she couldn't look away. His fire snaked its way into her, warmth that burned in contrast to the coldness she felt inside. His eyes widened and she felt parts of her inner being brought into the light, exposed.

"Ever since your mother disappeared," he said.

Every strand keeping Charlotte's body together tightened, pulling through her legs, her shoulders, and up to the base of her skull. She shoved away from the desk, away from the exposing light of Maimun's gaze, back into her comforting dark.

"Is this fascinating you?" she snapped, crossing her arms over her chest. "Am I a good case study? Enough to entertain you?"

Maimun backed away, causing shadows to creep out from the desk paraphernalia. The flames at the edges of his body flickered with green tips as the temperature dropped. The smoke from the floor smelled like burnt hair. "That was not my intention."

"No, but you have about as much empathy as a stray cat. You're treating me like a specimen. Do you want to be studied like that?"

"Some in your world have tried," Maimun said. "Few see me as anything but a vessel to their own selfish desires."

"How is it," Charlotte said, picking up a file from the stack, "that you're able to see desires so well, but so many of these wishes don't fulfil any of their desires?"

"I have learned that if I give people what they need before they ask for it, the results are disastrous." Maimun's light dimmed imperceptibly, his eyes slanting down at the edges. "I long for people to find that within themselves."

"Is that what you were trying to do with me?" Charlotte said. "Well, I'll tell you now, I've searched long and hard for my mother. She's gone. If she exists, she's changed her name, and made everyone forget about her. So don't think you can help me find what you think I need. I've already tried for myself."

"I could grant you a wish," Maimun said, his voice low. "As payment for your services. It doesn't have to be related to your mother." He bowed his head. "I apologize for pushing you in that direction."

"Why do you feel the need to push me in any direction?" Charlotte asked, ignoring the teasing prospect of a wish. *Not from him.* "I thought djinnis were supposed to serve the wishes of their masters, not shove their own agenda down people's throats."

"I told you before," Maimun said, biting each word, "I am not a servant."

"Isn't that part of the rules? Aren't you bound by a lamp?"

"I follow my own rules," Maimun said. "The lamp was a historical fixation of your people that became a convenient conduit to call my attention, and bring me from the realm woven into and around every space of your world. Almasi helped set up the rules, and encouraged the legend to spread."

A chill crept up Charlotte's spine. *How old is Mr. Almasi?*

Maimun no longer looked at her. He had turned to the side, and seemed as though he could see through the wall to some world beyond Charlotte's perception. Then he stiffened, and seemed to notice Charlotte again. "We are wasting time," he said. "I will honour your request for peace and solitude, and return in two days."

Before Charlotte could say anything, the office door flew open and Maimun glided out like a wisp of incense, star fire singeing the air behind him.

CHARLOTTE WORKED LATE that evening, determined to demonstrate how serious she'd been when she talked about her work. Delving into the file with all its intricacies provided ample distraction and pause from the painful memories the djinni had awakened. It also prevented her from thinking too hard about who or what Mr. Almasi was, and what she might have gotten herself into.

First she scoured Mr. Almasi's files to see if previous claims had been made under Maimun's name. If Mr. Almasi kept any history of Maimun's previous interactions, she discovered, he had hidden them very well. After that, she camped out in the office library, looking up historical cases and examples of anything close to what the djinni imported.

She focused on the dollar signs beside the desires of every one of Maimun's clients. $1000 for the perfect birthday party, $2500 for that first vehicle restored to its former glory. $8000 for a friendship rekindled. Not all the things Maimun imported into this world were material, but the material effects were surprisingly quite measurable.

Charlotte worked into the small hours of the morning.

TWO DAYS LATER, Charlotte should've felt proud after her breakthroughs, but she felt like the djinni's pile of documents had landed on and compressed her head into the desk while she slept. When consistent banging echoed through the office and circled inside her skull, she groaned and took a few weary steps into the hall. The light through the windows carried a bluish tinge.

"Morning hothead," she croaked. Maimun floated in the doorway, stirred-up clouds of dust obscuring the neighbouring buildings. If she didn't know better, she would have thought they were in the desert.

"Is this the time of day when you try to be funny?" Maimun asked.

Charlotte rubbed her eyes, and beckoned him in. "This is the time of day when I try to be anything."

"I don't understand."

"Just come in and turn down your brightness."

When she'd managed to coax Maimun and stumble her way into the office, Charlotte took a deep breath and let her mind sink back into the world of taxes and legalities. Maimun floated in a seated posture, eye to eye with her.

"This stack," she said, laying her palm on a pile of files as high as her computer monitor, "involves wishes such as weightless furniture, one hundred-league boots and apartment extensions. These were all destroyed shortly after the clients wished them into being—"

"They were all terribly impractical. I tried to warn them."

"You imported them, but they were destroyed," she continued. "So you don't have to pay any tax on these.

"Now this one—" she moved her hand to an even taller stack, "—involves goods that are considered charities, and actually qualify you for some deductions. Lifetime supply for the food bank, guaranteed election results that gave huge funds to political parties, that sort of thing.

"Now, we have this stack. I'm fairly proud of this one. All of these items are listed on a free trade agreement of some kind within various international agreements that exist between the United Nations. The principle of non-discrimination in all these agreements requires no most-favoured-nation treatment, meaning a country cannot discriminate between its trading partners. As a being partially existing in another realm interwoven in all the nations of the world, you can argue that you are a global citizen, and as such cannot be discriminated against. You are a part of all the member states involved in the free trade agreements, meaning you should pay no tax on all the items in this pile.

"There are a few that don't fall into any of the above categories. A thousand lifetimes of love is one of them, the happy feelings from when someone spends summers with their grandparents, the joy at seeing one's child for the first time—these ones fall into here. I mean, some of the tangible related items I could get exempted, but some of the abstractions were just too difficult to justify.

"In total, instead of upwards of five hundred thousand, you'll need to pay two-thousand, five hundred and seventeen dollars and fifty-eight cents." Charlotte sat back in her chair to catch her breath, and crossed one leg over the other.

The sound of crackling fire filled the space as Maimun leaned forward, glowing eyes wide, hands moving and making the papers float apart to see Charlotte's work for himself. The sight made Charlotte wonder if the gravity in the room were letting go, since all the papers gradually drifted into the air under Maimun's survey.

"Most impressive," he said at last. "It seems I won't be constrained to three wishes any longer. I'm sorry I underestimated you."

Charlotte's chest lifted. Although she hadn't expected Maimun's words to matter, the validation after how hard she'd worked still encouraged her.

"I must repay you for your efforts," Maimun said, letting the papers settle back into their original piles.

"Our standard fee is—"

"No," he said, "I will pay you in something much more valuable."

"That won't be necessary, I'm sure Mr. Almasi will—"

"I insist, Charlotte."

Charlotte thought back to his earlier offer of a wish. She'd seen some of the harsh realities of the wishes, but a part of her still wondered how she might make use of such a possibility, get something that wouldn't hurt anyone else. However, Mr. Almasi might be furious at her for not taking the regular payment—unless he had taken similar payments in the past.

"What did you have in mind?" she whispered.

Maimun lowered himself until he floated once again eye to eye with her. "I can show you your mother," he said.

Charlotte gasped. The heat no longer seemed to have a way out of her. "What?"

"Your mother," Maimun said gently. "I can show her to you, then grant you a wish."

"What, like she's a specimen or something?"

"No. I can open a window."

Charlotte's chest constricted. She took short breaths. "If you show her to me, will I know where she is?" she asked warily.

"I will answer as many questions as you desire after you see her."

She put a hand to her chest, willing her heart to slow down. "Okay."

Maimun waved his massive arm and one of Charlotte's monitors brightened into the view of a hilltop cottage with long grass swaying in the breeze. A woman in a blue country dress with a grey-haired bun walked up a dirt path carrying a wicker basket full of laundry. Her face was wrinkled with crows' feet and lines of happiness. She paused near the top of the path, closing her eyes and taking a deep breath before entering the cottage.

Mom, Charlotte thought. She dared not move for fear of

breaking the moment.

Inside the cottage, a man in a wheelchair rolled dough on a counter, flour spattering his clothes. He dusted himself off as she entered, then he and Charlotte's mother embraced.

"Where is she?" Charlotte asked.

"Rural British Columbia, Canada. East of Kelowna, in the Okanagan."

Charlotte watched as her mother and the man in the wheelchair held hands, and he showed her his latest batch of freshly-baked buns. They exchanged a few words, kissed again, and he patted her bottom, leaving a flour handprint. She swatted him, tried to dust it off, then walked with her basket of laundry into another room, shaking her head but keeping a smile on her face.

"Who is he?" Charlotte asked.

"Daniel Fitzpatrick." Maimun's throat crackled with words on the edge of utterance, then he added, "He was suicidal when I met him."

Charlotte turned her head slowly as she took in the words. "You *knew* him?"

"I found it in my old files when I sought an appropriate reward for you. I'd forgotten, Charlotte. I granted his wish. I'm sorry."

Charlotte's head felt light, the smoky air wanting to make her vomit. "W—What? Are you saying my mother disappeared . . . because of you?"

Maimun's form shrank, his fire flickering green as he dimmed. The smell of burnt hair returned. He nodded.

"You bastard!" she shouted. She picked up a purple-haired troll and hurled it at him. It vaporized. "You took her away from me!"

"I am truly sorry, Charlotte."

"After what I just did for you?! You manipulative, evil, g—get out! Get out now!"

"Charlotte, I—"

"This was your idea of a reward? Showing me how much of a shitbag you are? Thanks, Maimun. It's good to know the concept isn't confined to humans alone."

Maimun spread his arms. The room filled with even more acrid smoke. "Let me tell you his wish. Then I will leave."

"What, did he wish for a fine piece of ass? Someone to dote on him, look after him?" She wanted to throw the monitor at him, but grabbed one of the textbooks on the desk instead.

"He wished to meet someone who would love him as he is, and whom he could likewise love in return."

Charlotte's arm fell to her side, the book thumping against her thigh. She said nothing for a few moments. "Okay," she whispered. "And that love couldn't include me?"

"After your mother and father split up, she guarded against love. She would never have opened herself up to Daniel. Even if in time she had let her guard down, the damage ran too deep. It would have ruined her relationship with him." Maimun hung his head. "I did not understand the full effect of what I was doing. I thought the capacity for love was finite, and couldn't be healed in time. So I made her forget about your father, and you as well."

Tears blurred Charlotte's vision, and she sank along the wall to the floor, clutching her knees. Everything hurt.

"Charlotte," Maimun said, coming forward.

Charlotte sobbed. "Go away."

"Do you not see?" he said. "She never stopped loving you. She didn't abandon you. That was my fault, Charlotte. The self-doubt you've carried all these years . . . is based on a false notion."

"You took her away." Charlotte choked out the words.

"I can make things right," Maimun said. "You just have to wish it, and I will make it so."

Charlotte lifted her face, a mask of salty tears. It would be so easy. Just wish Daniel away, her mother back, and everything could be normal again.

But between her and the djinni sat the giant stacks of wishes, the catalogues of collateral damage induced by even the simplest of wishes. The paperwork barely scratched the surface of the ripple effects every wish had on the wider world.

"Is she happy?" Charlotte asked, staring through blurred vision at the monitor.

"Yes."

"Then we'll leave her that way," Charlotte said, shaking her head as a sudden weariness fell over her. "Maimun, you've done enough. Go. Please."

Maimun's cheeks lost their purple colour, and his glowing eyes closed, which almost looked like they vanished. "As you wish, Charlotte."

The room cooled and she knew he was gone.

FOR THE NEXT few days, Charlotte went to work early and stayed late, diving as deeply as possible into the accounting details. She felt raw and weak, as though at any moment she might lose hold of the fragile balance she had left. Her mind continually drifted back to thoughts of her mother living out a peaceful life in the Okanagan.

She's happy, Charlotte told herself. *That's something, at least.*

Something was churning in her mind, processing, and she felt like a child again, unable to investigate or understand what was happening to her. The sadness and weakness she felt after that first day had transformed into something else, but what exactly, she wasn't sure.

Charlotte began cold-calling clients in search of work, something she had dreaded before, but now found herself enjoying a small amount. One day as she hung up the phone after a surprisingly pleasant conversation, Mr. Almasi waited for her across the desk.

For the first time, she noticed the faint scarring on his arms, remnants of tattoos snaking up and around, buried beneath layer upon layer of tanned skin. His square jaw was speckled with hints of the curly hair covering his head, coloured a dark brown that shimmered grey and black in the light. A chain necklace hung below his collared shirt, hiding the outline of a circular medallion.

"Who was that, Charlotte? An old friend?" he said.

"No," Charlotte replied, glancing between him and the phone. "That's the first time I've spoken to her."

"You've finished all the outstanding work?"

Charlotte nodded. "On your desk."

"Wow. Terrific. I should go on vacation more often." He beamed, his grin stretching almost as wide as her computer monitor.

A week ago she would have remained thankful for her job and kept her head down to avoid arousing ire, but things had changed.

"Mr. Almasi, how old are you?" Her insides felt jostled, the sensations no longer familiar and comfortable. She wasn't sure whether to be excited or frightened.

“How old do I look?” he asked, leaning on one hip.

“Middle-aged,” she said, “but after what Maimun told me, it seems you’re at least a few centuries.”

There it was, in the open. She prayed she wouldn’t lose her job for it, or worse.

He looked her up and down, his expression studious. “Maimun came by, did he? The office is still standing so . . . it went well, I suppose?”

“As well as I could do. He seemed . . . impressed with how I handled his file.” She’d wanted to say *happy*, but the word died on her tongue.

“Great job,” he said, staring hard into her eyes.

There was a time when Charlotte may have been frightened by such a giant of a man looming over her, but she surprised herself again by holding his gaze.

“To answer your question,” he said, “I’ve been around for some time, yes.”

“Did you bring Maimun into our world?”

“Yes.”

“How did you convince him to come here?”

“Convince him? He came to me, and I helped him fill his need.” Mr. Almasi stepped back and laughed, his chortling filling the space. He levelled his gaze at her, and the questioning look had vanished. “Anyway, I’m glad you handled him so well. I knew you were the right person for the job.”

Charlotte sat straighter, still unable to discern what she felt as Mr. Almasi moved down the hall and away from her in a few strides.

THAT AFTERNOON, SHE asked Mr. Almasi how to contact Maimun. He pulled out an unmarred copper lamp from a locked filing cabinet, and told her to polish it.

Alone in the waiting room she rubbed its cool surface. Maimun arrived thirty seconds later.

“I . . . didn’t feel good about how we parted,” she said, coming around the desk to stand in front of him. His heat and smoke made her breath catch, but she felt it important to bridge the gap.

Maimun nodded. “Nor did I.”

She took a deep breath. “I know you did the best you could, and I realize it’s unfair of me to blame you.” She’d ran through the words a few times in the bathroom, but saying them now wrenched at a knot inside her. It untwisted with each word she spoke, and she was terrified she would disappear with it. "You—you were doing what you had to, in the best way you could." A tear rolled down her cheek. "It's strange, what you said about Mom never stopping loving me . . . I'm still processing it, but I feel . . . better, I think."

Maimun didn't move, but his flame brightened until there wasn't a crack of shadow in the oak panels. A purple halo grew beyond his body, and the smoke took on the deep and creamy aroma of sandalwood.

Charlotte was still intact, even though the knot had gone. "Your instincts are better than I give you credit for."

Maimun bowed his head, then shook it. "You were right about the collateral damage. And you are the first person who's turned down an offer for wishes, and who would deserve one most."

Charlotte frowned. The eternal temptation to ruin lives for the sake of her own. "I haven't changed my mind about that."

"I don't want you to," Maimun said, spreading his arms. "But you've made me change. I haven't the courage yet to tell Almasi, for he brought me into this world based on my need.

"Throughout my life, I had no sense of usefulness. No matter what job I tried, I wasn't good enough. The only skill I seemed to have was knowing what others wanted, but mundane jobs couldn't fill the need burning in me. I wanted to bring people what their innermost selves wanted, but they rarely asked for that. So I began granting wishes to strike at the heart of desire. At first I'd fulfil what wishes I could through material means alone. As my magic awakened from this newfound sense of purpose, I began to do all that you've seen in order to fulfil wishes. I paid a small price for the wishes, one that I didn't notice at the time—giving up my own desires. It was a job, a way to feel useful, a task of meaning that surpassed anything I'd known before, regardless of the unsuccessful results in the aftermath.

"I wasn't obliged to continue this lifestyle, but I did, especially after Almasi brought me here and created the expectation of my duties and a framework of rules, that this was what I did, this was the purpose of my existence. The more I did it, the less I wanted to do anything else. How could anyone see that I had other value?"

"You don't need others to tell you your value," Charlotte said, her voice just above a whisper.

Maimun nodded. "The words come easily, but true understanding does not. You've helped me learn, Charlotte. Shown me. My inner fire is enough. I don't need to give wishes anymore." He paused. "And I will never do to anyone else what I did to you."

Charlotte's voice caught in her throat. "W—what will you do now?"

"It's been so long since I've wanted anything," Maimun said. "But I think I will start by visiting an old friend—a troll."

Charlotte wanted to say something as Maimun bowed and headed for the door, but she could do nothing but stare as his fire concentrated into a white flame in his torso, and he passed into the dusty air and out of sight.

ON HER LUNCH break, Charlotte phoned Alicia and took her up on an offer to go to a poetry slam. Alicia sounded wary at first, then surprised. Mirrored in Alicia's voice Charlotte sensed the warmth they both felt in talking to each other again.

When Charlotte returned to work, Mr. Almasi walked through the hall, glanced back at her, then stopped and turned.

"Maimun must have rubbed off on you," he said. "You're glowing."

Charlotte smiled.

The Second Great Fire

Laura VanArendonk Baugh

IN THE COMICS I liked to read hidden behind an oversized *Look* magazine, heroes came by their superpowers via startling and novel means. Captain America was injected with a serum by Dr. Josef Reinstein. Superman was born on a distant planet where his literally unearthly powers are commonplace. Both Doll Man's shrinking to just six inches tall and Shock Gibson's electrical attacks were acquired via chemical formula.

I died for my power.

I'd left the States behind and gone to London, blithely confident in my youthful optimism that there would be no war. After all, the grim-faced men with the task of politics had all seen the devastation of the Great War and knew its repetition must be avoided. Neville Chamberlain insisted that if we left Hitler and the Nazis alone, they would settle and be quiet, and at home in the States most of the talk was of letting things work themselves out.

So I went to London in 1939 on the pretence of furthering my education, but really in search of a good time, and I found it. I met a man who said he knew a fellow and could get me a job at the Windmill Theatre, performing in their *tableaux vivants*, but that I would have to audition for him privately first. I scrubbed my skin raw and shining, chose the lingerie which was the best combination of flattering and easy to remove, and climbed upstairs to the projection room of the Folly Theatre. I hiked my skirt with practiced nonchalance to ascend the short ladder into the booth, never giving a thought to the thick metal door I had to pass through, or the iron shutters hanging over the projection ports facing the silver screen, or the chains which ran between the massive projectors and the shutters. All this meant no more to me than the machinery of the projectors themselves, and I had come only for Harry.

So he started the film and gave me the nod, as *A Girl Must Live* flickered over the heads of the audience below. We had twenty minutes before the reel change, and I began my audition for Harry.

I must have done pretty well, for I distracted him from the cigarette he'd lit in blatant violation of the sign upon the door. When he rose to come toward me—"a girl in the *tableaux vivant* must not move, no matter what, so let's test your resolve"—he let it fall to a stack of film canisters, one of many ringing the projection booth, but this one with a lid which was not quite closed over the coil of celluloid inside.

What I did not know then, but I know in exquisite detail now, is that nitrate film is very nearly the same substance as guncotton. It's relatively safe when handled properly, but it becomes volatile with age. It is intensely inflammable, and great care is generally taken to keep it from igniting via the carbon arc lamp in projectors.

When a burning cigarette touches it, it is a candle to flash paper.

The roll of film burst into flame, and Harry jumped backward, cursing. He struck the projector with his shoulder and grasped at it to stay upright. A tower of fire leapt upward from the canister, and around it ominous noises came from the adjoining canisters, warming in the sudden blaze. Celluloid ignites from mere heat.

Harry whirled and ran for the door, leaving me naked behind him. He wrenched back the heavy metal shield and fled through it, pulling it and the attached chain shut behind him. I stared, uncomprehending, hardly understanding the danger or that he had simply abandoned me to it.

The room exploded.

Fire raced around the walls, shooting out from stacked canisters. I snatched up my discarded skirt and blouse and tried to press out the fire, but I only burned my hands and arms. Celluloid creates its own oxygen as it burns; there is no smothering it. The heat fuses in the chains overhead burned through and the shutters slammed down, trapping me in the rising inferno.

Smoke poured from the burning film, nitric acid which began to dissolve my skin. I beat at the door, screaming, but it held fast, designed to seal solidly against a wall of flame and expanding with heat against its frame.

There was a fire grenade on the wall, a red globe filled with fire extinguisher. Its restraint melted with the rising heat and flung the globe into the rising flames. The glass shattered and its carbon tetrachloride spread over the fire, quelling the places it touched and transforming with the heat. The incongruous scent of freshly-cut grass swept over me, and I gasped the new-formed phosgene gas—the trench gas of the Great War—as I screamed.

I burned. I burned from nitric acid without, from phosgene within, from fire everywhere. The booth was filled with smoke and flame and my screaming.

Mistress.

The word seared my mind as the fire seared my flesh. I could not respond to it as I clawed frantically at the door, the wall, the flame-spitting forge of a projector.

Mistress. Come to me.

I turned, less in heed than in desperation, and saw a great black dog standing unaffected in the fire. It looked like something between a wolf and a great hound, tall and lean and dark against the flame, and it watched me as if waiting for something.

The blood waits, mistress.

I did not know what that meant, did not know where the words were coming from, did not know how I could see a dog where there could be no dog, did not know how to end my agony.

Breathe the fire.

I had been breathing the fire, had been scorching my lungs with acid and gas and flame. I cried in pain and frustration and fury.

Yes! Claim it!

I threw myself upright, clenched my blackened fingers into fists, and drank deep of the smoke and poison and blaze. I flung my head back in my pyre and poured out my crucible-purified rage in one incandescent scream.

The scream became a roar, matching the inferno in intensity, and despite myself I hesitated, surprised even in my anguish.

But the work was done. The fire continued around me, but my fingers uncurled, the skin uncracked, the charred black crumbling off into the carpeting fire to reveal pure skin. I gasped, and my lungs did not burn. I looked down at my unnaturally whole flesh, and my eyes did not water and peel.

I looked at the dog. It did not wag—this did not look like a dog who would often wag—but it somehow looked pleased.

Yes, good, mistress. You have done well. It cannot harm you now.

I tried to speak and found that I could form words with what had been my blistered lips. "What—what happened? What am I?"

The dog's ears moved back slightly. *You are a child of dragons, though the blood had weakened through generations of disuse. But it was there, and enough to be claimed.*

Child of dragons? I had a brief memory of Grandmother dragging me to sit through some part of *Der Ring des Nibelungen*, which had felt more like all fifteen hours of it. There had been a dragon. But I was still standing in fire and I could not think clearly.

Fire and poison are your birthright and your tools, the dog said to me, however it was speaking. *They cannot harm you once you make them yours.*

I relaxed my posture, gradually coming to grips with the fact that I was not burning to death. "Who are you?"

Brand.

The dog approached me, tail waving loosely behind him. Flame reflected in his eyes, or they were glowing with their own fire. I reached out and touched him—not giddily, as if he were a lap spaniel, but respectfully, as if he were a wolf-dog of fire.

The carbon tetrachloride was doing its work, and the nitrate film was burning out. But no one would enter the theatre soon, not with all the poison still in the air.

Brand went to the door. We can go before they *come.*

"I'm naked," I said. My clothes were ash.

His ears flattened in a canine grin. *Perhaps you should have considered that before disrobing.*

"I didn't know the room would catch fire!"

I, too, wear no clothes.

I resolved to steal one of the usherettes' overcoats on the way out, in the likely event one had been abandoned in the evacuation.

The cooling door slowly shrank in its frame, and I pulled it open with fingers that should have blistered from its residual heat. We left.

I DID NOT go back to the nightclubs, and I never went to the Windmill Theatre. That part of me had burned away in the projection booth, and now I craved purpose. Also, I did not want to see Harry.

I spent time in the public library, looking up all the reasons I should have died. I replaced the books on the shelves myself, irrationally afraid a librarian should wonder at my assortment and guess at something I could not myself identify.

The Prime Minister was wrong, and war came. A new prime minister replaced him. And then the Blitz began.

I joined the Women's Voluntary Services, aiding with evacuations, mobile canteens for the firemen, clothing and shelter for refugees, inquiries from survivors seeking those they hoped were survivors. It was hard, but worthwhile, and we did not bow beneath the bombs which fell so often on us.

Brand stayed by my side, and in daylight he looked much like any lurcher to be found in the English countryside, and few people gave him a thought beyond how much of my rations he must consume. By night, however, he took on the appearance of a hellhound, and he was careful not to draw attention to himself.

You are a dragon, he said to me one morning, as he did so often. *You have power to make war. And yet you stand here and make tea.*

"I am doing important work," I said, and I waved to a woman kicking fresh debris from the night's bombing off her doorstep as she retrieved the morning's bottle of milk. She returned the wave with a smile. "I do not wish to make war, only to survive it."

You are hiding from yourself.

That might have been true. I did not know what to make of my dragon blood, and alone in London I had no one to ask. Four times I had started a letter to my grandmother, asking about the dragon in the opera, and four times I had abandoned the half-filled sheet to the rubbish bin.

Christmas came. It was 1940, and much of London was rubble, although morale was still high and even the children were bearing up well. We at the WVS served refreshments and handed out toys to children, and I gave our Father Christmas a peck on the cheek to their great delight. We had gotten through the worst of the Blitz. Beginning in September, the nightly visits had come fifty-six of fifty-seven nights, and then the Germans seemed to have, while not given up entirely, at least exhausted themselves as much as their targets and to have slowed their attacks.

I'd treated myself to a viewing of *The Great Dictator*—it had been months before I'd entered a cinema again, and I was proud of myself for having done so tonight—and was heading home. I made a face as we crossed the Thames. The tide was exceptionally low this night, and the river stank with refuse and exposed muck. I went home to my flat, Brand at my side as always, and kicked off my shoes. It was Sunday the twenty-ninth, my night off-duty, and I meant to enjoy it. My flat-mates were away in their various roles, so I had the place to myself. There was an Anderson shelter in the back garden, should the sirens sound, but I meant to curl up in a comfortable chair with a novel and my windows safely blacked to hoard the light.

Brand curled into the matching chair beside mine, coiled into himself more tightly than seemed possible. I had not worked him out. He was a hellhound, he admitted that much, and he had recognized me for what I was when I passed him en route to that fateful cinema. Beyond that, he said only that he was adrift here much as I was. *We should be doing more than we are.*

"What more can we do?" I asked. "I cannot fly a bomber to Germany. I haven't the skill."

There are many women doing the war's work, he answered with a reproving tone even in my own mind, *and you have another skill.*

I did not like to speak of the time that a bomb had splashed fire onto the exposed wood of a pub and I had smothered the smouldering corner with my bare hands. No one had seen what I had done, as they were too busy fighting the rest of the fire, and that meant I did not have to face questions to which I had no answers—except from myself and Brand, and myself I could distract with a novel.

We must fight them, he growled.

"The Germans?"

Those who drive them. They are warg, outsiders, outlaws. Their spread must be stopped.

I did not know if he meant the Nazi party or something else. I did not ask. I opened my book.

Sometime near six, the banshee wail of the air raid sirens began to scream their warning, and I groaned my annoyance. Should I go out to the Anderson shelter, beneath the earth of the garden, or should I remain where I was? Most citizens sheltered at home, and there seemed little difference in results. The Anderson shelter would be crowded with other flat tenants, while here I had only Brand and myself. I turned the page and kept reading.

But this night was not quite like other nights. I heard the planes, and the booming of the guns trying to bring them down, but I did not hear the explosion of heavy bombs. Several times I heard what sounded like a scuttle of coal being spread through the streets, but there were no familiar whistles and booms. I read on; after over a year of constant raids, it needed more than a curious sound to draw me out.

An hour or two passed, with my attention primarily on the book and only vaguely aware of the continuing drone of passing planes. What eventually caught me away from the novel was not the shaking roar of explosions, but an ever-increasing light which pierced even my black-out blind. The bombs had ignited buildings. I glanced at Brand, whom I'd observed to sense fire as other dogs sense their master's returning footstep.

He was already looking at me. *We must go.*

I put on my uniform and we went out into an eerie London, with points of fire in all directions and planes screaming overhead, picked out by clawing searchlights.

Look.

I did not need Brand's instruction to note the conflagration rising through the city buildings, drawing the returning bombers with its guiding light. Its flames whipped into the air and whirled, caught in a fierce wind I knew did not blow over the rest of

London.

Firestorm.

I turned and ran ahead of the growing inferno. Telephone lines could go down in large fires, and the fire stations must know what was coming so they could meet it.

Wind pulled at me as I ran down the street, and I realized it was the firestorm drawing air even at this distance. At the fire's base it would be a howling torrent, screaming as it built the flames into a tower which leapt ever forward as its heat began to combust the buildings around it.

I looked ahead and my heart froze in an icy clench despite the fire. The dome of St. Paul's rose above the surrounding buildings, lit clearly for every German bomber to target.

Brand and I made it to Redcross Fire Station and I slipped inside the door. The electricity had gone; the office was lit with a few battery and oil lamps. "The fire," I gasped. "It's coming for St. Paul's."

The firemen inside, already soot-streaked and weary, nodded, not wasting time or breath to acknowledge what they already knew. Further within, firewomen worked at the phones, coaxing information out of failing lines.

"There's simply no more water," a woman said urgently into the phone. "The mains are destroyed. You must do something."

Another shook her head. "The river is too low," she reported in professional tones, as if she were not announcing the death of a city. "The pumps are drawing only mud and muck and are clogging. The fire boats cannot reach. The only water is what has been stored ready at the Cathedral."

A man finished his terse conversation with a woman and turned, and the firemen trooped out together.

I turned to the women. "Is help coming?"

"And the line's down," announced a firewoman with controlled frustration, putting down her handset.

Another firewoman, who by her sooty appearance had run through the street as I had, turned to me. "Yes, as much as we can. The Prime Minister has ordered all units are to concentrate on St. Paul's, saving it at all costs."

This surprised me. Yes, the cathedral was important, but it was a building like all the others. It was important—but was it so much more important than the rest?

She read my face. "Yes," she said. She leaned nearer me. "I came here from my own station when I could not remain any longer. The very asphalt had begun to burn around me. I came here, because I knew St. Paul's would need protection."

"But why at all costs? Why not try to save more?"

"Of course we will try to save more! But we must save St. Paul's." She bit her lip and frowned at me. "It is more than a building. It is a symbol—but it is more than a symbol. It is our hope."

"Our faith, certainly, and hope—"

"And our hope for aid." She held my eyes. "You are an American. You understand?"

I was an American, but I did not pretend to a knowledge of the complex politics between our countries. "I do not."

"My husband works in the Home Office. He says the talk there is that the Americans will not enter the war if they believe Britain is lost. If the continent is occupied and if they have no secure base, they cannot hope to succeed, and so they will remain well out of it rather than commit themselves to failure. If we want allies, we must not fall—and we must not appear to fall. There are photographers and reporters everywhere. St. Paul's is not just the cathedral, it is London."

"Then—if St. Paul's burns, the Americans will not join the fight."

"And if the Americans do not join the fight . . ." She did not say the rest. No one would say the rest. It was inconceivable that Britain would not triumph, with or without the Americans—but it was agreed that it would be easier with them.

I nodded. "Then St. Paul's must be preserved at all costs."

Brand barked once outside the door, a sound he did not make often, and I went out. The firestorm had reached the cathedral yard.

"God in heaven!" cried a voice from within the station behind me. "Cannon Street station reports an incendiary on the roof! On the dome!"

Brand turned and looked at me. *This is your task.*

"What?"

This is for you. Go and protect the Cathedral.

I looked about me, drew a breath of air to scorch my lungs, and ran for the gates.

THE WORLD WAS on fire.

Paternoster Row was ablaze beyond all hope of recovery or control, as maddened flames devoured the millions of books in the publishing houses. Ave Maria Lane was burning, but firefighters held their ground, struggling to wet the buildings with the weakened pressure of their hoses. The fires lit the street as brightly as day, so that I could clearly see the waist-deep rubble and pick my way across it as if in some monstrous children's game.

"Look at the dome!"

I shielded my eyes against the heat and squinted at the glorious, iconic dome, catching the bright smoulder of an incendiary lying on the sloped lead roof. I ran as best I could across the treacherous terrain, mindful of sliding debris and hidden flames. Brand bounded beside me, far more agile.

I could see members of the Watch scurrying about the Stone Gallery outside the base of the dome, hauling sandbags and stirrup pumps and rushing to several dots of fire scattered about the walkway. High above them glowed the lone incendiary, burning through its thermite.

When its magnesium load caught, its fire would grow to white-hot, turning the dome roof to butter beneath it and dropping into the gap between the outer dome and the hidden supporting dome, where it would immediately ignite the wooden supports and heat-crack the brick structure, dropping all into the cathedral itself.

That a single tiny device, less than the length of my forearm, should be capable of bringing down this great symbolic landmark brought me to fury. I rushed into the churchyard.

The Watch was spread thin about the buildings, fighting fires in the roofs, in the gardens, in the library. Incendiaries had lodged in roof timbers and narrow pockets, and sandbags and individual buckets had to be hand-carried to these all-but-inaccessible nooks to smother them before their magnesium could catch. Everywhere were shouts of alarm and of orders.

I climbed the stairs to the Stone Gallery and emerged into what should have been open air, but what was a view onto an inferno.

Nearly two hundred feet below, the streets of London were

yellow and orange, with abandoned fire trucks left where their tires had melted. Tornadoes of flame rose spiralling above the burning buildings, clawing high into the sky above me, as if to catch the German planes which had birthed them.

Buildings on either side were engulfed in flame. All across the roof of the cathedral, men rushed from place to place, attacking smouldering incendiaries and calling locations of devices spotted on other roofs, shouting through the roar of the fires and the crash of collapsing buildings and the hot wind which blew flame and burning embers across roofs to spread anew.

I turned and ran along the Gallery, looking upward for the incendiary on the dome. It was easy to pick out, burning against the solid backdrop of the dome itself, but I could not reach it.

Brand had followed me, unnoticed like me in the fierce concentration of the battling Watch, and now we stared up at the tiny, treacherous thing. It still burned only thermite, but even by only the orange light of the towering flames we could see the discolouring around it as the lead exterior softened.

I had once been inside the exterior dome, a private tour with a handsy guide. Great wooden beams spread across the gap between the decorative outer dome and the brick cone which supported both it and the seven-ton golden cross and ball above. I knew during raids the Watch patrolled along the open wooden beams, with careful balance of their buckets of water and little handheld stirrup pumps to throw water onto small fires.

There was no means of fighting a large fire there.

If an incendiary were to penetrate and lodge in one of the joints, there would be a brief scramble to extinguish it before the magnesium ignited and then the intense burst of heat and flame would be caught against wood and brick, and the three nesting domes would collapse together and drop onto the cathedral floor.

Melt it out.

I looked at Brand. "What?"

It lies on a slope, caught against lead. Melt the lead to the outside, so that it slides down the slope instead of burning through directly beneath itself.

The incendiary would slide downhill like a child's sled and drop onto the Stone Gallery, within easy reach of the Watch and their sand and water. "But—how can I do that?"

Brand's ears turned outward in irritation. *You are a dragon's child. Use your skill.*

I had no skill but survival. I had never had control of fire. Certainly I could not exhale it like the dragon tales of old.

Draw it. Pull it. Stretch it.

I looked up at the firelit roof.

You can feel it just as I do.

I knew Brand could sense fire. Could I? Could I—call it? Direct it?

The wind from the south-west drove a hail of sparks and embers across us, stinging against my cheek. I could only imagine how it burned the Watch fighting fires across the lower roof.

I concentrated on the incendiary, trying to grasp it in my mind. I had seen Brand alert to fire he could not see, but I had never seen him control it.

You can sense it.

Of course I could sense fire—I was standing on island of rooftop among blocks of devastated buildings. All around us was a sea of flames, broken only by the occasional spire of blackened stone which had not yet fallen. Smoke glowed orange and pink above us, a travesty of sunset.

Brand was insistent. *Reach for it.*

I took him literally and stretched my hand toward the glowing device, as if I could feel its warmth above the charring wind which swept the Gallery. I curled my fingers as if I could grasp it, and in my mind I pulled the flame like taffy, tugging it resisting toward me.

The flame flickered.

I did not think it was my doing. I had felt nothing, did not even know what I should feel, and there was a strong wind to pull it. But I continued, for there was nothing else to do and I would rather feel silly than helpless.

The burning canister slid a few inches, catching against a seam of unmolten lead.

Good, good, called Brand. *Bring it down.*

I still believed it the wind rather than myself, but there was no point to arguing. If I were doing nothing at all, at least I was not hurting, and there was nothing else to be done. I tugged at the fire, drawing it toward the lower end of the device, urging it to soften the outer ridge of lead before the sheathing below it. The wind blew a hot gust against my face, making me squeeze my eyes against ash and sparks, and when I opened them the device was a hands-breadth lower.

Bring it down!

There were voices near me, the Watch shouting to one another, but I did not let myself be distracted. I clasped my hands before my chest, squeezed my fingers as if I could actually catch the flame within them, and tugged.

The incendiary rode a smear of melted lead and rolled free, hitting the steep drop of the dome and tumbling to the Stone Gallery. My heart leapt with triumph, even if it were only my imagination that I had done it.

A host of cheers rose into the hot air, along with sharp cries of "Smother it! Smother it!" I turned and saw several members of the Watch converging on the device, crushing its fire with the pitiful remnants of sand they carried.

"It must have melted out, maybe the weight on the outside."

"Was that the only one?"

"Only one which stayed on the dome. There was a whole cascade of them what hit it and bounced everywhere. Still fires in the roof timbers."

"What are you doing here, miss?" This fireman, streaked black with smoke and sweat, was curious.

"I came to help," I said, trying to think of how I might be helping in a way which required less explanation. "I was carrying buckets. The mains are out."

He nodded. "No water to be had, that's the truth."

"Help!" This was from someone new. "Fire in one of the pocket roofs, and we have men trapped!"

We followed him to the fire. It did not occur to the Watch to warn me back; every capable hand during a raid was welcome. While men generally handled the pumps and hoses against the fires, women drove the trucks of petrol through burning streets to refuel the fire-fighting equipment.

The fire had caught in one of the pocket roofs, the space behind an arch, and penetrated to the timbers in the hidden space between the roof and the nave's ceiling below. The fire was contained, but only just; sand and water kept it from spreading across the roof, but there was a wall of fire cutting off the far end of the space. We hung back, shielding our faces from the heat.

"We've got them all out," called a Watch member as we

arrived, "all but one. Damned fool won't rush the flames to come through, but that means he's trapped for certain against the far wall."

"He's got to come out through that?" One of the men who had come from the Stone Gallery looked dubiously at the flames.

"We need water. No way to fight that down."

"He's afraid to come out through it," a man observed without judgment. "Sure, he'll burn if he does, but he'll burn if he doesn't. Least here we can catch him and smother him out. If he stays, he'll die there."

"Where's more sand? How much do we have? Can we make a path in?"

"We'll never find him in the smoke, if he's even still standing."

"We've got to try, haven't we? What have we got?"

As they conferred, eyes on their dwindling resources, I took a breath and stepped into the fire.

It took all my courage and more. While I remembered surviving in the projection booth, and while I had touched fire unharmed more than once in the past year, it still required an incredible act of will to step into flames my own height. If Brand had not walked beside me, I am not certain I would have done it.

Brand seemed to almost disappear in the fire, moving through it as if he were dark flame itself, so it was difficult to follow him and I had to press on in what I thought was a straight line. The smoke was so thick I could not see where I went, despite the flame all around, and what I breathed should have sickened me.

My blood rushed through me as if I were on a Coney Island coaster. I should have been terrified, should have been thinking of the poor man I'd come to find, and instead I felt a strange thrill or glory.

Here!

I found Brand beside the huddled figure of a man, clinging to himself on a patch of exposed brick against the outer wall. His stirrup pump lay abandoned beside an empty bucket. I rushed to them, wobbling as my shoes broke apart.

You know him.

I reached the man and seized him. "Come on! Can you walk? We have to go!"

He looked up at me, eyes wide with terror and surprise, and I saw it was Harry.

He recognized me, too. He saw the woman he had left to die in an inferno, who now had come for him in the flames at his own death. "I'm sorry," he whispered through cracked lips. "I'm sorry. I was afraid. I'm afraid now. I'm sorry."

For an instant I felt a perverse pleasure in his horror, and then I concentrated on the job at hand like the WVS woman I was. *If a job needs doing, it will be done.* "Get up," I said. "We've got to get you out of here."

He twitched away from my hand. "I don't want to go," he said. "Not where you're taking me. I'm sorry! I don't want to—"

I slapped him hard across the face. "Does that feel like a spectre's hand?" I snapped. "I came to help you to live. Sort your soul once we're out of this. Come on!"

I pulled him to his feet and steadied him; the smoke was taking its toll. Brand went ahead of us, passing through the fire, but I had to choose the less intense ways for Harry and myself.

He was terrified, and I had to drag him forward. "Hurry—don't give it time to catch you." He squeezed his eyes shut as we stepped into the flame.

I knew better now the stretch between us and the waiting Watch, and we burst free in a rush. Cheers went up as two men rushed forward to put out his burning clothing. Harry stumbled and went to his knees.

"Good Lord, miss," a Watch member said, "you put us all to shame. We didn't even see you go until you were already disappearing into the fire."

I smiled, patting out my blackened and smoking uniform. The wool had resisted catching fire, which made my lack of obvious injury slightly less implausible. "I didn't want you to try and stop me."

"I'm glad we couldn't. He's glad, too."

Harry was staring at us. "Can—can you see her?"

The Watch member laughed. "Did you think she was an angel, coming for you?"

Harry's face suggested he might yet think otherwise.

"Get them down to fresh air—what there is of it—and first aid," another man ordered. "And let's do what we can for this."

THE ALL-CLEAR sounded, which meant firefighters could work without fear of fresh bombs exploding over them. Dawn revealed the full devastation. The area around the Cathedral was ruins, a wasteland of rubble which, though contained, continued to burn for days. But the dome stood unvanquished, an island of faith and perseverance in the smoky sea of London.

They called it the Second Great Fire of London. Over one hundred thousand incendiary bombs had fallen upon the city, starting over one thousand five hundred fires which were visible in the night from one hundred miles away, and we had borne up under it. St. Paul's still stood, towering above the smoke. London could, as ever, take it.

A few weeks later, two men were waiting for me as I arrived for my WVS duties. They had the suits and undefinable air of government men. One wore aviator sunglasses. "Can I help you?" I asked, taking a notepad from a desk and a pencil from the incendiary tailfin we used as a holder.

"We understand you were present at the defence of St. Paul's," the man without sunglasses said, his hands folded before him. "Is that correct?"

"I was."

"You were seen near where the burning incendiary fell off the dome," he continued, his voice neutral, "and then you participated in the rescue of an entrapped Watch member."

"Yes, I was there." I did not know where this was going, but I was starting to feel wary. I did not know what I had to be ashamed of or conceal—but I did not know what I was concealing, either.

"You have a large black dog," he said. "Large for keeping in this time of rationing, and his coat is not long enough to be useful for the dog's-hair yarn you ladies use for refugee clothing."

Brand ate very little, in fact, but that was also a difficult thing to explain. "I have not overstepped my rations," I said, "and he's not been any trouble to anyone."

"I did not say that he had."

"What's this about, sir?"

"We should like to speak with you about doing special work for His Majesty's government. We understand you are an American, but arrangements can be made."

I blinked. "What sort of work?"

The man with sunglasses spoke for the first time. "Very specialized, and appropriate to your particular skills."

"Sir, I'm just a girl with the WVS, I haven't any particular training—"

He stepped forward and tipped his sunglasses down to look over them at me, revealing eyes with a peculiar orange tint to their hazel and curiously narrow pupils. "The training will be made available to you."

Those eyes. My heart quivered in my chest. "Do you—you know—do you know what—" I could not formulate the complete question.

"We are assembling a team," the first man said, "toward a specific end. That team will visit specific industrial centres in Germany. Hamburg, for example."

They knew. And they knew more than I did. And they wished to teach me to fight.

You are a dragon. You have power to make war. They are warg, outsiders, outlaws. Their spread must be stopped.

I thought of the thrill when the bomb had fallen from the dome, of the rush I had felt passing through the flames in the roof timbers.

"I'm listening," I said.

Bait

Krista D. Ball

Three Days After the Destruction of Borro Abbey by an Honest-to-Almighty Demon and the Bastard Cartossians.

(An excerpt from *A Memoir by Lieutenant Dodd of the Holy Father's Own Consorts, On the Destructive Nature of Demons, as Witnessed During the Borro Incident Aftermath.*)
(Unpublished and currently located in a trunk under Dodd's dirty stockings.)

IT HAD BEEN three days since the destruction of Borro Abbey. As I had been previously charged with the protection of Allegra, Contessa of Marsina and the Arbiter of Justice, I believed myself duty-bound to continue protecting her during the aftermath. I'd assumed she would want to escape to the Cathedral in Orsini, but she insisted on fighting the small demons that had escaped the abyss pit that had opened up inside the abbey. I was not particularly keen on the idea, but she was my charge and I felt in my heart that following her instruction was my most important task.

Walter Cram was with us, too.

Upon my advice, Her Excellency didn't use her innate elemental control over fire for the first two days. As an elemental mage, she was in violation of all manner of laws, both of governments and the faith itself, and I had no interest in her becoming a target of ill-informed farmers who didn't know the difference between a noblewoman and a cow shed. Cram was also an Elemental, but any man who introduced himself as Walter Cram, outlaw elementalist mage and demon whore, did not need my protection. However, Her Excellency insisted he be allowed to tag along, so I kept my objections completely to myself, as has always been my way.

We had successfully dispatched two demons—one I'd skewered on my sword with a well-timed thrust as it flew at my head, and the other died when Cram got a lucky shot with his magic and crushed the small creature with a tree—when Her Excellency finally decided it was time to make our way toward Orsini.

I was impatient to proceed as the Cathedral at Orsini was where I hoped Captain Stanton Rainier—my boss and Her Excellency's rumoured paramour—would have escaped to. I was also anxious for news about my fellow Consorts, especially my best friend since childhood, Lex.

However, Cram was brooding because he wanted to go spy on the Cartossian army because he had a thing against the Cartossian's general. Now, I'll be the first to admit that General Bonacieux was the biggest asshole I'd ever met. And, unlike Cram, I'd never been trapped inside a burning house that Bonacieux had torched in hopes of finding me. And, I admit, I'd not seen him murder his own Queen because he discovered she was an elemental. But *still* . . .

Plus, there was some personal history between the Contessa and Cram that I wasn't supposed to know about—but I absolutely did because I asked around back at the Abbey—so I didn't get in the middle of it when she said it wouldn't do any harm to detour from the faster route to Orsini.

"Take the lower road," Cram said.

"It'll be fine," Cram said.

Let this record show Cram didn't know what in the abyss he was talking about.

We did find lots of interesting things along the lower road—

cows, squirrels, a pissed-off goat—but nothing I felt would constitute useful strategic information that would justify this additional time on our journey. We eventually found ourselves outside a small farmstead chapel and that's when Her Excellency and Cram let loose, arguing back and forth about heading back to the main road.

That's when we saw it: the little bastard itself.

No, not Cram. I mean the demon.

It was a small critter, about the size of a bat. Like all of the demons I'd seen up to that point, it was a misshapen mixture of semi-recognizable features from Earthly creatures. Now, I'll be the first to admit I'm not the most dedicated member of the faithful. I certainly don't believe all of the rot they teach about mages being the spawn of humans mating with demons, and I certainly don't believe elemental mages are evil—excluding Walter Cram, of course, because all rules have an exception—but, every time I saw a demon, I always felt like I should be on my knees repenting all of my carnal sins. And I have committed many, many, *many carnal sins*. Forgive me, Lord God Almighty, for I have sinned *extensively*. And *enthusiastically*.

"Allegra, I think you should practice on this one," Cram said. "Dodd, don't kill it!"

I was being divebombed by a bat-sized demon, so of course I was trying to kill the little bastard. The demon. Not Cram.

"I'm not sure," Her Excellency said, looking about her. "There might be someone inside the chapel."

"Dodd, go look," Cram commanded me, like I was his servant.

"I'm kinda busy here, Cram," I snapped back. I was at that very moment trying desperately to untangle the damned demon from the feather in my second-best hat. I couldn't use my sword on the thing or I could end up (in no particular order) a) damaging my hat or b) damaging my head.

"Can you look for me? Please, Dodd?" Her Excellency asked.

My fist made contact with the demon's face, dazing it, and it collapsed to the ground in a little heap. I poised my sword to run it through, but Cram grabbed my elbow to stop me.

"Keep it alive," he said. "For Allegra to practice."

Now, I'm not sympathetic to the rights of demons. They're demons. They are evil. However, I wasn't convinced torturing any creature, even one from the abyss, was necessarily a right and just action. But, they asked, so I did it. Let this be a lesson to you, reader; never blindly follow orders.

I went inside the chapel, making sure to bless myself at the statue of Our Lady Tasmin upon the altar, and called out several times. There was no basement, just this main floor, and it was empty.

I turned to face Our Lady Tasmin, blessed myself once more, and headed for the door. That's when I heard Her Excellency shout and Cram swear.

An important note for all future experiences with a man like Walter Cram: if you hear a highly-trained elemental mage swear in surprise, run in the opposite direction. Do not look back. Do not investigate. Run.

I hadn't learned that particular lesson yet, and so I opened the chapel door, expecting (perhaps even hoping) to find the demon's clawed feet attached to Cram's ears. Instead, the demon flew right into my face and knocked me down.

A ball of pure fire flew through the air after the demon, hitting it square in the back. It dipped and ducked, but then regained control over its wings.

"Focus your thoughts! Aim, and blast. Again!" Cram shouted.

I had to roll out of the way to miss her blast of fire this time.

"Sorry!" she shouted.

The blast of fire seared the hair on the back of my neck, and a screech of pain escaped from the little demon. Now, I might be foolish to admit this part, but I confess there was a portion of me that felt bad for the little black malformed critter as it hit the ground in a puff of smoke and smoulder. It wasn't the little guy's fault that he got sucked into this reality by mistake.

The little demon wasn't done yet, though.

Now, I know you're not going to believe this, but it's absolutely true.

Without embellishment.

It sucked in a huge breath of the fire that had hit it in the face with a much deeper roar than usual. The creature expanded to the size of my head and its belly glowed red with flame through its flabby, black skin. When it opened its mouth, fire blasted out, returning all of the flames Her Excellency had sent after it.

And all aimed at me.

I pushed myself to my feet and ran toward the statue of Our

Lady of Tasmin, blessing myself like a good boy. "Can it even do that?" I yelled.

"Is that normal?" Her Excellency asked at the same time. "You never said they could do that."

"I didn't know they could," Cram insisted, in a very studious voice. "But, this leads me to believe that perhaps this is the cause of the teachings. If the demons can utilize elemental . . ."

"A little help, if you please," I said, very calmly, while being chased around a chapel's interior by a fire-breathing, now owl-sized demon.

"It shouldn't be able to do that!" Her Excellency insisted.

The demon demonstrated that, actually, it could do precisely that by breathing a line of fire down the length of the chapel, narrowly missing myself.

"Try hitting it again," Cram said.

I was screaming no, but they couldn't hear me over the sound of crackling flames, and Her Excellency hit the creature again. Again, it gulped the fire blast down. Its belly swelled and groaned, and the owl-sized demon became a pot belly pig-sized fire-breathing demon, with wings.

"Run, Dodd!" Cram shouted at me.

You might notice, dear reader, that at no point had Cram offered anything remotely helpful. Advice. A spell. Nothing.

Her Excellency's original fire display had caused this scenario, yes, but I could still easily take on an owl that spit fire. I could not, however, take on something half my size that could fly and breathe fire.

I completely and totally blame Walter Cram for the condition we found ourselves.

"Hurry, Dodd!" Cram shouted over the sounds of a burning ceiling beam collapsing.

As if I needed to be told to run when a fire-breathing demon was chasing me.

I cleared the chapel, and the demon chased me outside, happily breathing fire all over the place. I panted, desperate to catch my breath and get clean air into my lungs.

"He's getting away!" Cram shouted.

"Good," I said.

"No, we can't let it escape," Her Excellency said. "It could hurt innocent people."

"Perhaps we could find a way to harness it and . . ."

"No." That was it. I was putting my foot down. I would get the creature's attention so that the experts could kill it, but I was not risking my hide for Cram to put a harness on the thing like it was a horse.

No. I have limits and that was one of them.

"Fine. Fine. Don't be such a baby," Cram said. "Try to get its attention."

That part was easy. I threw a rock at the creature. It sailed wide, but the demon veered around and headed straight for me.

"Um, Cram?" I asked.

"Get inside the chapel!" Cram ordered.

"The chapel that is currently burning to the ground?" I asked, by way of polite clarification.

"Just run, Dodd! Do as you're told!"

I ran inside the burning, collapsing chapel, chased by a fire-breathing demon of our own creation. I blessed myself when I approached the altar, because honestly I needed all the divine luck possible as that damned demon happily caught the decorative curtains on fire along the back wall.

"Cram! Do something!" I shouted, dodging falling beams from the ceiling.

The demon and Cram both seemed uninterested by my situation and did nothing to assist. The demon's newfound power of fire was simply too exciting for its little brain to handle. Wooden pews went up in smoke. Wooden chairs did the same. Wooden chests for the worship items? Whoosh! It had found a new purpose in life, and while I was happy for its new discovery, I was against martyrdom as a general rule, and myself becoming one as a specific rule.

"Dodd!" Her Excellency shouted. "Run!"

"Run where?" I asked, since I was already running in circles as per Cram's original instructions. But politely, because I am a Consort and not some rebel elemental mage from the sticks.

"Run!" Cram shouted.

What in the abyss did they think I was doing in there? Serving the little guy tea cakes?

Then, I heard Cram shouting the litany he'd used when he tried to bring down the abbey. The bastard—Cram, this time—was going to pull the damn building down, open up the ground, suck the demon in, and then seal it up. With me still inside.

Run, indeed, I thought.

I ran for the entrance, dodging burning pews and beams alike. I was done with being bait. No more. Cram was literally an elemental mage on the run. It was in his title, so why in the abyss wasn't *he* in here chasing this stupid demon?

The floor shook violently but the demon didn't even notice—he was busy torching the place. Well, at least someone was happy.

"Hurry!" Her Excellency pleaded.

I was running as fast as possible, which was a difficult task when one was in a burning building with a newly-created fire demon. I only narrowly made it out by the grace of the Lord God Almighty, and by my own skills forged by training and wits.

I cleared the building just as a hole opened up in the ground and everything collapsed inside, demon, altar, Tasmin's statue. We will *not* discuss the loss of my second-best hat that I'd won fair and square without any cheating in a game of Three Card Poker against a bishop and two dukes back at Borro Abbey.

As I lay on the ground, panting and coughing, Cram said, "Good work, everyone."

"Good work? You two created a fire-breathing demon!" I exclaimed.

Cram shrugged. "I think this is important to know. The next time, we'll be ready for it."

I did not murder Walter Cram, demon whore, at that time, though I was sorely tempted. I will, however, take full credit in my persuasive and diplomatic ability, for twenty minutes later, we were headed toward the main road, toward Orsini, and toward safety.

(This is a true, accurate, and unembellished account of my dealings with a fire-breathing demon, Her Excellency Allegra, Countess of Marsina, and the self-described demon whore Walter Cram.)

Double or Nothing

Mara Malins

"ARE YOU SURE you want that to be your strategy?" Poole said, his sour breath wafting down my neck. I turned my head away, irritated, and focused on the hand. I shuffled through the cards once more, hesitating over two, before sliding one from the fan I was holding. I gave the figures listed at the bottom of the card a cursory glance (unnecessary since I had them all memorised) before tossing it onto the table.

Poole groaned in my ear. "You should have saved that one."

"Piss off, Poole, and let me be," I murmured, shoving him away with my shoulder. Poole immediately took a step backwards. His breath, soured by his constant chewing of salamander berries, was really distracting. I never chewed myself—precisely because of the bad breath—so having him breathe over my shoulder was starting to make my stomach turn.

Sitting opposite, the stone-like mass of Flick leaned forward to take a closer look at my card. He was so huge that watching him move was like watching an earthquake ripple through the Earth. Surprise rippled over his flat face but it was quickly shut down. "You sure you want to play that, old hoss?" His voice was as deep as a cavern.

I pushed my hair out of my eyes and nodded. "I am."

"You want to play the water hydra?"

"I do," I said, determined not to show the doubt starting to bloom in my stomach. As soon as I said the words confirming my move, the field over the table locked down. I heard it more than saw it. It made a high pitched *seeeeeuuuuutttt* noise, almost too high for me to hear. As soon as the table locked down, Flick grinned. My stomach started to clench.

"Oh man . . ." Poole whined. "He's got something planned."

"So do I," I said out of the corner of my mouth. Poole—an incredibly ugly man with acne erupting from the greasy skin of his cheekbones and temples—smiled. It was an honest smile, one he only ever used when he felt immense relief.

"You better," he answered, still smiling, "because I can't go back to the husband and tell him I've lost both of our ships betting on your sorry hide."

I didn't answer. Instead, I shoved my shoulder into him again, forcing him to move away. His breath was truly repellent and it was starting to piss me off. I stared over at Flick, who was staring back, a smile curling across his lips. The way he was looking at me reminded me of the way a hungry dog looked at a steak.

On the table, my card burst into flames, birthing a creature about ten inches high. I'd used this card only once before—and then only because the hand was certain—so I couldn't help but pull my eyes from Flick's stony face and admire the water hydra. It had nine wolfish heads, each snapping and snarling. Its legs were thick with muscle, its chest broad and strong. Water ran down its milky body in rivulets, pooling at its feet.

"What's your move, Flick?" I asked.

Flick took a quick sip of the oily black drink he was holding, then put the glass down on the side table. He selected a card and threw it down onto the table. Even before it hit the steel, I was leaning forward, craning my neck to see his choice. It was the Hiyoribō, the legendary spirit from Japan who stops rainfall.

I fist-pumped my triumph under the table, careful to keep my expression neutral. One of the things that aggressive card players like Flick *always* forgot was that the hydra's heads were separate beings. I was casting the equivalent of nine cards at once. It might not be the strongest card in terms of attack but whatever damage the hydra might take would only damage *one* of its heads. If it was enough to kill the head, well . . . *two* grew back in its place. Its defence was undeniable.

Behind him, I heard Poole whoop in victory.

The table gave another *seeeeeuuuuutttt* noise, locking both of our cards into the game, and Flick's Hiyoribō manifested itself as an old Japanese lady who carried an elegant Asian parasol over her shoulder. At the sight of her, my hydra threw back all nine heads and roared, though the sound was tinny, dampened by the shield. The old lady, hunched and crooked as she was, blinked mildly at the sound.

Flick raised his glass in my direction, saluting me. Then he raised his finger and touched the shield, starting the round. The Hiyoribō took a small step towards my great beast. Then another. Then another. When she got within a few inches, she held the parasol high into the air. I expected something hugely magical to happen, like a battle from *Lord of the Rings* or *Game of Thrones,* but instead a white mist started to creep from beneath the paper parasol. It edged towards the hydra slowly, like a fog coming down a steep mountainside.

As soon as it touched the hydra, an intense sizzling filled the air. The hydra's skin started to turn white and boil away. I watched with baited breath as the hydra roared in pain, gnashing its teeth in agony. The first of its nine heads melted away like a pat of butter in a pan, sizzling and spitting.

"My old lady never fails," Flick said, watching me and not the table. "I've been building her for years. She has the strength of nine hydra's . . . even if they all had nine heads."

Poole was moaning again, the victory he felt only moments ago already forgotten. "Just wait . . ." I whispered out of the corner of my mouth to him. "It's not over yet."

The hydra was still melting. The acidic mist had boiled away three of its heads and was showing no sign of stopping. I was starting to get nervous. "Just wait . . ." I mumbled again, more to myself this time.

Then it stopped.

The hydra had lost only four of its heads. And they were already growing back.

Over the table, I grinned at Flick, whose jaw was pulsing as he clenched his teeth in obvious anger. "Are you fucking kidding me?" He looked down at his glass and I wondered whether he might throw it against the wall.

On the table, the Hiyoribō bowed and took several steps backwards, her eyes lowered, waiting for the hydra's answering attack. At first the hydra just stood on the table, pawing at the steel with its foot.

"What're you waiting for? Stop wasting time." Flick growled at me. "Just do it."

I knew exactly what I was waiting for; the hydra needed all of its heads to grow back to ensure maximum damage. Did he think I was stupid, a level one player he could rush into making such a careless move? Not this time. Not with so much at stake. When the hydra was back to full strength, I raised a finger and touched the shield.

The hydra galloped forward, its nine heads snarling and snapping like rabid dogs. The Hiyoribō watched it come at her without flinching. Even as it tore into her, ripping the flesh from her muscles, she didn't utter a sound. When it was done, the hydra swaggered around the table. It hadn't left a single scrap of the Hiyoribō. There was nothing left for Flick to heal. He'd played that card for the last time.

"No!" Flick roared, clambering to his feet and throwing the glass he was holding against the wall, where it shattered into a thousand pieces. The viscous drink oozed down the bar brick, glinting beneath the florescent strips hanging overhead.

It looks like black blood, I thought. But even the unease I felt couldn't break through my triumph.

"Flick . . ." I started, then stopped when he whirled to face me, his expression tight with fury. I thought he might actually reach right across the table and pop me upside the head with his huge fist. I even squinted, waiting for the agony to come. But Flick's anger was always fleeting. *Quick to fight, quick to forget,* I thought, willing my heart to stop thudding.

He sat back down, already smiling that barely-there smile he had. "Double or nothing, old hoss. Double or nothing."

"No way," Poole hissed over my shoulder. "Tuttle will kill me. You know he will. For once, stop whilst you're ahead." The last was said in a lower voice, directly in my ear.

"What if I put up the fleet?" Flick asked, raising an eyebrow.

I swallowed. The need to meet the challenge was great, but Poole was right; I had to quit whilst I was ahead. I shook my head.

"Nuh-uh. I couldn't afford to run the fleet even if I won."

"What if I pay for the fuel for the first month?"

I shook my head, more hesitantly this time. "I'd still be as poor after the first month. I can't afford it."

"You can afford it, old hoss, I know how well you do at the games." His eyes locked on mine.

He was right; I'd become a very wealthy person over the last few years, winning round after round of the game. Partly because I was ballsier than any other person I knew and partly because I had a knack for playing the right card at the right moment. Most of the meatheads like Flick played aggressively, attacking on every round instead of alternating with defence when needed. It was like they wanted their cards to reflect the type of man they were; strong, aggressive, and violent.

That wasn't an issue for me.

"Maybe so," I said, standing up, as if to leave the table. "But I don't need your fleet."

"My cards then. How about winner takes all."

A silence so palpable that I could almost feel it descended on the room. Two other challengers nearby stopped their own game to listen in, their eyebrows almost meeting their hairlines in shock. Nobody *ever* wagered their entire stock of cards. The better cards took years to build up, and that didn't include the artefacts—the *rarest*—of the cards that could only be gifted to you by the mythical beast themselves, normally after a particularly strong game.

"Winner takes all?" I said slowly, as if I hadn't heard him correctly.

"Winner takes all," he repeated. He leaned back in his stone chair as if he was completely at ease—as if he hadn't just offered the wager of all wagers.

A wager I wanted to take.

"How many you got?" I asked, attempting to stall. I was stupid for even considering it, maybe if I gave myself a few moments I would see it for what it was and not want to snatch Flick's hand.

"Forty-eight in total."

I sucked in a shocked breath. That was a colossal number of cards! I had a large collection myself but at twenty-seven it was just over half of Flick's. If I wanted, I could sell half and spend the rest of my days living off the profits.

Flick was watching me. "How many do you have, old hoss?"

I swallowed. There was no way he would take the bet for my collection. "Twenty-seven."

Flick turned to Poole behind me. "And you?"

Poole held his hands up in a gesture of submission. "Count me out, my friend. I got my ships back, that's enough gambling for me for one day."

Flick's stony face rippled into what I thought was a smile. "How many?"

"Twenty."

Flick turned back to me. Now he was actually *grinning*. "Well, what do you know. Between the both of you, we have an equal wager. If you win, you walk away with an extra twenty-four cards each."

"And if you win, you have the biggest card cache this side of the planet," I said, my heart pounding so heavily in my chest I was sure the challengers either side of our table could hear it. I was like a junkie, desperate to take the hit of the bet. My mouth was actually watering at the thought. When I glanced at Poole, he was watching me warily, already shaking his head.

"No man," he said. "Count me out."

I grabbed him by the elbow and drew him over to the corner of the room, aware that every pair of eyes followed us. "Listen, Poole . . ."

"No. I know what you're going to say but the answer is no. Tuttle would kill me."

"You owe me," I whispered savagely, hating how ruthless the words sounded. Yes, he owed me but I'd promised I'd never call in that debt . . . and yet here I was, desperate to take the gamble. If I won, I would be the ultimate winner. There would never be another bet like this. Almost fifty cards? It's the stuff of legends.

"Think about it, man; there's no way a man like Flick would ever risk his cache unless winning was certain. He has something up his sleeve. You know he does. We *will* lose." We locked eyes for a long moment and I could read his agony there. Just like me, he *wanted* to do this, but he was too afraid. The smell of his fear was as ripe as his breath. I needed to reassure him.

"I never lose."

"Neither does Flick. Listen, I always back you. You know I do. But your need to win . . . it's too much this time. I can't back you.

Not against him."

"I'll use *it*," I said, my tone so low that I could barely hear the words myself. But Poole heard. His eyes widened.

"You will?"

I nodded. "It's made for times like this. We can't lose. Are you in?"

His face split into a huge grin, his fear burned away with the heat of my promise. "Fuck yeah I'm in. Let's do this."

"OKAY. THREE ROUNDS. Winner takes all." Flick said, announcing the rules to the crowd that had gathered around our table. There were at least two hundred people here—more than the room could legally hold. Every inch of space was taken, every seat occupied. Even the tables and bar were crammed with people, all elbowing their neighbours to get a better view. Nobody was really listening to Flick; they were too busy placing their own wagers on the outcome of the game with chancers who'd heard about the challenge. Others were shouting at the harassed-looking barman for drinks. I bet he'd never seen his hall so full of people.

Nervous, I sat at the table surveying the room and sipping a glass of burning liquid. Flick had poured me an oily fingerful of whatever he was drinking. "To calm your nerves," he said as he slid the glass over to me. It was vile, whatever it was, but it was free and the burning in my chest soothed my nerves.

The ultimate gamble.

Flick raised a spade-like hand and the rumble in the room quieted. The excitement was so electric that the air crackled like moments before a storm. "Three rounds. Winner takes all," Flick repeated.

"Winner takes all," I said, my lips numb.

Flick's eyes darted over to mine. The corners of his mouth curled up and I knew he was about to announce something unplanned. I held my breath as he said, "And we'll play the element of fire."

There was a moment of absolute silence and then the room broke into an excited roar. If we played the fire element, it meant only fire or ice demons could be used. Water and air would be nullified. Normally, that would cut any deck in half, if the player was savvy enough to keep the elements equal in his deck. I wasn't savvy; I liked playing water, which meant my playable deck had been reduced to a paltry seven cards.

Seven cards . . .

Shit.

Ironically, my blood turned to ice. My chances had been significantly reduced. I blinked, considering Flick's announcement. Poole met my eyes, his own fear as clear as day in his expression. He knew of my preference for water. Flick looked over to me, his expression smug. He was hoping that he'd unsettled me so, to prove a point, I gave an approving nod. "If that's how you want to play it, fire's more than fine with me."

I'm sure I saw his smile falter a little. Maybe I imagined it, I don't know. But even the thought that I'd unsettled him made my confidence soar. I could do this. I didn't need seven cards; I needed three well-played ones. I leaned forward, smiling. "Okay, your round first."

"Oh no," Flick answered, wagging a meaty finger at me as if I was a naughty school child. "You first, old hoss."

"Not a chance," I said, meaning it. I would walk away from the table before that happened. "The challenger always lays first. You know that. Besides, I went first in the last round."

Flick leaned back in his chair, one arm slung over the headrest. He looked calm, at ease . . . and yet I saw the beads of sweat gathering on his upper lip. "Very well." He pulled his cards out of his breast pocket and started to rifle through them. He organised them between his fingers like a pro-poker player, creating an ordered deck. Then he selected one, gave me a quick glance, slid it back into the pack and then picked another card instead. He threw it down on the table.

Every part of my body wanted to lean in and scrutinise the card like an overeager newbie but if Flick was going to play it cool then so was I. I darted my eyes to the card on the table, taking in as much detail as I could in the quickest time possible. My chest unlocked slightly at what I saw.

Flick had laid down the Santelmo, the Philippine spirit that roamed the world in the form of a fireball. The strength and magic skills were high, as expected, but the defence was mediocre. It was a good card, but Flick seemed to be sticking to his aggressive strategy.

"Are you sure?" I asked, giving him the chance to backtrack, though I wanted him to stick with this card. When he said he was, the table locked in with that high pitched *seeeeeuuuuutttt* noise. He touched the shield and the card burst into flames. The flames climbed higher and higher until they formed a vaguely human shape. A few of the people nearby gasped at the sight.

I drew out my own deck and pulled out all the cards I could no longer play, sliding them back into my breast pocket. I was left holding my seven cards. Seeing my poor hand, Flick's face broke into a smug grin. I ignored him. I read each of my cards over before selecting my choice; the Wondjina, the aboriginal weather demon that was element-less. I tossed it onto the table with a careless flick of my hand and whispered, "Fire."

With no fanfare, a humanoid figure climbed out of the card. It was strangely ethereal, with two huge black eyes that dominated the head. It was half the size of the Santelmo. Flick looked at my beast and threw his head back, barking a short and sharp laugh. "That's it?" he scoffed. "That's going take down my Santelmo?"

I didn't answer. I pressed my finger to the shield and activated the battle. The Wondjina walked towards the first beast with almost no presence at all. It looked as if a child was approaching an experienced fighter. I held my breath as it came to a stop before the Wondjina, the huge black eyes staring blindly through its opponent. Suddenly, it bent at the waist and charged. It struck the middle of the Santelmo, sending it flying into the shield, where it bounced off and crumpled into a fiery bundle. The room gasped, and then applauded, thinking it was over. But even I knew the Santelmo wasn't destroyed.

Sure enough, the Santelmo got to its feet almost immediately, though it staggered a little as it did. The Wondjina stood back, the fabric of its strange painted clothing smouldering where it had touched the Santelmo. I calculated the damage in my head; it'd probably lost around ten percent of its XP but that was okay.

"Here we go," Flick said, watching as the Santelmo approached my demon. Toe-to-toe, it came to a stop and started to move its limbs in a strangely elegant way. Even from outside of the shield, I could smell the flames in the air. It grew and grew until the beast flung its arms out, sending a huge ball of fire into my Wondjina. Beside me, Poole cried out in anguish.

Nothing could be seen on the table except fire. The intense heat washed over us like the aftermath of a bomb. I felt my hair tickle my cheeks. Eyes still on the table, I tossed my head back and flicked it away impatiently.

"Is it over?" Poole asked. "Did we get owned?"

"Absolutely not," I said with a confidence I didn't entirely feel. But I was justified; as the flames died down, the Wondjina was there. It was on its knees, its pale skin bubbling from the heat, but it was there. Flick let out a roar of impatience. I barely noticed; I was too busy calculating in my head. The attack had probably taken seventy—maybe eighty—of its hit points. With the ten it'd lost previously, it meant I *should* still have enough for the last attack.

Just as before, the Wondjina bowed from the waist and charged. Just like before, it sent the Santelmo flying into the shield. But this time it didn't get up.

"Fuck sake!" Flick pounded his fist into the steel chair he was sitting in. I noticed with alarm that it bent beneath his strength.

Poole was clapping me on the back, his happiness making him over eager. "Yes. One round down."

"Yes, one round," Flick answered, his eyes dark and hard. "But we have two more yet. That was just a warm up."

"Let's go then."

"Your draw."

I decided to play it bold and call the fieriest of all the fiery beasts; the salamander. I'd spent years building this card up. Salamanders were notorious for being defensive cards but mine was the strongest I'd ever come across. I threw it down and watched as my salamander, my faithful old friend, prowled around the table, breathing fire into the air.

"Look at the size of that," a man nearby breathed. "Mine own salamander ain't half the size."

"Size doesn't mean everything, old hoss" Flick said. There were a few good-natured cheers, and a few calls of, "depends what you got, Flick!" Flick ignored them all and tossed his card lazily onto the table. A huge fire giant—the biggest I'd ever seen—climbed from the card, immediately making a lie of his words. The creatures sparred back and forth, getting more and more aggressive as time went on, but eventually my salamander was pummelled into a fleshy pulp. It was close but I'd lost.

"Fuck," I yelled, leaping to my feet and stalking away from the table. I took a few calming breaths and then returned, my heart pounding in my chest. My stomach was squirming with anxiety and I wondered if I might throw up. I still thought I had this in the bag though, even if the last round hadn't gone as planned.

"Looks like this is getting interesting, no?" Flick said, rubbing his hands together.

I shrugged. "Well, I didn't want it to be too easy. People would say I'd robbed you."

"Robbed?" Flick barked that laugh again. "You sound confident."

"I am."

He picked up his glass of liquor and took a sip, surveying me over the rim. "Confident enough to up the stakes?"

"No," Poole immediately interjected.

I held up a hand to him, silencing him. "What's your bet, Flick? What could you possibly want more than our cards?"

"You, of course."

The silence in the room was absolute for a full ten seconds. Then sound crashed in around me so loud that I actually flinched from it. A wave of self-consciousness went through my body so cold that I froze. I stared at him blankly, my expression cold and stiff. It wasn't often that I was taken by surprise. "Me? What are you talking about?"

Flick was studying my face. "Come on, old hoss, you might play men's games but we can all see that beauty you try to hide. That *fiery* beauty," he breathed.

"What . . ." Then I shut my mouth with a snap. My blood ran cold when I realised that I'd been set up. Flick had deliberately goaded this challenge, had deliberately risen the stakes, to drive me to this point. He knew that I wouldn't turn down the challenge.

"If I win the next round," Flick continued, oblivious to my thoughts, "then you become my wife."

I cocked a disbelieving eyebrow at him, as if my stomach wasn't twisting unpleasantly. "And if I win? What on Earth could you offer me that would tempt me to make such a ridiculous wager."

"I'll not only give you all my cards but you can have every last penny of my wealth too." He held up his credit-stick, the device that held all his wealth. Not many people were so rich that they had to use a credit-stick. Most people, like myself, traded in food and fuel. On the rare occasion we had coppers, we didn't have them for long. A credit-stick like that would have pounds and pounds on it. My mouth practically watered at the sight.

But I made myself act cool. "You think I'm going to believe for one second that you'll hand everything over to me?"

His tone turned to ice. "I've just publicly declared that I would. And I always keep my word."

I bowed my head, as if thinking about his offer, but I knew in my heart that I'd already made up my mind; of course I would take the wager. I *always* took the wager. And this was the biggest one of all; my life. This would become legend.

"Don't be stupid . . ." Poole mumbled, his breath wafting down my neck. "Don't even think about it."

I lifted my head. "Deal."

ONE LAST ROUND. One last card.

Neither of us studied our cards. At this point, we both know what our strategy would be. We'd known it from the first moment we agreed to the wager. The first two rounds were warm ups only. It was this one that counted.

The room was so tense now that no man talked. All eyes were on our table, on our faces, trying to read whether they had bet on the right horse. But the books were closed. There could be no backing out now.

For anyone.

With a quick glance at Poole, I reached into my breast pocket and withdrew my wildcard; the artefact. It was the only artefact I'd ever seen first-hand, though I knew of people who said they'd had them and sold them on for staggering profit. I'd kept hold of mine, after being gifted it from my salamander years before. It seemed fitting that I use it in the battle where I'd lost my favourite card. This precious gift could only be used once but it would let me combine two cards together. I'd have twice the strength. Twice the defence.

Twice the power.

As soon as I withdrew it, the room *oooohhed.* Two people actually sighed at the sight of it, as if they'd never seen anything so beautiful when in fact it was just a silver disc, the shape and size of a coin. I flipped it high into the air—two hundred pairs of eyes following it—and then caught it again.

"Name your cards," Flick said, emotionless. I could almost

taste his failure.

I threw my cards towards the table; two high level dragons. As fiery as fiery could be. The cards fused in the air, snapping together as if they were magnets. It fluttered to the table, where it exploded into the most beautiful winged creature I'd ever seen. Its scales shimmered with every colour imaginable, its long, sinewy neck stretched out and breathed flames into the air. It glanced around, sniffing at the air, its ruby eyes searching for prey like a hunter.

"A dragon?" Flick said disdainfully. "A fucking dragon?" He rolled his eyes.

I shrugged. "You wanted fire."

"I always do, sweetheart." His eyes locked on mine and darkened. "Okay, let's make things interesting." He reached into his own breast pocket . . .

And my entire body froze.

Hell, the entire room froze.

Horrified, I watched as he withdrew his own artefact, flipping it into the air just as I had done. Where his face had been emotionless before, now it fucking *quivered* with smugness. He met my eyes, "You didn't think I'd risk losing, did you? With my wealth and a wife at stake?"

"Oh man . . ." Poole moaned. "Oh man . . ."

I swallowed down my rising panic. But even beneath the panic, I could feel my excitement. I would never admit it to anyone but *this was it*. The big one. Two artefacts. There would never be another round like this one. I swallowed. "Choose your cards."

He spent a long time deliberating over his cards, first sliding out one, and then another, until finally he tossed his selection down, one by one. "The Hikeshibaba," he announced as the first one fluttered onto the table.

The Japanese lady who extinguishes lamps.

"And the Metee-kolen-ol. The ice wizards."

His fusing wasn't nearly as dramatic as mine but it was more . . . sinister. A puddle that was as black and as viscous as Flick's drink started to spread on the steel of the table, sending out icy fingers. Out of the liquid came an old, withered hand. The fingers were short and shriven, the nails chewed bloody. It was attached to an even older and more withered woman who climbed from the liquid as if climbing out of a pool. The wizard followed next. He was as short as a dwarf and the shift he wore was grey and threadbare. They were holding hands, their fingers fused with ice.

The dragon saw them and backed up, hissing. Two short plumes of smoke burst from its nostrils like steam from a kettle but it didn't breathe fire. Flick's smile stretched further. "We can discuss surrender if you don't want to lose your cards?"

I shook my head. "Never."

"Then game on."

IT WAS SLOW. So slow.

The strange, stoic couple moved towards the dragon, their hands linked, their expressions mild. The dragon continued to back away, hissing and growling like an afraid dog. Its obsidian eyes were so wide that I could see the reflection of the wizard and the old lady staring back at me.

"Dear god . . ." Poole moaned, and for once I barely noticed the warm waft of his sour breath down the back of my neck.

As if at a cock-fight, the room started to cheer, boo, shake fists, swear, and scream—hungry for the battle to start.

But still the dragon had done nothing but snort smoke.

"What's wrong with it?" Poole asked.

My mouth was dry. I swallowed. "I . . ."

"You've made it too powerful, wife," Flick taunted. "It can't fight because the second it touches my creatures, it will die. Ice on fire will do that. And it can't use its fiery breath because it's so strong that it will end up burning itself up right alongside the couple," he said, pointing to where the couple were still making their slow procession across the table.

Shit, he was right.

The dragon, the most powerful card that was ever created, was powerless.

Agonised, I watched as the dragon took one step backwards for every step the couple took towards it. It hissed, warning them, but did nothing more. Soon, they were going around and around the table, nobody winning and nobody losing. Stalemate.

"Can't somebody make them fight?" a man to the left of me yelled. He was an ugly man with no front teeth. I wanted to punch what few teeth he *did* have remaining.

"They can't do anything on the table," another man answered.

On the table.

Adrenaline poured through my entire body, setting my nerves on fire. Had it ever been done before? Had anything ever broken through the shield? It was that dragon's—and my—only chance. I leaned forward and brought my fist down on the centre of the shield. Immediately I got a zap of electricity, not enough to hurt me but enough to make my fingers tingle. I did it again and again. The only time anyone could touch the shield was to lock in and start the round. But my action did the trick, the dragon saw me pounding the shield and started to rip at it with its claws.

"You can't do that," Flick roared, jumping to his feet.

"I bloody well can," I answered beneath my breath. Then, louder, "I'm not marrying you. Not for anything."

The shield was starting to lose power now, and was flapping around like a sheet on a washing line. It was then that I noticed the couple sneaking up on the dragon, linked hands outstretched. "Watch out!" I screamed.

But it was too late. Their clasped fingers lightly brushed the base of the dragon's tail. The dragon threw back its head and roared, sending a giant plume of flame into the air. The shield was so weak now that most of it got through, though it dispersed like smoke through lace. The heat was instant. Choking. Two people on the front row screamed and dropped to the floor, thrashing around in an attempt to put out the flames that burst to life on their clothes.

The dragon itself wasn't too badly harmed. The scales that had been touched by the strange couple had turned stark white, like frost burn, but I thought the damage was no more than fifteen or twenty percent. It's still had most of its XP remaining.

The dragon recovered swiftly from its agony. It looked around, locked eyes with the strange couple, opened its mouth and then . . .

Oh god.

The heat was intense. So intense that it took my breath away and the temperature in the room skyrocketed. Those of us nearest the table stumbled backwards, away from that burning wind. Through squinted eyes, I saw the angry fiery cloud envelop everything beneath the shield and then burst through it, shattering the forcefield as if it was glass.

I couldn't breathe! The one gasping breath I took burned the inside of my throat and lungs, and I started to cough, clawing at the skin of my neck. Through the choking smoke I could see several silhouettes scrambling away from the table. The fire raced up their arms, up their necks, consuming everything there was to burn. The smell of crisped hair—of crisped *skin*—hung cloyingly in the air.

The chair I was on suddenly melted beneath my weight and I crashed to the floor. I lay there, dazed for a moment, unable to breathe, wondering distantly if I was going to die, when a pair of arms wrapped around my chest and hauled me upright. "Move!" And I knew from the sour stink breaking through the smoke that it was Poole. I'd never been so glad to smell his breath in my life. "Move, goddammit, before we all crisp!" he yelled.

He half carried, half dragged me away from the table and towards the door at the back of the room. The entire place was engulfed in flames. Something swooped through the fire and dove at me, roaring. I felt something leathery swipe at my ear and I knew it was my dragon; it was free and it was angry.

Overhead, the lights shattered in the intense heat, sprinkling glass down onto the chaos, but it didn't matter; the room was lit by spears of ferocious flame jetting at the people over and over again. I heard screeching and wailing, so high pitched that it was impossible not to imagine the agony. I'm glad that I couldn't see through the acrid smoke. I'm glad I couldn't see the terror.

"Oh god . . ." I heard Poole almost sob.

I coughed. "W . . . what?"

"The door . . . it's too . . ."

I felt Poole slide to the floor next to me, his feet tangling with mine. I could hear him choking and gasping but there was nothing I could do to help him. I grasped at the door, desperately trying to find the handle. As soon as my fingers touched the burning steel I hissed and snatched my hand back. The handle was so hot that I was sure I'd left half of my flesh melted to the steel.

"Oh god . . ." I was sobbing now. I sank to the floor besides my friend, knowing I was going to die. There was nothing in the world except unimaginable heat and smoke. And the smell of burning flesh. Gasping for breath, I rolled onto my side and watched as the world burned.

WHEN I NEXT opened my eyes, I saw nothing but a greasy film

that had settled over my eyeballs. I had to blink once, twice, and then a third time before it cleared and I could see the destruction that I'd caused. The entire bar was nothing but a few melted steel beams sticking up from the ground. The stone walls were nothing but dust and rubble.

I was so weak. I raised my head, wincing as the boulders in my skull rolled around, to see a few others lying on the floor, some still unconscious, some awake and moaning. Of the few hundred that were in the bar, I could see maybe eleven or twelve still alive. The rest were blowing away on the warm summer breeze.

"Wh . . ." My voice came out as a hoarse whisper. I licked my lips and tried again. "What?"

"You're alive then, are you?" Poole said from beside me, his voice as hoarse as mine. I rolled my head to look at him; he looked as bad as I felt. What little clothes he had left were burned and hanging by threads. The skin on his face had blistered and melted until I could see the white bone peeping through. One arm had completely burned off, the other hung useless at his side. He was as bald as an egg, his hair crisped away.

"I guess . . ." I swallowed the painful burn in my throat. "The dragon?"

"Gone."

I nodded, expecting nothing less. "The old couple?"

"Gone as well. We released monsters into the world just so you could . . ." He coughed. "Just so you could win your fucking bet. Take a look around. Take a look at what you did. Was it worth it?"

FLICK WAS ONE of the first to die. Witnesses say he was still clutching the credit-stick when the dragon's flames enveloped him. Though nobody saw anything other than a great plume of fire, I can't help but imagine his clothes combusting and his skin melting from his bones. I can't help but imagine him drawing in a huge breath to scream but inhaling nothing but fire. I see it in my dreams.

Later, when the dust of the burned bodies had settled and the Night of the Dragon Cards became legend, I had to ask myself whether I knew what would happen when I combined those two cards together. I'd like to say categorically not. I'd like to say that I was doing nothing but playing the game, raising the stakes. *Placing the ultimate wager.*

But a part of me wonders.

I defeated him in the end. I am unbeaten. The ultimate card player. I hold the title and I doubt anybody will ever take it from me now.

Who will challenge me, knowing the lengths I will go to win?

A Girl, Ablaze with Life

Claude Lalumière

WAVES OF HEAT radiate from her belly; waves of sweat slither down her skin. A diffuse and fiery pain seeps deep into her bones, as though they were all about to shatter—but they never do. Instead, as she endures this cyclical ordeal, her skeleton eventually acquires a spongy quality, as if it were melting and making her body as malleable as that of her children.

The new one is coming. Flames burst through the pores of her skin and envelop her but do not consume her. She must fight the temptation to wholly surrender to these incandescent sensations; the process of creation requires her focused will, her engaged imagination. Her loins burn as her child tunnels its way into the world. At the precise moment of the explosion between her legs, all pain is extinguished. Creation leaves her weak, yes, but her body is resilient, and she remains the same as ever, bones unbroken, skin unsinged. Her body never deteriorates, never betrays any evidence of aging.

Her newborn hovers unsteadily above her, its fiery multicoloured wings flapping awkwardly to keep it aloft, its barbed tail snaking through the dawn breeze. The wisps of flame that tease out of its nose and mouth bespeak its fiery origins.

Even its eyes are ablaze. After a few moments, the girl's offspring gains confidence in its ability to navigate the air, and it flies away, never having given a moment's notice to its mother. It will find others of its kind; all of them will be considerably older. It has been many births since she shaped one of her children into a dragon.

The girl—the only human on Earth—sits up and settles into a lotus position, facing the water. The silky sand luxurious against her skin, she basks in the view and scents of the sea. She spends all day like this, ignoring the occasional pleading whimpers that escape from the dogs who not so patiently wait for her at the edge of the beach. Finally, as the sun sets and the temperature drops, she shivers. She gets up and walks toward her retinue of hellhounds. The dogs spring to attention, their tails wagging, the breath of their triple heads aflame with excitement and anticipation. There are so many of them. Unlike her other children, hellhounds never leave her side. Sometimes their ceaseless company is a burden, but other times it is her greatest source of comfort.

She nestles among her dogs for warmth. Around her the hundreds of dogs form a tight circle. The girl falls asleep and dreams of Fire . . .

. . . The girl's first memory is of waking to Fire, and Fire feeding her the flames of knowledge. Information came to her in disparate snippets, not all of which she has ever fully understood. This fount of knowledge replays itself incessantly in her dreams . . .

. . . Before the advent of life, Fire had raged across the world, creating and destroying, destroying and creating, with primal abandon, without purpose or plan. That primordial world of Fire underwent constant incandescent metamorphosis. The planet cooled down—slowly, gradually, imperceptibly, but over a long stretch of time it eventually cooled enough so as to dampen Fire's ardour, and it came to be that Fire slept. (The reawakened Fire is much tamer than its primordial incarnation, the girl muses in her dream.)

. . . The girl was born of a human mother, a woman more physically mature than the unchanging and unaging girl has ever been. She was born at the precise moment when Fire consumed the entire surface world; in that instant Fire fed the girl for the first time—fed her the flames of metamorphosis. For thirteen years, as her infant body matured to pubescence, the girl slept, the flames of metamorphosis remoulding her into a suitable mate for Fire. Once she awoke, her body stopped aging, and forever remained the same. (Sometimes, the girl wonders why she was chosen, among all the babies of all the creatures on the planet that were born at that precise moment when Fire consumed the world that was, but this question never lingers, because she knows the answer: Fire acts spontaneously, randomly, impulsively without consideration or design.)

. . . There are seven types of children that Fire urges the girl to create. Cherufes are not born fully formed; after a potential cherufe bursts from the girl's loins as raging fire, it only adopts its final shape once it merges with a sufficient number of rocks so as to fashion a body, at which point the bulky fiery creature starts tunnelling into the bowels of the planet, never to be seen on the surface again (what are they up to in their subterranean world?). The humanoid horned devils congregate in covens, whispering to each other in a language unknown to the girl (as babies, devils are the most adorable of all her children—with tiny horn buds, oversize hooves, and random patches of crimson fur—but as they mature they take on a terrifying mien). The dragons are winged reptiles who, once every century, hunt and feed on other fire children (nevertheless, the girl cannot resist the temptation to create these merciless yet alluring predators). The hellhounds never leave their mother (so loyal but so needy). The ifreets—born as living, flickering flame—grow to become mischievous pranksters whose shape is in constant transformation (an ifreet loves to disguise itself as any other types of firechild and sow confusion and discord with its aberrant behaviour). The phoenixes are firebirds of exquisite beauty, their fiery plumage displaying every colour of the spectrum (only rarely does the girl espy one of her phoenix children in the distant sky; each new phoenix stays with her until the next sunrise after its birth but then flies away for parts unknown). The salamanders are tiny fire lizards who scurry everywhere, even in the water (they feed on fish). (Fire had not imagined an eighth type, the girl's earliest children, whom the girl loves most of all, although they are rather dim-witted, with only scant traces of will or sentience.)

. . . The long-dormant Fire was reawakened by humanity, the species from which Fire plucked the girl. Human scientists from various nations raced to create a weapon more powerful than those of the other nations, so that their own people might reign supreme. Such a weapon was devised—a weapon of fire that drew its energy from Fire itself, although the human creators of the weapon did not fully understand what energies they had tapped into. And thus did the world end in Fire. And thus was the world reborn in Fire . . .

WHEN SHE AWAKES at sunrise, the hellhounds have scattered, intimidated by the presence of their father.

Fire teases the girl. Caresses her flesh. Ignites her senses. Stirs her hungers.

But the girl isn't ready. Not yet. Not so soon. She shoos Fire away. She runs to her dogs. The hellhounds run with her. All day long, the girl roams and plays with her pack of dog children.

EVERY DAY, FIRE presents itself to the girl. But the memories of the ordeal of creation overpower her growing hungers. Every day, she ignores Fire.

ONCE AGAIN, THE girl can no longer withstand the hungers. Her body growls for sustenance and for communion. Only Fire can satiate her.

Today, she does not spurn Fire.

Fire envelops her, its flames cascading across her flesh, it bursting into her orifices. It satisfies her needs for nutriments and pleasure and sparks life within her womb.

One lunar cycle from now, the girl will once again give birth, will once again give shape and life to a fire creature.

WHENEVER THE GIRL is pregnant from Fire's seed, the hellhounds are wary around her. They still follow her, but they don't nip at her heels, don't rub their coarse pelt against her skin, don't cuddle with her at night. What the dogs fear is unclear to the girl.

While climbing a scorched hill—the entire world, save for the seas and rivers and lakes, is scorched—the girl comes across a gaggle of some of her oldest children, from before she had perfected the art of wilful creation. Amorphous globs of floating fire, like miniature misshapen suns. She has never given a name to this most beloved species of her offspring. The name of the other species came to her with the fire of knowledge, and she knew then and forever that those were the children Fire wanted. But these shapeless anonymous beings . . . even though their creation required Fire's seed, they are hers and hers alone. Fire has no interest in them.

She beckons to her most ancient children, and they flock to her, bouncing on and off her skin. Their flames tickle her. She laughs, overwhelmed with joy.

The nearby hellhounds bark in jealousy, chasing away the primal children.

The girl reprimands the pack, but she knows they cannot help themselves. Nevertheless, she endeavours to lose the dogs, at least for a little while. In the distance, she sees a river. The dogs follow her to the shore. She dives and swims across.

The hellhounds shun water. They whimper at the girl. But she ignores their pleading. And away she goes. In time, the dogs will find her again. They always do.

Her next creation will not be a hellhound. She has enough dogs. More than enough.

THE GIRL LONG ago ritualized childbirth. She has once again sought a beach for the coming of her new firechild. The tangy aroma of brine and the gentle pulsing sounds of the waves soothe the inner fires that rage within her at the onset of creation. She seeks out solitude for these events. But occasionally, as in this instance, some of her children intrude.

In the distance, she hears the whines of her ever-needy hellhound retinue. In the sky above, a dozen-strong wing of dragons flies by. Fire-red salamanders pulse through the sand around her. And playing on the beach is a lone ifreet, mimicking and mocking her, imitating her shape, but with a pregnant belly of ridiculously huge proportions. The ifreet farts shoots of fire from its mock vagina.

She laughs at her ifreet child's puerile antics, but soon the ordeal of creation overwhelms her senses. Once again, heat radiates from her belly; sweat slithers down her skin. That familiar diffuse and fiery pain seeps deep into her bones.

The new one—still malleable, still unrealized—is coming. The girl must focus, must will her fiery foetus into a viable fire creature.

The pregnant girl thinks fondly of her amorphous early children; she wonders about the fate of her enigmatic phoenixes and the life of the subterranean cherufes; she wishes her devils would not spurn her so after reaching maturity. She has had enough of all of these. And enough salamanders. Enough ifreets. Enough dragons. And certainly enough hellhounds.

She yearns for a change in her long routine as firemother. The mimicry of her trickster child has given her an idea.

In a chaotic blaze, a new child explodes out of the girl's core.

A child in her own image. A baby girl, ablaze with life.

THE NEW FIRECHILD needs the girl's constant attention. For the first few days of her new motherhood, the girl is filled with love for the new being, this miniature fiery version of herself. But soon the intensity of the attention required by the baby, who is needier by far than even her relentless hellhounds, tires the girl. Has she made a mistake? This is not the change she had envisioned, this constant nurturing. Whenever the girl's attention wavers, the firechild cries, its wails strident and intolerable.

Still, she perseveres. Her previous firechildren of various species grew and matured after birth. So, too, will this one. Who knows what might happen then? The girl is consumed with curiosity.

And the new firechild nurtures her mother as well. Every night, as they fall asleep together, as the firechild nurses at the girl's small breasts, she inserts a finger, two fingers, sometimes an entire hand into her mother's mouth. Sparks of living flame escape from the child's fingers, feeding the girl.

FIRE WAITS LONGER than usual to come courting for communion with the girl but eventually the moment is here; the girl, however, has no yearning for Fire and Fire's attentions, has no desire for another child. Her new firechild is both all she can cope with and all she needs.

FIRE COMES AGAIN and again, always rebuffed by the girl. Eventually, by the time the new firechild is a toddler, Fire's patience comes to an end.

Fire ignores the girl's protestations. The sensuality of Fire's flames against her flesh tempts the girl; she almost gives in, but then she yells and pushes Fire away.

Fire leaves her alone. At least, for now.

The girl has lost track of her daughter. She looks to her hellhounds: there she is. Around her daughter, the hellhounds have formed layers and layers of protective rings.

THE GIRL'S DAUGHTER now spends much of her time playing with the hellhounds. What a relief to have the attentions of her neediest children focused on each other rather than on herself. Still, every night, mother and child nurture each other, feed each other.

IT HAS BEEN a year since Fire last visited the girl, and now Fire has returned.

Fire burns with fury and sets upon the girl with no warning, with none of the usual teasing play. This time, there is no sensuality to the contact of Fire's flames against her skin—only hurt. Try as she might, she cannot push Fire away. She screams, but Fire ignores her.

A horde of hellhounds attack Fire, freeing the girl from Fire's grasp. Fire burns with yet greater fury. Instantly dozens of the attacking hellhounds are reduced to cinders, the rest of them cowed into submission.

The girl runs to her daughter, takes her by the hand, and together they flee from Fire. The girl senses a change in her daughter. As they are holding hands, as they run, the firechild ages, until she becomes an exact fiery replica of her mother. The surface of their touching palms yields, as if there were no longer any separation between mother and daughter.

As Fire attacks, the mother and daughter complete the process of merging into one being. The composite firegirl screams, her screams made of such powerful flame that Fire is momentarily rebuffed.

Fire's rage mounts, strength and power building to an apocalyptic crescendo.

Now that mother and daughter are one, the firegirl is now connected to all her children. To her thousands upon thousands of offspring. And she calls upon them all. And they all come to her.

The ifreets steal portions of Fire's flames, diminishing their father's power.

A gaggle of her primordial blob children form a shield, protecting her from Fire's onslaught.

Out of the ground the cherufes emerge, lobbing mud and stone at their father.

Breathing destructive flames, the dragons soar toward Fire.

The remaining army of hellhounds chase Fire away.

Covens of devils chant various spells to contain and bind Fire.

The salamanders slither together to form a giant lizard that shreds Fire apart.

And the phoenixes, who had been flying the spaceways between planets, return to Earth to consume the last shreds of their sire.

TOGETHER, THE FIREGIRL and her children are building a city, a city that spans the breadth of the entire planet. A city of fire and earth. A city imagined by the girl.

The devils are the architects; the hellhounds dig the foundations; the chefures erect the structures; the dragons transport materials; the salamanders craft the fine detail work; the ifreets provide entertainment for the labourers.

And the phoenixes travel the universe, to guide space travellers to this new Earth, as potential citizens of the firegirl's metropolis.

As for those gaggles of primordial blobs, the firegirl's first and oldest children, they do the most important thing: they bounce around aimlessly, hovering near her, bringing her joy.

Light My Fire

Susan MacGregor

YOU'D THINK TIME would have little meaning for us. Those of us who are content to remain as we are, fiery butterflies who flit between sunlight and shadow, or demons who dip tongues into the nectar of mortality, aren't much affected by it. But time becomes a problem when you're ensnared by an even greater mystery than yourself. When that happens, wings falter, immortality loses its appeal, and you fade from what you once were.

Many of us were drawn to America in the '60s—a time of mass immigration. The diabolics, in particular, flew east to lap up the excesses of the Vietnam War. For me, blood held little appeal. The new music of California, the mind-blowing drugs, and the unfettered life-style were more exciting. I wanted to be a part of it, so I went to L.A.

Some humans burn brighter than others. He was one of the shining ones. All fae adore beauty—even the leeches who seek to destroy it. His eyes were close-set with pupils so huge I wanted to swim in those dark tides forever. His lips were as curved as a young god's—perhaps he had a touch of Dionysus about him, although the gods had long since departed from the world. For several nights, I watched him drop tab after tab of acid. He was trying to write songs, but the drugs kept getting in the way.

"Hello," I said, walking across the roof to his sheltered corner where he had been sitting before a flickering candle. It was twilight, a time of in-between, of magic. The breeze had come up. On the beach, the palms swayed, dancing free-form. The waves were white-capped, kissed by the wind. It must have seemed to him that I appeared from out of nowhere. I'm pretty sure he attributed it to the drugs.

"Whoa, get it on. Where'd you come from?" He squinted at me.

I'd taken on the guise of a Navajo girl, drawing from his memories. She was dusky, long-limbed, and black-haired. When he was four, his family had come upon a truck crash outside of Santa Fe where he witnessed the death of a shaman. He believed the old man's spirit entered him that day.

"Look inside. You know where I come from," I said.

He considered me a moment, then nodded. "Cool. Maybe I should have asked you *why*."

I settled before him on his blanket, cross-legged. "Every shaman has his songs. You're creating yours. I can help you."

He tilted his head to one side. "If I'm a true shaman, I don't need your help."

"Maybe not, but it's never wise to refuse a gift before you know what it is." I reached for his hands. At the contact, the world tilted.

We were on a wave; the roof lifting and dropping, floating us to the horizon. The sun slid into the ocean, wavering and molten, death in purple, orange, and gold. Then the moon came up, pregnant and gravid, dripping a silvery path across the sea. I kissed him, the taste of our lips flowering into hummingbirds on a midnight flight. There was music all about us—the stars punched the sky to the howl of guitars, and the earth groaned in a gut-wrenching bass. Then both earth and sea shattered and we made love, rocking in tandem to every quake.

It lasted for hours. When we were finally spent, he grabbed a pencil and scribbled madly. I drifted, exulting in every minute of his mania. Time stretched and shrank; he wrote and wrote. Finally, he came back to himself.

"Who are you?" He set his notebook down, then lay back on

the blanket, opposite me. I could tell from his thoughts he hadn't believed I was real, but now, as he stroked my arm, he wasn't so sure. My eyes were aflame, twin fires reflected in his.

"Why do you need to know?" It was dangerous for a fae to reveal her true name. Names meant control, and I would never relinquish that. "Names are nothing but someone else's definition of who you really are."

His own father had named him James Douglas MacArthur, after a five-star general.

"Truth." He grabbed a pack of cigarettes and fished one out. "I think you're an angel, come down to earth." He patted his knapsack for matches and came up empty. I flicked my finger. A small flame burst forth.

"Wow." He shook his head. "I'm still fried." He hadn't found his matches, but he'd found another sugar cube. "Let's keep this going. Wanna drop another?"

I smiled and sat up. "Later. You should eat."

His glance softened, as if touched I should care. "Had a can of beans yesterday."

"That was then, this is now."

He shrugged. "Can't. I'm out of bread."

"I'll take care of it."

"Really?" He gave me a quirky smile. "You're one trippy chick."

I said nothing, wanting to play it cool, but I wanted to wrap my arms around him again, keep him there forever. His admiration was ambrosia, honey from the gods.

He glanced at me side-long. "You show up out of nowhere, blow my mind, take me on the most amazing trip of my life." He nodded at his notebook. "I got pages of lyrics in there, great stuff."

"They're better than great. They're legendary."

"You think?"

"I don't think. I know."

His expression turned thoughtful. "Then they're because of you. You're the music, baby. You're my muse. That's what I'll call you—Muse."

I kissed him, not wanting to admit how much that pleased me. Then I dressed and coaxed him from the roof, so we might fill his belly. We spent the next three nights as we had the first—

tripping, making out, and talking about life, death, and other worlds. Then he'd write like a fiend possessed. We were in heaven.

"You're going to be famous, Jim."

He gave me that lazy smile I'd come to adore.

"Yeah?"

"Uh-huh. Together, we can do anything. We'll *do* everything."

"Everything? So, you'd die for me, Muse?"

The question left me unsettled. From our conversations, I knew he had a strange fascination with death. It was as if the spectre of it watched him from the corners, a dark and hulking killer that would one day take everything from him. He gave it the finger, while dancing on his grave at the same time. He was death's clown, death's fool, both victim and psycho-pomp. I attributed it to the drugs, but I suspected his asking me if I would die for him was also a test of my devotion. It ticked me off. He shouldn't have doubted. I'd been with him for three days; it felt like three eons. "Don't talk shit, Jim. Keep it up, and I'll go."

"Chill, baby. You know I wasn't serious."

But he was.

On the fourth day after he finished his lyrics, we headed for Olivia's, a diner on Venice. I didn't have any bread, but we fae are nothing if not lucky. I knew if we timed it right, we'd show up just after Olivia threw out the trash behind the restaurant; there'd be half-finished hamburgers and cold fries. Enough for Jim until he sponged some cash. Most of the pan-handling we did went to booze, smokes, and dope.

Sure enough, Olivia had just finished dumping a bag into the dumpster as we arrived. She didn't see us and stepped back into the diner. Jim headed for the garbage, wanting to get whatever was in there while it was still good. He was so intent, he didn't see the body further down the alley, slumped against a wall with a needle in its arm. Three grey shadows were hunkered beside it, amorphous clouds that kept swelling and shrinking. I didn't have to look hard to know what they were—leeches, sucking up the soul of a soon-to-be-dead junkie.

I grabbed Jim and pulled him around the corner, hoping they were too involved in their feeding to see us.

"What's the deal, Muse?" I'd yanked him hard. He was hungry, strung out.

"We need to split."

"Why? I wanna scarf—"

"So we'll go somewhere else."

"Hell, we will." He pointed at the dumpster, never one to waste anything if he could help it. "There's perfectly good food in there."

"Listen to me. This place isn't cool, right now."

"You're tripping."

"Whatever. There are things down that alley. Bummer shit. They'll come for you, especially if they see you're with me."

"Let 'em! Didn't you say we'd experience everything together, Muse? Bring 'em on! We'll fuck 'em up together."

"I'm *not* kidding, Jim!"

He saw how freaked out I was and began to laugh and laugh. I didn't care. It was enough to get him out of there. After that, I left him to fend for himself for a time. He needed to miss me, realize what he had lost. Besides, I feared the leeches would follow him. A type of diabolical, they like nothing better than to destroy our favourites. They sniff them out like hell hounds on the hunt. A fae in the company of a mortal is a sure give-away.

I didn't leave him completely alone, though. I watched him from a distance, and I kept busy. I'd made him a promise—to make him great. He needed friends to help him get there. A month later, I made sure he ran into Ray.

Ray was solid; they'd been together in film school at UCLA. Ray played in a band. He was what Jim needed. After a few minutes of rapping, Ray coaxed him into singing one of his new songs, "Moonlight Drive".

"That's far out, man," Ray said, and with that, they were on their way. They began to rehearse. John joined the band as drummer, and later, Robby, as guitarist. They called themselves "The Doors" after the William Blake quote: "If the doors of perception were cleansed, everything would appear to man as it is, infinite."

They got gigs at the London Fog, which didn't pay much, and later, at the Whiskey A Go Go, which did. I liked the Whiskey. The place was hip, all red exterior and black awnings, with a psychedelic marquee that vomited names in tie-dye colour—The Byrds, Buffalo Springfield, Van Morrison. Inside were cages for the go-go girls who shimmied and shook, and red patent leather booths that swallowed you whole and made you their oyster. Everybody who was anybody made the scene at the Whiskey.

On stage, Jim kept improving, overcoming his shyness. In leather, he was mesmerizing, sometimes an electric god, sometimes the shaman who paid homage. He made love to the music, hypnotizing us with it. His words, with the organ, guitar, and drums in steady syncopation, lulled us like a drug, and then he'd explode, slay the crowd in a screaming orgy of love, lust, and hate—all of it pure and potent and real. It didn't matter what he sang, the crowd dug him. And it was my influence behind it all. The whole band was better off because of me.

When Jim sang, "Hello, I Love You," he'd look right at me. All the girls thought he was eyeing them, but his gaze held mine, deep, hooded, and huge. It was his way of honouring our first night when I said "hello" and refused to tell him who I was. As for the leeches, there was too much fire inside the Whiskey for them to tolerate. They kept to the edges, sniffing and floating about dark alleys where deals were made, urine pooled, and blood smeared.

My own addiction for Jim kept growing. I didn't realise how bad it was until she came onto the scene. A perky red-head, too pretty for her own good, it was easy to see Jim was into her. It's true what they say: we fae are a jealous lot. I was possessive of him. He was mine.

He didn't agree. Or maybe he still thought I was just a figment of his imagination. All I know is when he finally balled her it tore me up. I wanted to burn her to a crisp and torch him in the process. I did neither. I might be made of fire, but I never let it burn away my ability to think things through, to strategize.

She kept a bungalow in Laurel Canyon. The next time they went there, I followed them. Jim was unaware of me, too stoned or oblivious, which was the way I wanted it. I watched as they giggled and clung to each other as they climbed the long stairs into her house, both drunk on whisky and high on acid. In the living room, several people had already flopped. A joint, now cold, had rolled from an ashtray to the floor. Jim ignored the sleepers, and swept aside the beaded curtain that passed for her bedroom door. They collapsed on her bed.

She pulled at his clothes. He clawed at hers. And then he was between her legs, doing it. It gave me some pleasure to see she wasn't happy. No foreplay as she expected. Jim wasn't concerned about it. As he thrust his way to climax, I slipped inside her, willing him to open his eyes.

He did. He saw *me*. She was no more. I lay in her place, a fae of fire, spread-eagled beneath him, consuming him as only fire can, my hair a torch of orange and yellow, my eyes, red and glowing, rubies of fury and desire.

Who am I, Jim? I forced him to say it.

"You're Muse," he muttered.

Fucking right. Don't forget it, or I'll leave you forever.

"What are you saying?" Beneath us, Pam heard him. I felt her need, her longing for him to love her.

I hated her. *Tell her to shut up.*

"Shhh, baby," he replied, a far cry from how I wanted him to say it.

She did, good little groupie, that she was.

LATER, PEOPLE THOUGHT his song, "Love Me Two Times" was about a dude leaving for the Vietnam War, or the band leaving their girlfriends to go on tour, but I knew better. Jim was mine. I gave him what no one else could. If I had to take her place whenever they did it, I would. *She* was the usurper.

On Sullivan, they wanted him to change the lyrics of "Light My Fire" to "Girl, we couldn't get much better," but he spit the real words at the camera with such venom that the suits said he'd never appear on Sullivan, again. I think that was the point I started to feel differently about him. I was jealous and possessive, yes, and flattered by his acknowledgment that I was his muse, but this feeling was something different, something I'd never felt before. It was softer, warm, like a banked fire. I started to think about death—his—and it terrified me. I didn't want him to die. I had to find a way to make him immortal.

With his belief in me finally set, he felt he could do no wrong. And perhaps that was the downside of hanging out with a fae—fire made him dangerous. He took risks he shouldn't have. He didn't play safe, on stage or off. He and Pam began to fight, shouting matches I encouraged and enjoyed. She suspected there was someone else. And when he trashed the president of Elektra Records' office, people said he was possessed.

It wasn't me or the acid. He was allergic to whisky and didn't know it. As for the acid, hallucinogens fall under my element, fire: the visuals and rushes are pure mental and physical energy. Alcohol is the opposite—heroin too, especially if injected. Mainlining was something the leeches liked, watery vampires, they sucked the souls of their victims dry.

It was around this time Pam started to chip smack to numb her heartache, but I didn't care. Jim had more women, and I had enough to contend with, slipping in to take their place. When he was aware of it, he would just laugh.

I drew the line at the witch, though.

He was fascinated with her; she was a link to his shamanism. Perhaps he went with her to better understand me. I admit, she had some ability. There was no slipping into her; she knew how to ward herself against interference. The worst I could do was to knock over candles in the hope they might set the bed on fire. As a last resort and to punish him, I turned him impotent. Bitch countered it by having him drink her blood.

One night, after he had finished with her, I had it out with him. My fires were burning so fiercely, I thought I might burn out; jealousy riddled me, my fingers left fiery after-images wherever they passed. He had vacated the bedroom, leaving her to sleep so he could toke up in the garden. It was three in the morning, and the moon was full. They'd been celebrating Imbolc, the Spring Sabbat. Outside, tiki torches were burning beside the pool. He stood, mesmerized by one, staring at the flames. As usual, he was tripping, so it made it easier to reach him.

I appeared in the torch, a face aflame. He startled briefly, then took a long pull from the joint he had been bogarting, staring at me all the while. He'd been expecting me.

I delivered my ultimatum. *Her or me.*

"You know, I never did like pushy women." He exhaled the smoke in a long, even breath and looked away.

I'm no woman. You know it.

He turned back to me, irritated. "And you know what else, Muse? I don't think I dig you, anymore. You're a downer. A real drag."

I could hardly believe what he was saying. I'd given him everything I'd promised on that roof in Venice Beach. The lyrics, the fame . . . and here he was, dumping on me, as if I were nothing.

Maybe fae are nothing, when no one believes in them.

You bastard. I go now, I don't come back. I take it all away. Your inspiration, your voice. You'll have nothing, be nothing!

"Yeah? You said that before, and here you still are. Good riddance, you god-damned firefly. Screw off! The world loves me. I do just fine on my own."

You don't mean it.

"I fucking do!" He grabbed the shaft of the tiki torch as if it were my neck and started to throttle it. His hands didn't hurt me, but his hatred did. I felt the punch of it like a blow. Something inside me cracked and broke. I felt as if I were made from glass, that I was shattering into a thousand pieces. Every shard cut me more, severing my wings from my back and leaving them in tatters on the ground. And then, as if to douse me from his memory forever, he threw the torch into the pool.

We were done.

I came to with barely enough energy to keep myself alive. I was an ember, smoking at his feet. He didn't see me there. He blinked once, as if not quite knowing why a tiki torch was on the bottom of the pool, and then he stumbled for the house, grabbing a bottle of whisky from a table as he went.

After he disappeared inside, I lay there for a time. There was a dampness about my eyes, and for a while, I thought the water had splashed me which was why I couldn't move. I finally realized the impossible had happened. The wetness was tears. I was a fae, made from fire, and I had shed tears.

How could that be?

With the question came the truth, and it stunned me. I actually loved him. And he had spat on my love as if it meant nothing.

Fae don't love. If they do, they become less than what they are. Something closer to a mortal. With the potential to die.

Why did he loathe me so much? Every morning, the fires of the sun renewed me. Dawn was a few hours away. I would have to wait to recover until then. I stared up at the moon and stars and took what comfort I could from them.

If *I* loved him, why hadn't he loved me in return? Was he as incapable of love as I had been? Or was my attempt to keep him tied to me not a loving thing? What *was* love, anyway? I understood desire, and passion, and jealousy. If he came back out of the house and said he'd been wrong, I would forgive him. Why was I so quick to do that, even now? Was that love, or was it something darker—addiction?

I *was* addicted, plain and simple. And the only way to deal with it was to go through cold turkey. There could be no Jim. I would do as I said—more for my sake, than for his. I would leave him.

And I did for a time. But like any addict, the lure of the drug is almost impossible to resist. I'm fairly certain that in his song, "When the Music's Over", I was his butterfly's scream.

WITHOUT ME, HE drank more than ever. Whisky now seemed to be his drug of choice. By the time the band hit Miami he was out of control. Back then, Florida was still part of the Bible Belt. Jim hated the repression it represented. In true form, he insulted the crowd by telling them they were all "a bunch of fucking idiots", and then later, invited them to take off their clothes after a fan doused him in champagne. Several people claimed he exposed his penis while on stage. At the trial months later, he couldn't remember if he had.

Through all of this, the witch disappeared, but the groupie remained. Finally, faced with jail and hard labour, she convinced him to go to Paris while he waited for his appeal.

I should have been there for him. He needed saving. I should have protected him from the full-up junkie she'd become.

When I finally relented and looked in on them at their French apartment off La Rue Beautrellis, I was horrified by what I found. The place was lousy with leeches. Slug-like and amorphous, they gibbered in corners, slid across the floor like swill, and hung off *her* like she was some kind of blood sausage. She was so riddled with them she lost focus; I couldn't see her beneath their putrid grey cloud. They hadn't attacked him, yet—I suspect because Jim hadn't yet fallen prey to her blow—but they eyed him, waiting.

He had put on weight, as if the extra mass gave him protection, or perhaps he knew on some level, he was surrounded by a swarm. He'd grown a full beard, another way to hide. I could see he was sick. The whisky and the drugs had taken their toll.

I was at his side in a moment. Hissing their annoyance, the leeches drew away from him. As much as I try to avoid them, it also costs them to tangle with me; fire and water don't mix. Their touch might snuff some of my fire, but I also have an adverse effect on them.

Baby, I'm back, and I'm sorry, I told him, sick at heart. *I'll never leave you, again.*

He closed his eyes. I don't know if he heard me. I'd like to think he did.

I'll make it right, Jim. I promise you. I love you. I tested the word on my tongue. Because, yes, I could finally admit I'd given in to my own addiction. He *was* worth it, even if it meant I was less than what I was. *We* were worth it. I needed to get him right again.

I nudged him and poked him, a hovering, frantic presence, and convinced him to take a walk the next day, although I know he thought it was his own idea. He needed sun and fresh air. So did I. I especially needed to get him away from her. She let us leave without a fight, likely because she wanted to drive a spike up her arm. The leeches let us go, content to remain with their food supply.

It was a beautiful July day. The weather was perfect as we walked down a narrow cobbled lane. He'd had a couple of beers for breakfast—not great, but I wasn't able to talk him out of it. At least he wasn't high on acid although it made it harder for me to reach him. On our walk, he paused before a jewellery shop. A glass Star of David dangled in the window, catching his eye.

It might be the only opportunity I had, so I took it. The Star was a mirror of sorts—a religious symbol for Jews, representing God and the teachings of the Torah and Israel. In broader terms it was also a symbol of the divine permeating and providing existence to all worlds. I straddled two of those worlds—Jim's and mine. As the sun caught the Star's bevelled edges, I slipped inside the glass, willing my face to form.

He gasped as he caught sight of me. His eyes tightened as if the Star was too bright, or perhaps my fires were hard for him to endure. I could see his pain reflected in his gaze. "Muse," he murmured. He reached a trembling finger to touch the window. It was a stroke, a caress.

I'm here, Jim. My throat grew thick.

He nodded, swallowed, and didn't say another word. To my shock, tears filled his eyes and two wet lines spilled down his cheeks. I felt my own eyes spark as my heart burned. All was forgiven between us. He had missed me as much as I had missed him.

Someone hailed him, snagging his attention—his friend, Alain, I learned later, and sent by her to keep an eye on him. Before Alain could draw him away, Jim insisted on going into the shop and buying the Star of David. Alain thought he was buying it for Pam, but I know he bought it because of me.

They spent the afternoon at a café, drinking beer and whisky. I hovered over him, fretting when he suffered a bout of hiccoughs that came and went. By the time Alain walked him home, he was spitting blood.

She was clear-headed enough to be beside herself, seeing the state he was in. "We should call a doctor, baby," she kept saying, dabbing at his bloodied lips. "This isn't good." Jim waved her off. He needed to sit, he had overdone it at the café. As she steered him to the couch, Alain cautioned her to call if things got worse. Then he left.

The leeches crowded in on them, sensing a feast. I struck them away, shrieking warnings like a banshee. They'd retreat for a few seconds, then hem us in, again. At their wet contact, I began to sizzle, their touch snuffing me bit by bit, but they also paid the price by turning into steam. Their stench filled the room in a foetid smog. Where others disappeared, more kept appearing. There were too many of them for me to defeat.

Pam shook a powdery white line along the top of the coffee table. "This'll make you feel better, baby," she murmured. She spilled another and scraped it with a credit card.

Jim glared. "I told you, I don't like it in the apartment. I *told* you to quit using."

"Jimbo, I hate to see you like this! It'll help you! Make you feel better. You can sleep a while—"

Leave him alone! I shouted at her. *You'll kill him!*

"—and the spasms will stop."

"I said I don't like it!"

"You've never tried it, so how do you know?"

"God, I feel like shit—"

"This will help—"

"Screw it! All right! Just to stop your bitching at me!"

Jim, no! I screamed.

He grabbed a rolled franc and snorted the smack, tossing it

back like he might a shot of whisky. She joined him, and then snuggled beneath his arm, as if content she'd finally convinced him to do the right thing.

You stupid skank! I shrieked at her. *You bloody junkie!*

Of course neither of them heard me. Over the course of the night, she woke him several more times, and they snorted more lines together. The leeches were so thick about them, I had to retreat to the balcony. Jim was fading, his soul guttering like a candle going out. Heroin was a doorway for leeches, and they had come crashing through.

My heart burned down to a hard, round coal. I felt faint, dizzy. I couldn't catch a breath. I knew if I left him, he would fail.

Another hour passed. I remained where I was, praying for a miracle. He'd collapsed. I willed him to rouse. Perhaps it was enough. He came to, vomiting whisky and blood. I don't know how he found the strength, but he stumbled for the bathroom and collapsed beside the toilet. After a moment, he swiped at his face and poured himself a bath.

In the bathroom, the leeches dangled from him, bloated gourds that clung to his body. Unaware of them, he shed his clothes and climbed into the tub. He lay there, his heart hammering and his pulse jumping in his neck. The slugs weighted him down like malevolent buoys. Suddenly, he scrabbled at the sides of the tub, heaving blood and fighting for air. He jerked once, then seemed to fade and sputter out.

I dove for his chest, tossing leeches aside like so much offal. I had never possessed him in such a way, preferring to appear before him in his acid-fused dreams or taking the places of others so we might love.

I chased him down a long, dark tunnel. It was a little brighter at the end, but not by much. He was already at the brink.

"Jim, wait!"

Hearing my voice, he paused. I drew up alongside him. We teetered on an edge.

Before us stretched an infinite black space. There were no stars. At our feet, a silver pathway floated, a shining artery of light that pulsed and branched, dividing into smaller and smaller forks. Who knew what it was or where it led? Would it take us to other realms or leave us stranded nowhere?

He looked at me, his eyes hooded, intense. He was no longer

ill, but as I first knew him, whole, happy, perfect. He was ready to go, to leave the tunnel and never return. He stared into the vastness, as if confronting the greatest of mysteries. I think we saw our deaths there. "Would you die for me, Muse?" he whispered, his voice low.

He had asked me this once before. I glanced down the tunnel behind us. There was a tiny pin-prick of light at the other end, my salvation if I decided to return. For him, the only option was to go on—into annihilation or whatever came next.

He was my drug, my addiction. I loved him.

Which meant I was no longer truly fae, because the fae don't love. As much as I had made him into a superstar, he had also turned me into something else. Was I willing to grieve for him for an eternity, or go with him now? Would we travel the cosmos or disintegrate into dust? Suddenly, time was crucial and had meaning for me in a way it never had before.

I took him by the hand. "Yes," I said, knowing it was the only choice. "I would."

We regarded the mystery before us, black and shining. The promise of a new life or a spectacular destruction.

There was no turning back.

With one last breath, we took the final step.

AUTHOR'S NOTE: THE following songs by The Doors inspired me while writing "Light My Fire". I suggest the reader listen to them during the story, or shortly thereafter:

Hello, I Love You
Moonlight Drive
Light My Fire
Love Me Two Times
Soul Kitchen
Riders on the Storm
When the Music's Over
LA Woman
The End

Ring of Fire

JB Riley

PELE WAITED.

Other than the small Demons who lived within the cinder peaks along its chain, the Aleutians were home to no fire dwellers. Meeting here was neutral territory; it removed the need for hosting duties and eased territorial concerns, but she had still determined to be the first to arrive. There was power in being last—of making the others wait upon her pleasure—but Pele decided instead to claim the gathering place as hers before anyone else could.

But that meant she had to wait. Pele hated waiting.

She was pacing in frustration when an amused voice behind her made her jump.

"Trying to stay warm, Little Sister?"

Pele whirled around to face the huge, gold-eyed beast who had spoken. Its desert-coloured coat stood out from the Arctic Waste around them.

"Coyote." Pele curled her lip and turned her back again. "You do not belong, either in this place or this meeting." She felt power shiver past her, then a tall man dressed in caribou skin garments with dark hair and the same gold eyes walked past her and sat on a nearby rock.

He shrugged. “I heard of the gathering, and was curious.”

“And so you decide to mock me?”

Coyote spread his hands. “That’s the curiosity, again.”

“At how I might kill you for the insult?”

“More likely as to whether you would rise to this one’s bait.” A third voice spoke, deep and full of gravel, fitting the squat, roughly human-shaped creature that moved slowly out from a nearby fissure. Steam rose from its shoulders and back in vast clouds, while glowing ribbon-like cracks of lava appeared and were re-absorbed across its naked form.

“Cherufe,” Coyote inclined his head respectfully. “You have travelled far.”

“Too far to listen to younglings while they bicker.” Cherufe stopped moving, its legs flowing and thickening to form twin pillars anchored to the cinder rubble of the ground.

A shadow crossed the ground. Pele looked up to see a huge Frigate bird circling above them, spiralling downward with each slow pass.

“Land on the Old One,” Coyote yelled up, pointing at Cherufe. “He’s feeling particularly mellow today.” The other’s ribbons of lava flared brightly in threat or warning, though Pele didn’t know if it was toward Coyote’s brashness or the bird that was setting down on the flat, frozen beach just below them.

Another flare of power and a very tall, slender man stood where the bird had landed. His skin was dark copper, his intricately braided hair was darker still, and despite the bitter cold he wore only a red shuka wrapped around his hips and over his left shoulder, plus thick strings of beads at his wrists and bare ankles.

“Greetings, Pele. Greetings, Cherufe.” When he turned to Coyote, his voice took on an edge. “As for you, Trickster . . .”

“Wow, just looking at you makes me colder,” Coyote shivered theatrically, wrapping his arms around himself. “It must be nice to carry Kilimanjaro around inside of you, Kibo. Although I’m not sure it would be as nice if we were all meeting in the desert, now would it?”

“Why are you here?” the other asked bluntly.

“Same as I told the lovely lady over there—I heard about the gathering, and was curious.” Ignoring a basso grunt of irritation from Cherufe, Coyote skipped in a circle. "Tell me, are your meetings as interesting as ours?"

"One Trickster is bad enough," Pele responded, ignoring the kiss Coyote blew in her direction. "I wish to hear nothing about a collection of them."

"Nor I," the voice carried from past the beach. An intricately carved wooden boat was almost to shore. A small blond woman in furs stood at its prow, one hand grasping the long neck of the snarling wolfhound that made up the figurehead. As the boat ground ashore she leapt nimbly over the side and waded through the shallows to join the others. "We have bound our Trickster under the Earth in iron chains, Coyote. You can join him if you wish."

"Hekla!" Coyote bowed, sweeping off an imaginary hat and grinning. "You are as charming and lovely as ever." She looked at him with pupil-less jet black eyes but did not respond. "Wow, tough crowd. Well, at least you're dressed for the weather."

"Why *are* you here?" Pele snapped.

"Simple: I heard about the gathering and—" The ground shook suddenly and steam exploded from fissures that opened in the earth as the other four glared at him.

"Whoa! Easy there, volcano gods." Coyote picked himself up from where he had tumbled when the ground started shaking. "Don't be angry at me, it's not my fault. You haven't asked the right questions."

Pele held on to the edges of her temper and spoke through gritted teeth. "What are the right questions?"

"Quickly," rumbled Cherufe when Coyote hesitated.

"*You're* telling *me* to do something quickly?" Coyote asked, then crouched as the ground started to move again. "Okay, okay. The right question is *who* did I hear about the gathering from?" He straightened and looked at them expectantly.

The other beings just stared at him.

Coyote sighed. "Can't get a straight line to save my life, can I? All right so if you ask me 'O Coyote, Wise and Handsome, from whom did you hear about this gathering of Fire Dwellers?'" He paused briefly, then shrugged and continued, "I would respond 'That is an excellent question. I heard of it from the Lord of the Rising Sun. He told me.'"

"But—" Kibo shook his head. "Why?"

"Because we have need of him." Pele felt the voice more than heard it, so deep was the sound. The dragon had arrived.

HE APPEARED SLOWLY out of the Western sky, bright red skin under pearlescent scales chased with tiny bits of green flame. His eyes were burnished copper, his lion-like mane was bright gold and his mouth lit deep orange by the fire that burned within him. Where his claws dug into the frozen ground it steamed and hissed, and he took up most of the small beach. Then in the blink of an eye and a rush of power that made Pele's red-feathered cape rustle as it passed, the dragon was gone and a small man with a long white beard and dressed in red ceremonial robes stood on the beach.

"Fuji-san." The others made gestures of respect. Even Pele—who recognized no being as above her—bowed her head in deference to the great dragon, who nodded to each of them in return.

"A grave time of war is coming, guardians." Though he spoke softly, the dragon's voice echoed like passing thunder. "My people shall face a terrible fire, one that—once lit—shall burn evermore in the minds of men greedy for destruction. I come to petition our council: let us change this future. If it is agreed, this Young Trickster will serve as our vessel."

Coyote had wandered off to dance along the edge of the surf. Kibo gestured toward him. "That one? Really?"

The dragon chuckled. "Coyote is far more serious than he may appear. He also moves freely among the world of men, which not all of us can easily do." He gestured toward Cherufe, who grunted and spoke.

"We are bound to our fires. Already I feel the pull of my mountain." Cherufe looked down the beach, where Coyote was running in and out laughing as the waves crashed in. "Coyote is bound to nothing, especially not common sense."

Pele was also aware of the distance she had travelled from her home. It was an itch on her skin that she knew would soon become need, its pull irresistible. She resented Coyote in his freedom, and this shortened her already-strained temper. She swirled her cape around her and strode forward, chin up. "What is this grave time you speak of, Ancient One? And why should we trouble ourselves? We are above the wars of Man."

"Not this one," Fuji-san replied. "Watch, witness, then decide." He swept his arm and fog rolled up out of nowhere; on that fog images appeared. They watched.

WHEN THE IMAGES finally ended the fog dissipated on the ocean breeze as they stood, stunned and silent. Cherufe spoke first. "I understand now why you chose this place. The battles of Attu will be . . ." he rumbled to a stop and shook his head.

Hekla was ashen, glowing red tears running down her face as she swayed slightly on her feet. Kibo stood with his legs braced apart, head bowed. Fuji-san took a deep breath, then spoke. "The war will cause terror and suffering across the world. But the fire which will rain down on my people must not be allowed its release. On behalf of the world, I ask: let Coyote once more steal fire to save the human race. Not to bring warmth and safety, but to prevent this dread burning." He looked around him.

"Aye," rumbled Cherufe.

"Aye," whispered Hekla.

Pele took a step forward, hands balling into fists. "Your people will attack me? *Me*?" There was a surprised yip from the surf line as the waves rose to twice their size and roared up the beach. "They pay the price for their error!"

"Yes, but it is too terrible—this fire beyond even our imagining." The dragon spread his hands. "Please, Pele. Surely you can see the need."

"Need?" Pele laughed without humour. "Where is the need when your people rain fire from the skies into the loveliest of my harbours? Why not have Coyote stop that?"

"It is too much—there are too many pieces for the Trickster to control. But this 'atomic bomb' . . ." The Dragon rolled the words around as if tasting them. "Coyote need only change one of numerous small events to steal its fire."

"Bah!" Pele waved her hands. "What of Hekla's people? They shall burn each other! Why not have Coyote steal that fire, so those accursed ovens never light? And where is Gorynych? The Guardian of the Steppes should be here. His people shall face horrors too, in this war you have shown us."

"The Slavic Dragon still mourns the death of his mate at Tunguska," Kibo murmured. "And Pele, you speak with passion, but Fuji-san is correct. This fire is beyond our control, beyond even our understanding. It must not come to pass. I say 'aye'."

Pele sneered and lifted her chin. "And I say no. Your people pay the price for their folly, Fuji-san. It is no more than justice."

The Lord of the Rising Sun bowed his head and closed his eyes. Then he shimmered into his dragon form and with a great leap launched himself into the sky. Cherufe simply sank into the ground as with a puff of steam the fissure in which he had arrived closed up again. Still weeping, Hekla pushed her boat into the surf and jumped aboard without a backward glance.

Kibo and Pele faced each other on the beach, neither speaking, for some time.

"Well?" Pele finally challenged.

"You do the world a grave harm, in your anger and caprice." Kibo stared down the beach where Coyote sat upon a large piece of driftwood, skipping stones into the surf. "But all creatures must be true to their nature. You, me, even Coyote."

Pele snorted. "I don't think he could have done it, anyway."

Kibo raised an eyebrow. "I think you underestimate him," he said, and climbed onto a rocky outcropping before shimmering into his winged form. The Frigate bird stretched its wings wide and balanced there for a moment until a wind gust pulled it aloft. It flapped a few times as it rose, then circled in farewell before heading South. Pele watched it fly.

"Ah, alone at last."

Pele jumped, startled, and spun around again. "If you sneak up on me one more time I will burn you!"

"Sorry." Once again a coyote the size of a timber wolf stood on the beach behind her. "Will you travel safely home, Little Sister?"

Pele nodded. "I shall go underground and run the waves of lava with my Papa Holua sled. Soon I will be within my islands."

"And will you be okay, Sister?"

She glanced at him sideways. "What do you mean?"

"Untold deaths will be laid at your feet."

Pele shrugged. "Fuji-san was incorrect. You cannot steal this fire, Coyote. You do not lack the cunning, but humans must be true to *their* nature. Just like the flames, they carry destruction within them, and that cannot be changed. If not this great atomic firestorm then some other, or another, or another still until they finally change their nature or destroy themselves."

Coyote bowed his head toward her. "Pele is wise. Now, if you will excuse me?" He smiled his lupine smile, long tongue dangling, then spun and sprinted into the surf. Three great bounds in, he leapt into the air and with a flash of silver scales was a salmon cutting into the waves and then gone.

Pele looked around. Attu was quiet around her, though now she could hear the battles to come. A stomp of her foot split the ground (rattling windows in Petropavlovsk six hundred miles away) and she leapt onto her koa wood sled to ride her waves of lava home again.

Aladdin's Laugh

Damascus Mincemeyer

WHEN HENRY FIRST spotted the lamp it was hidden behind an old fur hat. In the dim light of the antique shop's corner, it looked tarnished and old and there were engravings along the side, from long spout to curved handle, in a flowing script Henry didn't recognize. Part of him wondered if it was some sort of fancy oil can, but he knew Marie would appreciate its strangely blemished elegance, and as he went to pay for it, Henry tried to think where in the house she'd like it placed.

At the cash register a young woman with black hair streaked with shocks of pink and smeared, raccoon-rings of eyeliner rimming her eyes looked at the lamp and smiled. "Someone finally bought that piece of junk. It's been in the store since I started working here, and that was a long time ago."

"How long's *long?*" Henry asked. The girl shrugged, giving him his change.

"A year. I've been stuck here a whole year already. It's creepy sometimes, all the dead people's stuff they bring in." She paused, looked around the store and repeated quietly, "A whole year."

"You're right. That *is* a long time," Henry chuckled facetiously, taking the bag with the lamp from her. "I worked for the postal service for a year. Longest year of my life. It lasted four decades."

The girl said nothing at the joke, just popped her eyes wide while Henry went to the door, which made him chuckle all the more.

As was his habit on Fridays, Henry stopped by the doughnut shop on the way home and had a bear claw with a cup of coffee. Sometimes he'd see Joe and Mac there and they'd shoot the breeze about the old days, but that afternoon he was by himself except for the Crazy Cuban, who always sat in the corner mumbling in Spanish while he read the paper. Being by himself was fine with Henry; he could savour his pastry without a bunch of old ghosts flitting around in his head. That was the problem with the past: if you let it, it would take over your present until you were mired waist-deep, like a bog. He'd seen it happen to some of his buddies from Korea, and even Joe and Mac to a lesser extent. You couldn't do that. Life went forward.

He finished his bear claw, sipped his coffee and left, nodding to the Crazy Cuban, who just scowled and muttered as Henry went out the door. Going home, Henry passed through the neighbourhood he'd grown up in, and as usual, was impressed at how well it developed after he'd moved out. New buildings had been constructed, replacing most of the shabbier tenements of his youth, yet the people still hung out on the steps and sidewalks and music still played from a dozen different windows. A few people, old guys like Jack the Man and Stu Budgie, even called out to him as he passed by the bistro where they sat playing cards.

Henry's house was two neighbourhoods away, out where the apartment buildings shrank and mingled happily with regular houses. It would have been faster and easier on his hip if he'd taken the bus, but half the fun of Fridays was tramping down the sidewalk, seeing the life, feeling the sun on his face. No bus ride could accomplish that. The house itself was small and comfortable, and the first thing Henry did once he got inside was open all the windows, letting the stuffy air out and the warm June breeze in.

When he pulled the lamp out of the bag, he took it directly to the living room to show Marie. He walked over to the big photograph of her that hung above the curio, from when they visited Paris years before. Her golden hair was just getting its first wisps of grey then, but her smile was enough to light up the Champs-Élysées. Proudly he held up the lamp to the picture.

"What do you think?" he asked, looking at the antique. "Not too tacky, I hope?"

Henry turned from the photograph and peered at the living room, eyeing all the places he could display the lamp; there weren't many remaining spots available. He'd always been a sucker for antiques—other people's rubbish, Marie would say—and had filled rooms with old vases and clocks, chipped pottery and tin boxes. Finally he decided to leave the placement until after he'd cleaned the lamp up.

It proved filthier than he thought. A coat of grime took an hour to scrub off, and after drying, Henry grabbed the metal polish, daubing it all over the lamp. By then he'd pulled out a beer and turned on the radio to listen to the Red Sox game. They were down 2–1 against Philadelphia, bottom of the fifth, and he swore every time the Phillies got a hit.

He had the lamp upside down, rubbing the side with the cloth in a vigorous circle when a tiny bit of dust sprinkled onto the table from the long spout. Henry stopped, wiping the dust away, but as he continued, more fell out, all over the tabletop in unbelievable amounts. In a heartbeat—half, even—the dust rose from the lamp, gathering into a cloud above the table and swirling around faster and faster like a miniature whirlwind. Pushing his chair back, Henry darted across the kitchen, snatching up the baseball bat he stashed behind the door for protection. He didn't know what was happening, but he'd be damned if he'd survived Inchon to let some glorified dust devil take him out in his own house.

The eddying dust coalesced into something more solid, like a ball with two thick tendrils spreading out from the top, two more from the bottom, and while Henry watched it took a shape he recognized as human. A second later the dust dissipated and there, standing in the kitchen, was a man where moments before there had been nothing. The man was short and stocky, with a dark complexion, piercing emerald eyes, and a black moustache that drooped on either side of his mouth. His clothes were loose-fitting, more wrapped around his body than worn, and the dome of his head was wrapped with a topaz-coloured turban. From both of his ears hung round, gold hoops that shined in the kitchen lights.

Henry stared, wide-eyed, but said nothing. The man clasped his hands together, bowing his head before speaking with a resounding bellow.

"O blessed mortal, the Lord of a thousand Heavens has smiled upon you, and with each of three wishes shall I fulfil all of your desires."

Henry blinked, his mind racing. *Fulfil all your desires?* He didn't like the sound of that coming from a man no matter how he sliced it. Slowly he raised the bat.

"Look, pal," he said, voice wavering. "I don't know who you are or how you got in here, but you better get the *hell* out of my house before I clobber you upside the head."

The man—if that's what it was—frowned. "Mortal, I bid you no harm. I merely am an agent to fulfil—"

"Yeah, I *got* that part," Henry took a cautious step forward. "There will be no fulfilling of desire by some Nancy-boy who fell out of a dust cloud in my kitchen."

The man's frown deepened. "Did you not rub the engravings of my lamp?"

Henry furrowed his brow. "What? How'd you know I—" He glanced down for a second, swearing under his breath before looking up again. "That's a genie's lamp, isn't it? And son of a *bitch*, you're a genie, aren't you?"

The man smiled broadly, exposing gleaming teeth. "I am indeed of the djinn, mortal."

"Stop calling me that, will you?" Henry balked, keeping the bat high. "I *know* I'm that. You don't get to be my age *without* knowing that, so there's no need to rub it in."

"Then what am I to call you, if not mortal?"

"Henry. Henry Reinhold."

The genie nodded. "Very well, Henry Reinhold. You have been graced by virtue of awakening me to any three wishes your heart desires."

Henry laughed and lowered the bat. Then he laughed some more, going from a small chuckle to a wild guffaw and back again, more than once as he plopped down into the chair he'd abandoned. When the giggling finally wore down, the genie still stood there; it, however, did not look amused. Henry held up a hand to the djinn.

"Sorry about that, buddy, but I was kind of hoping you were some kind of hallucination. Thought maybe the Crazy Cuban slipped something in my coffee when I went back for extra cream." He paused, studying the genie. "This is real, though, isn't it?"

"Indeed, Henry Reinhold," the genie smiled again. "You should feel blessed. Few get the opportunity to fulfil—"

"Yeah, yeah, their heart's desire," Henry interrupted. He prodded the lamp on the tabletop with a finger. "You really live in here?"

"It is a paradise beyond all conception of mankind, truly. Rivers of milk and honey, swaths of desert oasis filled with fruit, and palaces of women," the genie leaned in closer. "And all of its like can be yours, if you choose. *Anything* can be yours, if you desire."

Henry sighed, leaning back in the chair before propping the baseball bat against the edge of the table. "Well, that's just perfect, isn't it? Especially since I don't really desire anything that I can think of."

A perplexed expression crawled on the djinn's face. "Pardon?"

"Well, I've pretty much got everything I need," Henry replied. The genie's confusion doubled.

"There is nothing you desire?"

Henry shrugged. "Well, I'd desire you to get back in your little lamp-house and get the hell out of my life if that's at all possible."

The genie frowned. "I could, but that would leave your other wishes unfulfilled, and I am bound to you until you make them."

"So you're not leaving, then?"

"I cannot."

Henry twiddled his thumbs. On the radio Philadelphia scored another run and the Sox were down by two with an inning to go. After a bit, Henry looked back to the genie. "What do most people wish for?"

The djinn swelled with pride, as if it were readying itself for wish-granting. "Most go directly to the sensual delights. Forbidden sex and lust are *very* popular."

Henry scratched his chin. "I'm afraid that's not going to happen. My, ah, equipment doesn't function all that well these days, if you follow me. Besides, it would feel weird unless it was with Marie." When he saw the genie's brow crinkle, Henry clarified: "She was my wife."

"She has passed this mortal coil?"

Henry nodded. "Ten years back. Ovarian cancer."

The genie snapped its fingers. "There! I can bring her back to you, just as she was the day you met—every hair and eyelash, each whispered sweetness, all alive once more!"

Henry launched a sour scowl in the djinn's direction.

"Now you just wait one *damn* minute! That's nothing but perversion, you hear me, and I won't even entertain the notion. Things happen in a natural order, and you just can't go dicking around with them, all right? That's off the table. Off. The. Table."

The genie stroked its moustache. "I confess I do not understand, but I shall heed you." After a pause it asked, "What of riches? Surely no one would turn down the lure of treasure?"

Henry thought about that before shaking his head. "I get a pension that suits me just fine. Haven't starved yet, anyway."

"Revenge against one's enemies? It is quite satisfying, from what I've heard."

"Enemies?" Henry mulled the thought over. "I don't think I have any." He shook his head again, exhaling a frustrated breath. "Look, buddy, there's a hell of a lot more people in the world worse off than me who could use the sensual delights and riches you're waving around. Why don't you pick on one of them and let me listen to the game in peace?"

"I cannot do that, Henry Reinhold. We are bound."

"Right," Henry stood up. On the radio the announcer despaired as one last, lousy pitch cost the Sox a winning run, and with it, the game. Henry turned the radio off and glared at the genie. "I'm going to bed. I don't want to see you here when I wake up."

He flipped off the kitchen light and exited the room, leaving the djinn standing like a shadowy sentry, its eyes glowing green in the dark.

THE NEXT MORNING when Henry came down the hall, the genie was nowhere to be seen. The lamp remained on the kitchen table, tipped on its side where he'd left it. Before making his breakfast, he conducted a search throughout the house, double-checking everything to make sure the djinn hadn't hidden itself away. *A fellow who lives in a lamp could be anywhere,* he reasoned, and dutifully opened all the cupboards and closets, checked under the bed, upturned each sofa cushion, scrutinized the pantry and even peeked behind every stack of dinner plates before spying down the sink drains, just to be sure. After half an hour Henry was satisfied the genie was gone, or better yet, had never existed to begin with. He hadn't thought hallucinations a particularly *good* thing, but to his mind it sure as hell beat the alternative. With quiet relief he wrapped the lamp in the cloth of metal polish he'd used the day before and set the thing in the trash outside.

Afterwards Henry made himself some bacon and eggs and coffee, relishing the peace and quiet. He set the dishes in the sink and passed through the living room, saying good morning to Marie as he went, before heading down the hall to the bathroom. Henry ran the water in the shower, getting it nice and hot before stepping in. That first blast was relaxing like few things were, and he smiled, lathering up. A few seconds later he began whistling.

Above the tuneless melody, Henry heard a deep voice from behind him speak in puzzlement. "Why is it that mortals sing as they bathe?"

Henry shrieked and spun around; there in the shower with him, arms crossed, stood the genie. Henry yanked at the shower curtain, covering himself. Surprise had his tongue tied, and beyond shielding his nudity, Henry just pointed and stammered like a madman.

"You . . . You—" he grimaced, annoyed, before clenching his fists. "You were *gone!* You left!"

The djinn stared impassively. "I did no such thing. As I said, we are bound, Henry Reinhold, and as such I heeded your tone and left you in peace as you asked. I thought perhaps you had to reason out what your desires were, and would be thus prepared to cast your wishes to me."

Henry ground his teeth together, jabbing an angry finger at the genie. "Weren't you listening yesterday? I've got everything I need and I've had a good long life. Had a great wife. Two great kids. A steady job. I even travelled the world a little bit. The point is, I don't *want* for anything. Everything that makes me comfortable I've already *got*. Now I'm telling you somewhere on this planet there has to be *someone* who wants what you're selling but, for the last time, it ain't *me*."

Henry stepped out of the shower then, quickly wrapping a towel around his waist before heading to the bedroom. There on the bed sat the djinn. Henry exhaled an exasperated breath and went to the closet, pulling out some clothes.

Just ignore him, Henry thought, rifling through his plaid shirts. *It's like an annoying kid. Give any attention at all and it'll just get worse.* He glanced back to the bed and was surprised to see that the djinn had disappeared once more. With a satisfied grunt, Henry turned back to his wardrobe, only to cry out when he spotted the genie standing imposingly in the closet, a tie flopping down from the shelf onto its shoulder.

"You must make a wish, Henry Reinhold," the genie commanded, its voice growing so intense the hangers and bins in the closet rattled. "I tire of waiting."

Henry ground his teeth again, obstinate childishness rising in him. "No!"

He went to grab his shirt from the bed, but the genie was there, standing by the dresser. Henry ignored him, put on his clothes, and stormed from the room. Out in the hall the djinn was waiting for him.

"Would you not desire a larger abode, Henry Reinhold?" the genie asked, gesturing to the living room. Henry staunchly shook his head.

"I like it fine. Anything bigger would make the electric bill sky high."

"Then would you desire more wealth to pay for it?"

"I told you, my pension's solid," Henry glared at the genie. "*I'm* going out."

Henry stomped out of the kitchen to the back stoop, but there was the genie, pulling its discarded lamp from the trash. Its eyes glowed with anger, but it simply set the lamp on the porch railing before glaring at Henry once more. "Perhaps you desire a larger rubbish bin, in order to dispose of my shrine more effectively?"

Henry didn't even bother to reply. He took off down the sidewalk at a fair clip, hoping to outpace the genie, but the djinn persistently clung to his side, pointing to everything it saw on the street—a dog, a fire hydrant, a skateboard, a stop sign, *everything*—and offering it to him. Henry stayed silent, clenched his jaw, and tried to tune out the genie's constant prattle. It was a code of silence he maintained while he was at the corner bistro despite the fact that the genie relentlessly badgered him.

"Would you desire a larger sandwich?" it asked. "Or a different sandwich? Or a delicatessen of your own to craft sandwiches whenever and wherever you choose?"

After he ate, Henry saw Jack the Man and Stu Budgie playing cards at the café out on the sidewalk. Budgie waved to him, but Henry just nodded, keeping on course. He was afraid if he said anything it would make the genie worse.

His stoicism did nothing. The whole time Henry was at the corner market, and the fruit stand outside, and all the way home, the djinn kept going like a wind-up toy that never slowed. Even as Henry calmly put away his groceries, the tirade did not cease.

"Would you desire a better oven?" the djinn hounded. "Or a new sink? A factory of your own, perhaps, to manufacture ovens and sinks in any way you choose?"

Henry clicked on the radio, turning it up loud to try to drown out the djinn. It was the second of the series against the Phillies, and for a long while the game was tied at two before going to extra innings. The Sox tried to rally, but come the top of the eleventh Philadelphia's best hitter smacked a home run, and that was that.

When evening rolled around, Henry decided on some television. Sitting on the sofa, the genie nestled down next to him, still chattering away. Henry settled in to watch a show about people enthusiastically demolishing a family's house in order to rebuild it with somewhat less excitement. When the first commercial break came on, the djinn suddenly halted its verbal assault. Henry had gone so far into himself in order to endure the genie's blather that it took a few seconds for him to realize it had gone silent. He looked at the djinn. Its gaze was transfixed on the television, childlike, captivated by something on the screen. After a bit, it motioned to the TV.

"Now *that* must be desired by millions," the genie said flatly, looking at Henry. "You cannot tell me it does not stir longing in you, Henry Reinhold."

Henry hadn't even been paying attention to the commercials; they were one of the few things more annoying than the genie's incessant yammering. Now he focused on it, and groaned.

"It's a *Victoria's Secret* commercial, you dope." Henry shook his head as half-dressed waifs shimmied and sauntered and pouted on his television—he hadn't seen that much skin in Seoul's red-light district—however the djinn, for the first time, appeared distracted, even mesmerized.

"Even in the harem of my lamp's paradise there is rarely such exquisite beauty," it rhapsodized. Henry grunted.

"Plastic surgeons are rich for a reason, kid."

The genie's puzzlement returned. "And you are still adamant that even their beauty is not desirous to you?"

"Is it to you?" Henry countered. The genie raised its hands, palm up, and shrugged.

"What *I* desire is irrelevant," it said. "My function is to fulfil the wishes of others, not my own."

"Hardly seems fair. You should be able to have what *you* want once in a while. Maybe I'll wish one of those models here for you."

"Is this what you desire?" The djinn looked again to the screen, restrained eagerness on its face.

"I desire to shut your ass up," Henry shot back. "And if one of those peep show pageant girls will do it, you're damn right it is."

"Then it shall be done." The genie smiled its gleaming grin once more, crossed one arm over the other, and bowed its head. Before Henry knew it, an impossibly tall, impossibly tanned woman with the tiniest waist he had ever seen appeared in the living room in front of the television, wearing high heels, barely-there lingerie, and nothing else. It happened so fast, Henry hadn't even blinked; one second, nothing, the next a person in his house. The supermodel looked in bewilderment around the living room.

"Where am I?" she asked, her voice a thick stew of an accent, before motioning to Henry and the djinn. "And who are you?"

Henry stood up, pointing to the genie. "*He's* a jackass, and *I'm* going to bed."

As he walked away, Henry heard the djinn's voice behind him. "You still have two wishes, Henry Reinhold."

"Isn't that a shame?" Henry replied. Looking back he saw the supermodel in the spot Henry had occupied on the sofa. Gently, Henry reached up and grabbed Marie's photograph from the wall, tucking it under one arm. "Whatever you two do out here, my wife doesn't need to see it. She was classier than that."

Henry went down the hall to his bedroom, propped Marie up on the night stand, and went to sleep.

WHEN HENRY WOKE the following morning, he couldn't believe the wreck the living room had turned into. Pillows and sofa cushions were strewn haphazardly across the room, a table lamp had been knocked over, and an antique vase lay on its side, part of the rim cracked; a pair of woman's panties was draped over a potted plant, and a bra hung from the television. Henry shook his head. He'd done the right thing taking Marie with him, after all.

He heard voices talking in the kitchen, and when he entered, Henry saw the genie and the supermodel sitting at the table. The supermodel had on Henry's bathrobe and was drinking a cup of coffee, her thick auburn hair tousled. The djinn spotted Henry and smiled widely.

"O blessed Henry Reinhold, may the Host of the Thousand Firmaments shower you with unending good tidings and joy."

"Mm-hmm," Henry said. "I see you experienced some joy yourself last night."

At the table the supermodel squirmed with obvious embarrassment, but the genie's leer intensified. "It was an excellent wish, Henry Reinhold. May your other two prove to be just as interesting."

Henry nodded before leaning in towards the djinn. "It goes like *this*. I want you *out* of my house. I want you *out* of my life." Henry pointed a finger at the supermodel. "My second wish is for her to go back to where she came from, and take her unmentionables with her."

The genie's features slackened with sudden surprise before disappointment gave way to a weak plea: "Is there no way you would reconsider?"

"It is my desire," Henry answered forcefully. The genie folded one arm over the other almost involuntarily and bowed its head, frowning while it did so; instantly the supermodel disappeared, the empty bathrobe crumpling to the kitchen chair. The djinn glumly looked at Henry.

"That was unwarranted," the djinn sighed. "She was Brazilian, you know. They are a festive, enthusiastic people."

"I'm sure they are." Henry picked up the bathrobe; it still smelled of perfume. He peered at the genie then, staring right into its emerald eyes. "I know my third wish, too."

"That is wonderful news, Henry Reinhold," the djinn said, chuckling nervously. "And what is your desire?"

Henry told him and the genie's laughter doubled. After a minute it stopped, scrutinizing Henry. "You are serious, aren't you?" Henry nodded, and the genie's spirited face sank once more. "Of all the things of Heaven and Earth at your beck and whim, and this is your choice? Not riches or women or power or revenge or reshaping the world in your image, but *this*?"

"It is my desire," Henry repeated, smiling. The genie slowly nodded.

"Then it shall be done."

"Does this mean you'll finally leave me alone?"

The genie nodded again. "My obligations to you are thus fulfilled, Henry Reinhold. May your desire be what you hoped."

The djinn again folded one arm over the other and bowed, and a second later Henry saw the genie's visage begin to fade and disintegrate into dust, rotating back like a whirlwind to the rear kitchen door leading to the porch. The door opened and the dust cloud careened through the air to the stoop, narrowing into a stream and flowing into the long spout of the lamp that sat on the porch railing. A heartbeat later, everything was still.

Henry sighed, grabbed the lamp and set it on the kitchen table before making breakfast. While he ate his eggs, he idly wondered what would happen if he rubbed it again. He tried it, but unlike before nothing happened.

"Limit one per customer." He smiled, finishing his breakfast.

He spent the rest of the morning cleaning the living room, putting everything back into place and vacuuming before he brought Marie back out from the bedroom to hang on the wall. She always had loved a clean house.

As afternoon rolled around, Henry took the cracked vase to the kitchen and attempted to fix the ceramic with hot glue and clamps. He turned the radio on. It was the third of the series between Boston and the Phillies, but this time the Sox came out swinging from the first at bat; by the top of the fourth they were up on Philadelphia 5-0 and at the stretch had doubled the lead. In the ninth, with bases loaded, the final Sox batter walked up to the plate and knocked a Grand Slam clear out of Fenway. The announcer was beside himself with excitement, and kept calling it the most amazing game of the season. Historic. Unbelievable.

"We couldn't have wished for a win this big. It's just crazy," one of the players said in exhilaration after the game. "Somebody out there was really looking over us today, you know?"

Opening up a cold beer, Henry smiled contentedly at the radio for a moment before turning his attention back to the vase.

Phoenix Rising

Heather M. O'Connor

TWO OLD FRIENDS, one plump and grey, the other as frail as a bird, share a bench in the park, grateful for the summer sunshine.

"How is she today?" the plump one asks.

"Not good, Rose. I've just come from her side. I don't think she'll live out the day."

"Don't fret, Viv. Death is part of life. The endless circle." Rose pats her shoulder. "Clara is going to a better place. No more pain and suffering. We'll see her again soon enough."

"It's not that." Viv's rheumy eyes leak tears. Her lower lip trembles. "I just—I wish it was me."

Rose hands her a handkerchief.

"Thank you," Viv says, dabbing at her eyes.

She pauses a moment to collect herself.

"I never wanted to grow old, you know. I wanted to burn fast and die young. Now look at me. We were never meant to live this long. I'm so tired of being old and grey."

She fumbles in her purse.

"Viv! Put that away. You know you can't smoke here!"

"You can't smoke anywhere anymore!" she says, showing a spark of her old fire.

"Come on then. Let's go for a walk."

They hobble off, holding onto each other for support. A crisp carpet of pine needles cushions their steps. Rose points to a bench deep in the trees, and they settle, breathless.

Pines tower above them, filtering the heat. Viv shivers. "I wouldn't say no to a nice toasty cremation. The summers are getting hotter, but I'm always chilled."

She roots around in her bag again. "'Stop smoking,' they said. 'It's dangerous.' Ha! What do they know?"

Rose nods. "Not many pleasures left at our age. Need a light?"

"Please."

A spark flares. Tendrils of smoke curl around them.

"I was quite a beauty when I was young, you know. Men worshipped me."

"I remember, Viv. Quite the catch."

"If they could catch me." A mischievous smile flickers then fades. "But now . . . People don't even see me anymore. It's like I don't even exist. Don't you ever get tired of it?"

"Of course I do. Not so much losing my looks. It's the attitude that really burns me up," says Rose. "Hmph. I may not be a spring chicken, but I'm not dead yet."

Viv breathes out a cloud of smoke. "Wasn't like that when we were young."

"Mm. People respected their elders. Didn't think they knew it all. They listened, instead of flapping their gums all the time."

Viv nods. "Try to tell them that today."

They shake their heads.

"Bunch of tree huggers," says Rose. "What do they know?"

Viv sniffs. "Moderation in all things. That's how I was raised."

"Remember Smoky the Bear? 'Only you can prevent forest fires.'"

Viv titters.

"They think they're so clever, putting out fires before they begin. Now it's out of control. First Fort McMurray. Now the BC Interior. When will they ever learn?"

Viv breathes in. "Look." She points to a column of smoke rising in the distance.

"Clara."

They hurry into the woods, following the drift of smoke to its source. Already the fire pops and sparks. Flames dance along the forest floor and soar to the treetops, leaping from pine to pine. Rose and Viv glow ember-red and amber in the blistering heat.

Bathed in wildfire, a child wails. "Clara darling," Rose coos. "You must be famished."

Cold Comfort

Gabrielle Harbowy

IT HAD ALL been about a boy.

It had never been about a boy.

It *started* with a boy, but that isn't the same thing at all. It's easier, telling myself the boy is to blame. It hurts less than admitting it's always been about Nuala.

Frostbite hurts. The humiliation of frostbite stings long after fingers go numb and black. I draw mine through the living flame of my hair, by long habit. Though I no longer expect the gesture to warm me, I'm disappointed every time when my hands emerge still cold.

It hurts, but curses are supposed to hurt.

My prison is the plane of ice, an endless terrain of caves and snow. Or, if it has an end, I've yet to find it. The caves, I formed myself. I have no interest in mapping them. If I want out, I can just melt my way.

Even the ice elementals are bored of me, and mostly leave me alone. Occasionally some plane-bound creature explores my caves, perhaps on a challenge or a dare. They melt from my heat before I can draw near enough to ask.

At least they don't leave behind corpses to compound my guilt, and a few of the items they leave behind in their puddled remains have proven useful to me. The chronometer, scavenged from the mortal plane, is a beautiful thing of metal and glass and dials. It withstands my heat, as long as I'm careful, and seems to be of the same make as the portal frame, resistant to tarnish, brute force, and corrosion, as well as the elements.

With the chronometer, I know when the portal will come to life. I have set the device so that both wands are pointed upward when the cycle begins. Upward, for hope.

The frame is powered by aether and steam. It gets hot. Because it's a heat I haven't made, I can feel it. I must be close by when it starts up so that I can wrap my hands around a column, press my body to it like a lover, and soak in those burning moments while I can. It makes the chill worse, but the indulgence is worth it. Besides, curses are supposed to hurt.

Demons emerge from the portal. My birth mother first, then a dozen or so children, then my mama. The heat of their skin reacts with their new environment, and steam wisps from their bodies. The ghosts of tethers encircle one ankle of each child, tying them to their home plane.

"Stay close, little sparks," my mama says. Mother helps round up the stragglers and keeps them still while Mama counts them.

I've slipped behind the post, pressing my back to its waning heat.

"Who here knows what a curse is?" Mother asks. About ten scarlet hands shoot up. I don't have to see them to know it. It's the same every time.

"It's what happens to you if you're very bad," one little ember says.

The metal is nearly cold. I press my cheek to it and peek round it to catch Mama's eye. The look she gives me is sad. It's a look I know well.

They're teachers, my parents are. It's the only way they're able to come and see me.

"That's right. Everyone has to be fair to everyone else, or they could get cursed."

A curse is a funny thing. There's no defence against it, and no way to bypass or remove it save by following its conditions exactly. Some creatures are just so powerful that their decree can reshape reality. Nuala knew she had that power. At first, I comforted myself by believing that she hadn't known; that she had spoken in anger and hadn't meant it. But I knew better.

"Come out, Izelle," Mother calls. As always, I consider what would happen if I didn't obey. I'm already here, powerless . . . it's not as if they could punish me much further. But the little joys are all I have, and seeing Mother and Mama is one of them. Even if it comes at the cost of a handful of gawking children.

The littlest ones gasp and stare when I emerge. My frostbitten fingers and tail are as black as my hooves, and the rest of my skin has faded to pale pink from exposure and cold. I barely look like one of their kind anymore. I can see them all thinking it.

"The thing about curses," Mama says, "is that there's always a trigger that removes them, but only the one who places the curse knows what it is. She can tell the target or not. She doesn't have to tell anyone. She can tell the target and make them unable to tell anyone else, or put them in a situation that would make the conditions of releasing them impossible."

"What do you think?" Mother asks them. They're all still staring at me. "Is that fair?"

"Punishment doesn't have to be fair," one of the littles says. Mother calls them sparks, but I think of them as embers, their optimism burning brightly, but easily snuffed out.

"What's your curse?" another asks me. My parents share a look. They're supposed to address their teachers, not me, but because I've been asked, I can answer. Do my mothers fear what I might say?

"My own fire will never warm me." It's been a long time since I last used my voice. I expect it to be hoarse, to sound unpleasant in my ears. It doesn't. "Only when my body is back to its normal temperature will the portal allow me through. I may speak only things I am asked to say."

"What about fire you kindle?"

"Even a fire I make by physical means, yes." I look around pointedly. "Not that there's anything here to burn."

There had only been my clothes. I had learned by burning my clothes.

"What did she *do*?" the first young one asks Mother. This one has remembered not to speak to me.

Mother considers a moment, then surprises me. "Izelle, what did you do to earn this curse?"

I can recite the stock answers the teachers always give, or I can speak in my own words. In opinions. Do I dare to?

"I angered a summoner."

They all gasp. Glances are exchanged. No one is quite sure what to say next.

Some mortals, powerful ones, can summon us. The embers wear the tethers to keep them from being summoned too young but most of us can choose to resist the call. To me, Nuala had been radiant, full of life and ambition. Perhaps she had been powerful enough to compel me to her, but I would have gone to her by my own will in any case.

No one has told me to stop speaking, so I go on. "We were familiar for a long time. Long enough for her to grow from girl to woman. I was her pet and servant and companion. She compelled me to share my thoughts, my opinions. But I had a strong opinion she didn't like. She was—that is, I *thought* she was—in danger, so I warned her. I tried to protect her. She was so angry at my interference that instead of just dispelling me, she cursed me and banished me here, to the plane of ice."

Silence, but for a distant howl of wind. I can read the children's moods by the subdued colours in their fiery hair, all oranges and yellows. A dozen or so pairs of eyes are fixed on the snowy ground.

"This is why we no longer heed the plane of mortals," Mama says quietly.

What? I try to speak it, but she hasn't asked for my reaction, so I can't. I spread my hands, hoping the supplicating gesture will do. The few moments of speech have spoiled me and now I keenly feel its loss.

Neither Mother nor Mama look at me now. Mama has let herself say this to the children so that I can hear it. I'm sure of it. So she must intend to follow through. She *must*.

She doesn't.

The portal opens. Through it I see a world of fire. My home. I yearn to reach toward it but I know I'll only be knocked unconscious if I try to rush the aperture, or even draw too near—I can only approach the structure carefully, from the side.

My parents gather the children and shepherd them through, without another word or glance to me. They can't let on that I'm their daughter around the children. That would shift focus from the lesson they're meant to learn. I'm a cautionary tale, not an object of pity or a damsel to be rescued. If any of them should be compelled to rescue me, they must come to it on their own.

But they will not. Ours is a race of passion, not compassion. Fire devours and cleanses all in its path. It gives no consideration to the unwary.

Be wary, my presence here teaches them. *Look on this freezing wretch and remember her. Do not slip your tethers. The mortal plane is not for you.*

The rest have all gone through when Mama, bringing up the rear, pauses. "Close one, today," she says to no one in particular, and then steps through.

Silence rings loud in my ears.

I turn and walk idly toward my caves. I need to think.

What do they *do*, then, in this new demon utopia where the threat of summoning by mortals has become obsolete? Do they keep their tethers all their lives? Do they still train in the arcane arts? Do they still hone the strength of their mental self-control?

In my youth, I learned how to resist a call, how to accept one, how to throw another demon into a summon if I did not want to go. How to defeat a summoner and return home at will. Without these things, what is there? How does society function if no one is ever swept away without warning?

If I ever get out of exile, will I recognize the world I return to?

I sleep fitfully and dream of bonfires. Even in dreams I'm never warm.

I wake with the words "Close one, today" ringing in my ears. Hope is dangerous. Hope distracts me and makes me weak.

Nuala knew just what she was doing. The curse can only be broken by one who does not know how to break the curse. One of those little shits has to feel sympathy for me and want to warm me of their own accord. But I've been cast as a villain and deprived of the voice to explain myself, so that may never happen. I'm unlikely to ever inspire kindness, Nuala's words loudly implied.

This was the reward for trying to save a summoner's heart. Look on it, little children, and meddle not in the affairs of mortals.

Let them burn.

DAYS GO BY without another "close one," but I still see that moment every time I shut my eyes. I don't need to sleep, but I like sleep. It helps to pass the time. Without it, time passes slowly and thoughts zip about like embers, singeing wherever they settle.

When I see the dark shape in the snow, I assume it's a hallucination. Not a mirage, because mirages require heat and the only heat in this place is me.

Closer, carefully closer. I'm positive I'm losing my mind, I've finally cracked, because it looks like a person. It looks like the one person it can't possibly be.

I kneel in the snow, hands hovering but afraid to close the distance. If this really is a torment made in my own mind and my hand goes through her, I may never trust my own senses again.

Yet, that's still better than whatever it might mean if this is real.

I'm losing feeling in my legs. It's time to decide. I lower my hand, and—

Solid. Wet, limp silk, sweat-soaked hair freezing in crisp clumps like arctic lichen.

Nuala.

Time has touched her. There are lines at the corners of her eyes. Someone has touched her, too, and not gently. Burns crust her face, raw and oozing. Burns decorate her body, wherever skin is visible.

I lift her, surprised I have the strength to—either I am not as weak as I thought, or she has very little substance left—and I carry her into my caves, out of the wind. I warm her. At least my fire is of use to someone, if not to me.

Holding her while she slumbers floods me with memories, all overlain by her face, twisted with rage, when she pronounced my curse. It hurts more than frostbite, more than solitude. I wonder if this is a test of some kind. Of my compassion, maybe, to see if I've been punished sufficiently yet. It could well be, but I find that I don't care. I will do what I will do for my own reasons, no one else's.

Different voices are loud in my head now. These voices, at least, let me sleep.

"Izelle."

For the first time in an age, I don't know what I'm going to see when I open my eyes.

"Izelle, I know you're awake."

She always could tell.

"You were right about the boy. Lenzhen. The dragon. Whatever he is. I'm sure that's what you want to hear. Well, it's true. He hurt me. He was too much. Too cruel. I thought I could tame him the way I tamed you."

It stings right to the quick. And she hasn't asked anything of me, so I can't retort. I huff and elbow her in the side. She ignores both.

"I thought you were just jealous of him. Now I understand what you saw. What you tried to warn me of. Dammit, I'm confessing to you. The least you could do is look at the wreck of me."

No, if I'd done my least I would have left her where I found her, to freeze. I've already done more than the least. When she cursed me, she dismissed me. She has no power to compel me anymore. I leave my eyes closed.

A confession is not an apology.

She huffs and turns over, shutting me out. I wonder if she remembers the limits she put on my speech. Is she deliberately avoiding questions to keep me from talking, or has she just forgotten?

Or is she that accustomed to giving orders instead of asking?

She's muttering to herself. ". . . send you to wherever you sent your demon wench . . ." and ". . . see if anyone keeps *you* warm." She sounds delirious, but from her grumblings I can piece together a chain of events.

She is not here for me. I'm meant as her punishment and that is how she sees me. Karma made flesh, nothing more.

I withdraw my heat from her.

"Don't you dare stop," she snaps at me.

She has no control over me. I stop.

Nuala rolls onto her back, wincing, and shrugs. "Fine. Cold is good for burns, anyway."

I watch her until she starts to shiver in silence. She could ask for my help. Request it. She doesn't.

I turn away.

BY THE TIME my chronometer signals the arrival of the next class,

Nuala's wet clothes and raw skin have frozen to the ice. Fused to it. She screams when I rip her free. More than frozen silk stays behind.

I don't press myself to the portal. I savour the cold. It's colder for Nuala, because she could be warm at any time for the small cost of a little kindness. It's colder for Nuala because she's only endured one night of it, and considers that equal to the eternities of torment to which her words sentenced me. Were they careless words? I still don't know. It doesn't matter. That's what I've learned. Whether she meant the curse or it was a heated response to a heated moment, she's never regretted; never had remorse.

Knowing this . . . I'm not comforted by it, but it's enough.

Mama comes through first and halts in her tracks. The first little ember bumps right into her before she remembers her hooves and moves out of the way.

When Mother comes through, Mama grasps her hand and clings to it.

Silence. Long moments of it.

I imagine what this must look like to Nuala. A cluster of crimson-skinned creatures, most small, led by two stern women. If she thinks they're considering how her frosty white flesh would taste, she's not far wrong.

I tighten my fist in Nuala's stringy hair, forcing her head into a token bow. She wavers on her feet, so I let her fall to her knees. I keep hold of her hair.

"Izelle," Mama says carefully, "who do you bring us today?"

"This is Nuala, Mama." The mortal stiffens. "She's the summoner who sentenced me here."

Now she knows she's not just before a jury of my kind, but a jury intimately connected to me.

The children have never seen a mortal, but they all know to fear the word "summoner." Many of them take an instinctive step back, even though this summoner is in no condition to pose a threat. They can't know that, I suppose. Those tethers they wear: have they ever been tested?

Nuala is still. She says nothing, having lost her urge to complain before a greater audience.

"Tell me more, Izelle. How did she come to you?"

"She was cursed to be exiled to wherever she'd sent me."

"Ah. Are you pleased to see her?"

I'm uncomfortable suddenly. I don't want to analyse my thoughts on this, and I want to admit to them even less. But I've been asked.

"I always thought I would be, but I also thought she'd be remorseful about how she'd treated me. But she wasn't, so . . . no. Her presence adds to my torment."

Mother appears to consider this, but I already know what she's thinking. Suddenly it all plays out before me. And I smile a toothy smile. "Children?" She turns to the embers.

Nuala twitches. Now she sees the road before us, too.

"Set her on fire," one ember squeaks. "Can we? Can we do it?"

The rest bounce on their hooves, excited. "Can we?" It becomes a cacophonous chorus. Excitement sparks from child to child; it blazes alight.

"Go ahead, sparks."

The children are glowing. Pent up energy spills out their eyes and fingers. Their hair blazes.

I miss the first spark. I don't know which of the children sets it off. Nuala's hair catches first. She almost seems to welcome the warmth for a moment. Then the flames reach her skin. I'm still behind her, holding her by the hair, and by hell, she's warm. I'd forgotten what heat feels like. It's absolute bliss. Like sinking into silk.

The children stare. My parents stare too, with teary hope in their eyes. When I pull back and make a show of toasting my palms on her flaming hair, they see. They can't show extreme emotion before the kids.

The colour returns to my skin. My arms darken, changing from frost pink to my natural crimson.

It's working.

It's *working*.

Nuala thrashes weakly. Flames crackle up my arms, warm my torso, lick at my chin.

Someone who didn't know how to lift the curse set a fire. And it warmed me.

"It's . . . It's broken, I think," I say, experimenting. The words come out, so it must be true.

I'm reluctant to let go of Nuala's burning corpse, as if the snow will quench her and the curse will return. I add to it, making my own flame, and I *feel* it.

I keep my hand in her hair while Mama and Mother rush up and embrace me. They add their heat to mine. The embers circle us, dancing and cheering.

I drop my tormenter's body only when it's time to go through the portal. I consider taking her with me, but she doesn't deserve my home. Her corpse will freeze, preserved on ice. I leave her as a visual aid for the next generations of students.

"Close one, today," I say to no one in particular as I step through.

Aitvaras

R.W. Hodgson

ANNA OPENED THE door of the small cottage to find four neat stacks of coins on the stoop glinting in the last rays of the summer sun. She shut the door and pressed her back against it. Her blood ran cold.

There was a tremendous rush outside like the sound of a windstorm, though the branches of the tree beyond the yellowed window did not move. Then the knock came again. *There will be no hiding from this.*

She took a slow, steady breath and opened the door. She could see nothing but feet, belly, and a tip of a snout. A black dragon drummed long charcoal talons on her wooden step, its scaly lips parted over inky teeth. It emitted a growl with a tone that could only be described as "satisfaction".

Anna kept her head upright and her eyes forward though her legs were shaking. The dragon dissolved into a puff of dark smoke that skidded around her skirt and into the small cottage. In front of the hearth it re-formed, as a cockerel, ebony from the top of its comb to the tip of its claws, save for five long tail feathers of flame. There was a burst of fire to her side as the money materialized on the table.

The creature paced along the back wall, light from its plumes making shadows dance across the floor. It brushed its tail over the hearth, lighting a pile of neatly stacked logs.

"Good evening, Anna," it said. The beak did not move, the deep voice emanated from every wall.

Anna swallowed. "Aitvaras, you have returned."

"I have. And, in honour of our new home, I have brought you a gift."

Anna inched towards the table. Two stacks of gold chervonetz, another two of silver roubles all on top of two ten-chervonetz notes. More cash than she'd seen in one place in five years, perhaps even in her life.

"Where did you get it?"

"That does not matter; it is yours now."

She shook her head. "We've been bartering for everything for a year. Adomas had to save for weeks just to scrape up enough money for his ticket to Kaunas. And what would I do with this?" She turned a coin over in her hand. "Waltz into the village and hand over a gold chervonetz to buy a cow? Wouldn't that seem strange? But that's the point, isn't it?"

The aitvaras cocked its head.

Anna scooped up the money in one swift motion, opened the front door and tossed it out. "Well, I don't want it."

With another puff, the money re-appeared on the table.

"And yet, it is for you and for Adomas."

A knot wound in Anna's stomach. Adomas had gone to Kaunas five months ago, at the risk of being discovered, to find a girl he had met in the resistance, marry her, and bring her back to this small spit of a village. Anna had stayed to hold their place and to make this shabby cottage into a home. Last week Adomas had finally sent word he'd be returning with his new wife. They were to arrive tomorrow morning on the overnight train.

Anna was also married, or, at least, she had been; the Soviets had deported him in 1940 and that was the last she'd ever heard of him. But a wife for Adomas meant life for all of them: a home, children, and perhaps even a bit of happiness. Anna's eyes swept the meagre, one-room cottage, which she'd slaved to clean and prepare; then shifted back to the aitvaras strutting the floor. *It might have been a nice home, but now it might as well be ash.*

Anna grabbed her kerchief from her bedpost and knotted it

behind her ears. She gathered up the money again and pushed out the door of the cottage. The aitvaras followed, its head bobbing with each step. As soon as it was beyond the threshold, it regained the form of a dragon and its footsteps shook the ground underneath her feet.

She found a spot where the earth looked soft and dug with her fingers. She was used to this. She had worked on the local collective farm in the months her brother had been gone. Tools were few and far between, so it was sticks or rocks or her own bare hands that she used to work the earth.

The aitvaras sat next to her, hot breath on the back of her neck and a wing stretched over her like a canopy. She knew it could not hurt her directly, but its presence made her mouth dry and her heart beat faster.

During her childhood, she had only seen fleeting glimpses of the aitvaras as a dragon, but as a rooster the creature had been ever-present. It had strutted the rooms of her grandfather's farmhouse, hopping up on the furniture, pacing the mantle, peering down at her with a shiny black eye from atop the clock in the hall. Back then, she had tried to chase it—a shadow with a candle for a tail—but her mother had caught her round the waist and whispered in her ear that it was an evil thing and would burn her if she touched it.

Though she was never courageous enough to test her mother's word, it remained a strange and almost joyful thing for her to lay eyes on. That was until the morning she woke to find her mother crying and her grandfather and father standing solemnly by her uncle's bedroom door. Her uncle had always been a drunkard, kept mostly dry by his personal poverty. The aitvaras had granted him the gift of a whole cask of wine and he'd drank himself to death.

Later, in 1928, the entire village's crops failed and bags of grain appeared in their pantry. Her grandfather refused to accept them even though the whole family was starving. He took the bags into the village to return them, but the rightful owner was not the type to listen to reason and stabbed him. He never made it home.

Then there was the gold watch that appeared by her eldest brother's bedside. He had been much more cautious in trying to find the owner, but was trampled by a runaway horse and cart with the accursed thing still clutched in his hand. From then on, Anna had tried to frighten the aitvaras away when her mother wasn't there to scold her, but to it the waving arms of a little girl were nothing.

"Why did you leave?" Anna said softly—barely loud enough to be heard over the creature's breath and the din of cicadas. Anna couldn't say precisely when it had left, but one night, after they were forced to leave the farmhouse and were sleeping huddled in the forest, she realized she couldn't remember the last time she had seen it.

The rumble of satisfaction sounded again. "I have laboured at my revenge for centuries, thinning out the ranks of the descendants slowly, as is my nature. But there are times when it is quicker for me to step aside and let history take its course."

"Ah, so it was easier to leave us to the Russians and the Germans," she said as she dropped the money into the hole and covered it with earth. It spoke the truth; her parents and five of her brothers gone in less than five years. She rose to her feet and stamped down the spot.

Night had fallen and the only light was the fire in the cottage. Anna dusted her hands as she entered and the aitvaras skidded back to rooster form, black wingtips whispering by her legs. The dirt was still under her nails but the money was on the table, clean and neatly stacked. It was not surprising, but still her heart sank.

She sat down with a sigh and began to shred the chervonetz notes, over and over again. Each time she let them fall to the tabletop, fire lit the edges and they reassembled.

"I still don't understand," she said, caught up in the rhythm of tearing. "I know we're the descendants of some warlord who once supposedly controlled half of Lithuania, or some other embellishment I've never benefited from. But what my mother never explained to me was *why*. What is it that you are taking vengeance for?"

There was a pause, the aitvaras' shadow was long in the light of the hearth, the reflection of its tail stretching across the floor like fingers. "Long ago I brought that warlord success," the walls said, reverberating in her chest. "And for that I was worshipped—by him, by his children and his children's children. But then the new god came and the old were forgotten. I was called a devil and they tried to drive me from my home."

Anna gave a short, bitter laugh. "Haven't you heard? The Soviets are here, there are to be no gods, old or new."

The creature didn't answer.

"So this is because you felt slighted, is it? How pathetic. It's been six hundred years; your revenge is too slow."

"And yet, once you and Adomas are dead, it will be complete."

How long do we have before this money brings fate crashing down on us? Will I talk to my brother across this table? Will he have a night to rest with his new wife in the small bed with the red blanket? Perhaps a few of my brothers deserved their fate, but not Adomas.

Anna cocked her head to the side and the rooster cocked its head along with her.

She grabbed one of the ten-chervonetz notes and half the coins, carefully creased the face of Lenin, folded up the edges of the note and wrapped them around the coins until she had a neat, secure little packet. She then repeated the process with the second note. She held one in place with a thumb against each palm and strode slowly towards the hearth.

She stared into the flames where they danced along the cracks in the logs. The heat pulled at the skin on her legs and the smoke touched her nostrils. The aitvaras paced beside her, alternating flashes of black and fire. From it, there was nothing: no heat, no scent.

Laughter came from the walls and the aitvaras shook its jet comb. "Go on then," it said, pointing with its beak. "Throw them in. Let's have this over with."

"If you have brought us this gift," Anna began softly, "it means you know there is nothing outside these walls that will kill us, at least before we bring the next generation into the world and render your revenge incomplete."

The aitvaras flapped its wings and its tail glowed brighter.

"No matter if we are sent to the Gulag or fight for the Forest Brothers or get hit by a runaway carriage, Adomas and I will not die. Or else you would not be here. If you did not put this money on our table, in wait of the Russian you stole it from, we would live."

Anna looked at the packets and back to the fire. Her mother's voice rang in her head: *Don't touch it; it will burn your fingers.*

She bit down on her lip so hard she drew blood. When the creature turned for another strut, Anna whirled on her heel and grabbed a hold of the fiery tail feathers with both hands.

The aitvaras screamed.

It started as a chicken's squawk but then grew deep and powerful. The walls shook so much she feared the cottage would come down around them. Anna screamed too, but the sound was lost like a match in a wildfire. Her hands blistered and tightened, the money turning molten in her grasp.

The aitvaras ran on its rooster feet, pulling her behind it like a ragdoll around the cottage.

The pain in her hands was unbearable.

Her skin burned off in layers down to the raw nerves, hissing and popping as it went. Then, to her relief, she couldn't feel them anymore.

She fought to gain footing on the wooden floorboards, then pulled back her shoulder with all the strength she had. Three tail feathers pulled free in her left hand and burst into sparks around her before fading into the darkness. She clung to the remaining with her right.

The aitvaras' screams took on new vigour, changing tone as it reached the doorway and the dragon form washed over it. In an instant, Anna's feet were above the ground as the creature took to the sky. She dangled behind it by her right hand which was fused to the two remaining feathers. Her hand floated inside the shadow of a black dragon tail unable to solidify.

The aitvaras crested in the sky. It made no attempt to shake her: it could not cause her death directly, but it cursed her liberally to the heavens.

The air was cool and growing colder; the stars bright and beautiful. Her left hand hung limply at her side; it throbbed at the unnaturally straight line where char met flesh. In the quiet she could hear the sound of it sizzling. Her fingers were black as coal, forever burned into a claw around a fistful of ash and slag.

She smiled weakly. She was shivering and there was something warm in her mouth. Far below her, the countryside stretched like a black blanket. Pinpricks of light were rare, save for a great cluster off in the distance that must be Kaunas. She saw the lights of a train snaking its way through the forest. And she saw Adomas. He was sitting at a window seat, staring into the night, a woman asleep on his shoulder. She had an honest face and hands used to work.

They were almost home.

She lifted her stiffening left arm and pushed her elbow into the leathery hide of the aitvaras. With her leverage in place, she pulled the remaining tail feathers.

She hung for a second in the summer sky above her homeland. The tail dissolved, the aitvaras screamed, and the air burst into flames and wrapped around her.

She was free.

"HEY, YOU," NIKOLAI said, grabbing the collar of an old man they met on the village road. "My money has gone missing, do you know anything about it? Justus?"

The translator spoke with the man in Lithuanian. Nikolai could tell by the head shakes and hand gestures that the answer would be no.

Nikolai let the man go and Justus took up his conversation with the soldiers about the fireball in the sky last night. They'd talked about nothing else their whole walk from the last village to this one but Nikolai had more important matters than meteorites on his mind at the moment.

He had found nothing but frustration since he'd been sent here from the smoking rubble of Stalingrad with a medal pinned to his chest to work as a collective farm supervisor. Migration had been heavy in this area, there weren't enough people, there weren't enough tools, and no one spoke a word of Russian.

He had to get his money back. It was a small fortune he'd hoarded during the war in gold chervonetz, bills, and roubles, one he didn't want to lose and one he didn't want the higher-ups to find out about.

He grabbed a second man passing by, a younger one, both arms weighed down by carpet bags and a woman by his side.

"He says he doesn't know a thing. He just got back into town this morning on the train," Justus translated.

The woman searched her clothing and produced the stub of a train ticket.

"I don't care what anyone says," Nikolai said with a sharp chop of his hand. "I'm going to search every house in this village from top to bottom until I find it."

Justus thought it necessary to translate this to the young couple, who shrugged.

Three men huddled together by the side of the road caught Nikolai's eye.

"What are you doing here? Justus, ask them what they're doing here."

Justus raised an eyebrow as he translated their answer. "They say that one's old rooster laid an egg."

"Rooster? These country idiots! Did you tell them roosters don't lay eggs?"

"I did, but they still insist."

"Here, let me see." He squatted in the midst of them and snatched the egg. He held it up to the sunlight. As Nikolai stared at it, he saw flames dancing below the surface. His mouth went dry, the farmers were crowded around him but he couldn't make out a single face.

"Let's go and start the search," Justus said, his voice sounded far away, drowned out by the buzzing in Nikolai's head. "We want it done quickly, huh?"

A warmth spread through his chest, Nikolai waved his arm. "Aw, don't bother, I'm sure I just misplaced the money." The flames leapt at the back of his eyes, more consuming than the sun. "This, I'm keeping."

Midnight Man versus Frankie Flame

Chadwick Ginther

HUMANS HAVE BUILT fires and shared stories of what lurked in the dark for our entire existence. If they only knew why midnight was a time to dread.

I smiled.

Midnight.

The witching hour.

My hour.

I'm the Midnight Man. I put the monsters back to sleep.

EVEN BEFORE FRANKIE Flame had been cremated alive the old mortuary and its adjoining church and graveyard had been weird. The church was haunted in locals' eyes in the way most old buildings were—people felt the weight of its history, not spirits from the Kingdom interacting with our world. The complex was up the hill from Mort Cheval; a little city with a big appetite for the odd. Frankie Flame wasn't my problem's real name but it was what I called him. I liked to name my villains. Francis MacDonald had lost big betting Calgary would win the Stanley Cup. Oh, and he'd been an arsonist who specialized in insurance fraud with a side business in murder.

Legend says he jumped from the furnace and ran to the church, burning all the way and bringing it down around him. Same legend says Frankie's spirit, still burning, now runs to escape a fate he'd already succumbed to.

When Frankie's ghost had first appeared, it'd been no big deal. He didn't have the power to kill. Not then, or at least, not yet. And since I didn't have the power to summon him, Frankie had always sat on my backburner. A death on the grounds early in the morning—or late in the night, depending on your reckoning—had changed all that.

The decedent, one Todd Bickle, had been a cameraman on *Ghost Walkers*, a bullshit ghost hunting show. My police contact said Bickle spontaneously caught fire, and nothing could put out the flames. After thirty minutes of dousing, smothering with blankets, and Todd screaming, the fire died, as if it'd never been. The *Ghost Walkers* crew had obviously caught some spookier action than they'd hoped for.

Either Frankie had levelled up, or somebody had made a long distance call to the Kingdom. *That* meant a necromancer. Which meant it was my job. The bad guys—villains all—called themselves necromancers, called their gear necrotech. I usually called them dead. At least, I did after I was done. Only problem with killing necromancers: given their skillset they often weren't done after they were "done."

The first thing a necromancer does after they roll into town is take over a mortuary or funeral home. It gives them cover and access to raw materials. Next they go after their competition, whether by buying them out, or more commonly, burying them.

That's how *I* joined the Fight, when necromancers killed my family.

Before I'd joined the Fight, there'd been no one to battle that evil for me. Now the Midnight Man fought for everyone else. Ever since I'd retaken my parents' old funeral home and made it my hideout, I'd held Mort Cheval from all comers.

Tonight's mission couldn't have come at a worse time. I was low on gear. The last necromancer I'd dealt with, The Black Crown, had exhausted my reserves—the curse of scavenging their necrotech and not being able to make my own. I had two clips of tombstone bullets, a ball-and-chain bomb, my Hades cap, and my Grave Sight goggles. It was unlikely my Colt Model 1911s or remaining gear would do any good with a pure spirit like Frankie Flame, but I had to try.

THE CHURCH AND graveyard predated Mort Cheval's founding and the old church was a hotspot for Mort Cheval residents. Wedding photos. Grad photos. That's why there's been so many Frankie sightings. People hoped to catch him in their special moment.

No one had been buried here in a long time. Grave stones, toppled by time or the teens who congregated here to drink, lay prone in the tall grass amid branches, rocks, and swarming ticks. I did a quick scan—never underestimate the willingness of late night mourners, partiers, or tourists to muck up a mission. I saw no one.

I wasn't worried about being seen. My Hades cap kept me hidden from the living as long as I wished, providing there were shadows. Unfortunately it was the dead who worried me, not the living, and they were everywhere, and saw everything. You also never knew who they talked to. If one warned Frankie, my part-time fireman gig might be over before I could get the truck rolling.

I slipped on my Grave Sight goggles and the world turned red.

Unlike the necromancers I usually hunted, I couldn't see into the Kingdom beyond, but my goggles kept spirits from surprising me. They also showed me where their power connected them to the Kingdom, and how I could best dispatch them.

In the penumbral grey of my Grave Sight, the old church was still whole, still ruined, still burning all at once, its three states superimposed over one another. A typical sight when the Kingdom is overlain with our world. Shades stood and wept all along the cracked causeway leading into the old church's walls. A phantom bell swung in a phantom tower, but only the roaming spirits could hear it sound.

The crematorium was where I needed to go. It remained mostly intact; a conical roof clad in cedar shakes topped octagonal walls. Three rectangular windows on each facing had long ago lost their glass. Broad steps—the width of its facings—lead to an arched double door entrance. Trees had infiltrated the stairs and entrance; slender trunks and creeping ivy formed natural bars over the doors. Hints of landscaping survived, but wildness had dulled those edges.

I pushed through the foliage and shoved at the doors. Rusted hinges protested. If anyone waited for me, they'd hear me coming.

I trailed my hands over the walls, taking in the graffiti and scratches, scoring the soot left behind from Frankie's last trip out of the furnace. With my Grave Sight goggles on, I saw that old fire, fresh as if it still burned. I could almost feel its heat. Time to find whoever'd taken Frankie Flame from light show to murder show.

It didn't take me long, the chanting drew me in. Even if I wasn't in the know, I would've suspected him for a necromancer. He looked like your typical bugeater: dressed all in black with greasy hair; long fingernails on digits encrusted with rings. Although I supposed I couldn't point fingers when it came to the "none more black" sartorial choices, considering my head-to-toe black leather and the Jolly Roger emblazoned on my Hades cap.

"Francis MacDonald, come forth and burn again," a man's voice, raspy from too-enthusiastically calling on the dark powers, said. "Francis MacDonald, come forth and burn again."

Whatever the necromancer's plan to raise Frankie Flame's spirit, I guessed each repetition of Frankie's true name brought him closer to success.

Braziers burned with coals and he upended something—no doubt an unpleasant something—into the last one remaining unlit. The braziers ringed a rectangular hole in the chamber's centre. That hole, once the elevator to take bodies to the fire, was my ticket to the furnace room—to Frankie Flame—assuming this chucklehead didn't kill me first.

"Howdy," I said, firing my Colt.

Tombstone bullets kill dead things deader. Usually. Tonight, the bullet pinged off an invisible ward my Grave Sight goggles couldn't penetrate.

The bugeater whipped around, and I added sallow skin to his necromancer's ID package. He had a number of magical geegaws, but I couldn't tell which had stopped my bullet. His Grave Sight gave his sunken eyes a milky corpselike cast as he probed me for any exploitable weakness.

If I got too close, he'd use his death magic to end me. There was no telling how close was too close with thanatomancy, either. Effective range varied necromancer to necromancer. As did strength of effect. Maybe he could only make old wounds—sore knees, dislocated shoulders, a thousand aches and pains, distract me. Maybe he could stop my heart. Give me a stroke.

The necromancer smiled. Evidently he'd seen something. I put my back to the wall. I saw something too. Him. In my sights. I had twenty-five more rounds. And if both clips couldn't break his wards? I'd dust off my knucks. Few necromancers liked fisticuffs. That's what they had meat puppets for. We circled the chamber.

He had a Zippo in his hand. One brazier unlit.

He smiled again.

Damn. He wasn't trying to kill me. He wanted to stall me. To call and bind Frankie. He wanted to watch me burn.

"Drop your gun," he said. "It'll have no effect on me."

"Obviously, you don't know who I am."

He snorted. "You're a deluded fool who thinks he's a hero—a paragon. A fool who believes he can stop the inevitable by dressing in a ridiculous *costume*."

Okay, he *did* know who I was, and he was being purposefully hurtful. Costume. My *uniform* was iconic.

"If you knew who *I* was," he said, smirking, "you'd run screaming."

I shrugged. "I may not know you yet, but I'll happily name you after I kill you."

I fired at his face. He flinched despite his protections. I leapt over the hole in the floor. The necromancer started and backpeddled. Right into the wall. Nowhere to go. I punched him in the nose. Hitting him was like hitting steel. Slammed his head into the stone. He didn't drop. His ward—a cloak pin—blazed in my Grave Sight. I snatched it and elbowed him in the temple. This time he slumped, groaning.

One more tombstone bullet and a red flower bloomed on his throat. Blood streamed as he gurgled and gasped. The lighter and something smaller, also metal, tumbled out of his hand to clink and clatter over the floor.

"Who's the deluded fool now?"

He didn't answer, but there was someone else who might. Life pulsed into view through my goggles: someone alive—and hiding—down the entrance hall. An innocent who'd followed me in, or an apprentice?

"You may as well come out," I called, turning on the flaring lights in my jacket's double M logo. "I see you."

Shuffling, cautious steps inched closer. I recognized her despite the arm held over her eyes. She'd been the one in the film crew with the blue hair. Jennifer . . . something.

I turned off my lights so she could see me and demanded, "What are you doing here, Jennifer?"

She jumped at the mention of her name. "I'm sorry. I'm so sorry."

Fingers knotted behind her head, Jennifer's eyes drifted from the fallen necromancer to me. "Did you kill him?"

"I sure hope so."

"He . . . he was in the crew. Our new PA." She took a step back. I shook my head and she froze.

"He's a necromancer. *Was*. The one who killed Todd Bickle."

I knew how nuts my explanation sounded. This wasn't the first time I'd had to give one. I didn't care how I sounded to civilians. Not anymore. Only the Fight mattered.

"Todd burned to death. An accident. A terrible accident." Her voice said she didn't believe that last part. Ghosts were one thing, but necromancers were obviously a bridge too far. "Electrical short in his camera."

I holstered my Colt and gestured at the necromancer. "An arsonist's ghost this creep stirred up caused the fire."

"And that's why you're dressed like a superhero?"

Close enough. I also would've accepted black mask or vigilante. Comic heroes were my inspiration. Their black and white goodness, their purity, kept me going when I'd lost my parents to real evil. An origin story I shared with my inspirations.

I tapped my logo. "I'm the Midnight Man."

Oddly, she didn't find me crazy. Maybe she'd heard of me. Or, considering what she did for a living, she saw a new reality show in the making.

"What's with the deal with the Jolly Roger?"

"To scare the bad guys."

She furrowed her brow. "You fight ghosts and necromancers. Why would they fear skulls and bones?"

"It took them time to get the point."

"Which is?"

"Death comes for everyone. Even the undead."

And those who raise them. *Especially* for them.

"I wanted to see for myself," she said, "the place where Todd died."

She had spunk, but she was also ignorant of the Kingdom and ghosts in general—let alone Frankie Flame. There's no hell. No heaven. Only aimlessly wandering the Kingdom until something worse ate your spirit. I didn't have the heart to tell her. Not yet, anyway.

"We stopped the necromancer. We figure out how he planned to wake Frankie Flame and the deaths should stop."

"Frankie Flame?"

"My name for Francis MacDonald. The arsonist's ghost." I shrugged. "I name my villains."

"Villains." She rolled her eyes. "And if the deaths don't stop?"

"I stop him too."

I almost didn't hear the flick of a lighter being ignited, didn't smell the butane, or see the small guttering flame as the Zippo arced toward the unlit brazier. The brazier ignited the instant the lighter landed. That couldn't be good.

"Francis MacDonald come forth and do my bidding. Francis MacDonald come forth and burn again," the necromancer rasped, smirking, as he stood. My bullet oozed from his body. "I've three lives left, *Midnight Man.*"

I hate necromancers.

But his boast also gave me his name. *Triple Tombstone.*

I couldn't wait to carve all three of his markers. Later.

Triple Tombstone held a clenched fist toward Jennifer and she doubled over in pain. "Release her."

"No." He laughed and held a knife to her throat for added insurance.

I might've been able to tag him, but I couldn't count on it. And if he wasn't lying, tagging him might not do any damned good.

There was a racket from below as the furnace started. Frankie was awake.

We did our little dance, me trying to get a shot off, him hiding behind Jennifer. He'd kill her, I knew. One way or another. But if his boast was true, and I shot through her to kill him, he wouldn't be done, and she'd be dead for nothing.

Besides, I wore the double Ms to kill necromancers, *not* add to their body pile.

Triple Tombstone glanced downward. Something had caught his eye. My chance. I had a shot but Jennifer took the option from my hands. She snapped her head into bugeater's nose. He shrieked and she shoved him away, diving to the side. I fired but I couldn't tell if I'd hit him.

Frankie Flame stirred and I had a civilian running around. Now that Frankie was crackling, in the next thirty minutes one of us would die.

I ran toward the exit, barely stopped before Triple Tombstone's ward trap would've fried me. He gambolled over the field toward the graveyard. I didn't follow. I couldn't. Tricky creep made a ward passable from the outside. Anyone who came looking for Frankie tonight would've been stuck, same as me. My Grave Sight goggles showed me the wards, but I couldn't unthread them. I had to laugh. I could see the exit, but the invisible barrier was solid real oak.

We were locked in. My bullets *weren't.*

I fired. Triple Tombstone fell. I watched for him to get up. When he did, I shot him. The third time he tried to stand, he didn't rise again.

Maybe he'd actually told the truth about his three lives. If he hadn't been such a braggart, he might've left here with two in the bank and a score to settle.

"Mister . . . Midnight?" Jennifer said.

"Midnight Man," I corrected.

"Is he dead?" Her voice quavered at the question.

"I think so." Unfortunately, if I watched his corpse until satisfied, we'd join him. Trust a necromancer to make me waste my life to confirm their death.

Jennifer wiped sweat from her brow. "I don't feel good."

When she brushed her hand aside, I saw a ring. *That's* what Triple Tombstone had dropped with the lighter. Frankie Flame's ring. Thick gold band. Fire opal centrepiece. Three rubies on either side. It'd been Frankie's pinkie ring. Jennifer wore it on her thumb. His lucky charm, except the charm—or his luck—wore off. On the plus side, now I at least knew which of us would die *first.*

"Where'd you get that?" I demanded.

"I found it. After I hit the necromancer."

"You shouldn't have put it on."

Her face turned ashen. "Why?"

"Cause it'll burn you alive."

"Like Todd."

"Yes."

She jerked at the ring and screamed as if already aflame. Jennifer hit the ground with a thud; an ash cloud billowed.

I knelt at her side. "For what it's worth, I'm sorry."

"You'll stop him? Right?" She held out her hand. "Stop *this*?"

"Yes." I nodded, pulling her to her feet. What I didn't say: Not likely before you die.

UNDER GRAVE SIGHT ash cloaked Jennifer like a shroud. Embers glowed underneath her skin, and with every second they brightened. I asked, "How do you feel?"

"Terrible," she croaked, coughing. "My head pounds. My body aches. I can barely catch my breath."

"I don't blame you."

She regarded Frankie's ring. A flash reflected in her eyes. Fire. Smoke. Pain. Knowledge. "I don't remember putting it on. I remember . . . They burned him alive. Alive. *Oh God*." She looked at me. "That's waiting for me, isn't it?"

No point sugar-coating it. "If you live through this, you might be able to control that fire."

"Then what?"

I shrugged. "Join the Fight? Keep dead things in the ground?"

She considered and nodded. It was hope. A *mad* hope. The belief she could fight against what waited in the night. I knew the look. I saw it in the mirror.

"I'll need a name."

I *loved* naming duty. Her name was Jennifer. She had blue hair. "How's 'Blue Jay?'"

She pulled a face and shook her head for emphasis. "*Ugh*. That's *terrible*." After a moment, she murmured, "Acetylene."

I didn't like "Acetylene" any better than she'd liked "Blue Jay," but I supposed it was *her* name to bear. "You do you."

TRIPLE TOMBSTONE'S ZIPPO still burned in the final brazier, unharmed, arcane runes blazing blue against the orange and yellow flame. A dangerous trinket in anyone's hands except mine. The Zippo or the ring had woken Frankie; they might put him back to sleep. I kicked over the brazier and spread the coals with my boots. No fires died.

I snatched the lighter. Its heat seared my hand through my leather glove; I snapped it shut and the fires flickered, as if I'd denied them air, but didn't die. I tucked the lighter into my belt and affixed Triple Tombstone's cloak pin to my coat.

"What now?" Acetylene asked.

I pointed to the hole in the floor's centre. "Down we go."

THE FIRES IN the basement were no longer phantom flames reflecting the Kingdom. No longer visible only through Grave Sight. They were real. And growing. The furnace room floor was a twelve-foot drop, but only seven or eight to the casket table. I lowered myself, dropped the final span and hoped my weight wouldn't collapse the table. It creaked, holding.

I gestured for Acetylene to follow. When we were both in the crematorium's bowels, I breathed easier. Acetylene couldn't stop coughing. I jumped off the table and ash puffed around me. The pillars supporting the crematorium tower were caked in it. Every crack in the building's foundation glowed like hot embers; tongues of flame crept, slithering vines, hunting new fuel. Litter snapped with ignition and new fires spawned in every corner.

I drew my Colt, though I didn't know what to shoot at.

"Is that a magic gun? Can it kill ghosts?"

It was, and it could. Sort of.

"Can I have one?"

Not the reaction I'd expected. And an intriguing one. She *was* ready to join the Fight. Another shooter would be handy, but I didn't trust strangers' trigger discipline. There's no such thing as a flesh wound with tombstone bullets. "No."

When Acetylene's time was up, Frankie Flame would make sure she took me with her too. His fires would cross over from the Kingdom and bring the crematorium down around us. And then he'd be free to return to his old business.

I could've found a way out. There's always a way out if you'll pay the price. The price for tonight's freedom: let Acetylene burn. Deal with Frankie Flame and Triple Tombstone later. A choice which would've made me the same as the necromancer who'd killed my parents. I've made tough calls, bad calls, and sketchy calls, *this* one was easy.

The furnace's rumble took on a human cast, the groan of an old man who'd sat too long, and yet must rise. The groan changed pitch, becoming a scream. Acetylene covered her ears, shaking her head, as if the sound was something beyond the physical realm.

Frankie was fire in a man's shape; his eyes were as blue as Acetylene's hair, and his body mimicked a once-powerful build. His flicker and glow showed he ostensibly wore the clothes Frankie had died in—a power suit, complete with a fiery tie. When he saw us, he screamed again. Fire shot from his body to fill the chamber.

My clothes frayed and smoked, but the leather held, and Triple Tombstone's lighter and pin protected me from burning as the heat in the crematorium grew unbearable. Frankie's ring protected Acetylene—as it had Frankie in life—and would until he killed her or took it back, but no trinket would keep us safe forever. Sweat pooled on my back and beaded from my scalp, streaming from my Hades cap and into my eyes, stinging.

"My ring," Frankie snarled. "Give it to me."

"Do *not* do that," I yelled over the crackle of flames.

"Yeah," Acetylene said. Flames gathered around her arms and she hurled them at Frankie. "No chance."

The furnace fire snapped, cracked, and roared Frankie's displeasure. Any trace of Frankie would've been long burned to ash, but the furnace was a direct conduit to the Kingdom and Frankie's rage. If I jumped in and survived the trip, I'd have a path to where the monsters came from.

"Always outnumbered, never outgunned," that's my motto. I wasn't ready to make that jump today. Throwing my life away for revenge meant Acetylene would die and Frankie would burn Mort Cheval to its bones. The Fight—Acetylene's life, and every life in the city—outweighed my own desires. *Snuff Frankie. That's the job.*

Binding his spirit with a ball-and-chain bomb probably wouldn't work. Frankie had no meat to be locked into. Normally when you kill the necromancer you don't need to worry about summoned things. They run back to the Kingdom or they go *poof* but Frankie was just warming up.

Tombstone bullets wouldn't stop him. I fired anyway. Frankie's heat envelope was so intense, it cracked my granite bullets, turning them into birdshot before they reached his "body."

He screamed though; while my shots didn't end his manifestation, they hurt him. I was an irritant. Pissing at an inferno. Assuming the bullets' enchantment survived their breaking, they might slow him down. Or they might make him *really* irritated. Considering he already wanted to burn me alive, I wasn't sure I wanted Frankie Flame angry.

I shot again.

Since I'd been lucky with the bullets, I tried a ball-and-chain bomb. Its eggshell-thin casing burst, releasing a puff of silver dust. The dust sparkled as it coated Frankie's body. Now he roared. Grave Sight showed me why: the bombs had worked, if not as expected. Normally ball-and-chain bombs locked a spirit in whatever meat it'd possessed and my bullets sent it back to the Kingdom. My bombs had severed the connection between Frankie and the Kingdom. When his fuel extinguished, he'd be snuffed.

Unfortunately, we were currently standing among his fuel, and I doubted he'd be inclined to let us leave.

He slapped me across the chest with a heated backhand that was palpable for all he was not. I reeled backward from the impact, skidded into a burning trash pile, and rolled away trying to keep the flame from igniting my uniform.

"My ring!" he roared, burning brighter, growing larger.

I needed another tactic.

"Francis," I said. He turned back to me. His name had been used to call him. It might put him back to sleep. "Francis MacDonald."

He advanced, orange flames going white. The echo of his screams still remembered his name, but no one in that much pain couldn't easily find slumber. Not without more help than I knew how to give.

I gripped Triple Tombstone's lighter before me. "Francis MacDonald, rest again in your ashes. Burn no more."

He wavered, before turning to Acetylene and advancing on my nascent sidekick.

She scrambled away from him, creating a fiery wall to obscure her retreat. A fast learner. I liked that. I gave her cover, snapping off a rapid succession of tombstone bullets, interposing myself between them. Both furnace and Flame roared.

There had to be a way. Acetylene's ring. Frankie's name. The lighter. We had the means. Somewhere. I caught a wild-eyed look from Acetylene in my peripheral vision. Frankie had found her.

I snapped open the lighter, flicked it on. The fires seemed drawn to it. Frankie turned to me as I repeated his name. I snapped the lighter shut. Smaller pockets of fire died.

"I have an idea," I said.

Acetylene hurled a ball of white hot flame at Frankie. *Fire with Fire*. "I hope it's a good one."

"Get upstairs."

I hurled another ball-and-chain bomb, holstered my Colt, and cupped my hands for Acetylene. She ran to me, setting her foot in my locked fingers. I alley-ooped her out of the basement as the crematorium crumbled in on itself. We needed the ring and lighter both, working in concert to wake, or snuff Frankie. And since Acetylene couldn't take off the ring . . . I'd die quick and ugly without the lighter's protection. Triple Tombstone's cloak pin may work against fire as well as impacts, but I couldn't be sure. Still, no choice at all.

Her life or mine.

I hoped she'd take up the Fight when I was gone. I only wished I had time to show her the hideout. And my car. Especially the car.

In the distance, sirens cut through the night. I couldn't count on the Mort Cheval fire department to free us.

I held up the lighter. "Take it!"

I wouldn't last long without it. But we didn't have long left anyway. Acetylene was sharp. She'd figure it out. I tossed it to her and the moment the lighter left my hand, the heat in the furnace room dropped me to my knees. Soon the smoke would suffocate me. My gloves caught fire.

Over the flames, I heard the snap of a Zippo opening; the rasp of striker over flint. Despite the smoke, burning butane filled my nostrils. Frankie ignored me. I had nothing he wanted.

A fiery ladder formed with a gesture from Frankie, and he ascended like a risen god. One plus: he dragged the heat and smoke with him. I could almost breathe. I rolled, beating out the flames that'd caught on my leathers. I'd live long enough to deconstruct the mess I'd made tonight.

The Zippo clanked shut and Acetylene yelled, "Francis MacDonald. Rest again in your ashes and burn no more."

Frankie flickered and his fire dimmed.

Acetylene repeated her chant. Again. Again. Once for each overturned brazier. With each repetition, Frankie's fire guttered as his brightness faded. With the last, his ladder collapsed and he fell back into the furnace room.

His defiance and raging roars became a slow hiss; a whining keen as his form lost coherence. His afterlife had been pain, but it'd been all he'd had. Fire's alive in a way. It needs to breathe. It can grow. Be nurtured. And it can die. Nothing remained of his flame body except a shimmering heat mirage, until that, too, was gone. Peace at last. Even if he hadn't deserved it.

"Goodbye, Frankie."

Despite Frankie's death, the natural fires still burned. My uniform had taken the brunt of the damage, but I'd definitely need to replace my kit. First, I had to get out.

Acetylene asked, "Midnight Man? You alive?"

"Toasted, but not toast," I called back.

She sighed with relief. "You look terrible."

"I've been worse."

I hauled myself from the furnace room and walked Acetylene out of the now ruined crematorium. Fortunately for us, the door where Triple Tombstone had set his wards had burned up—we were free to leave, and wouldn't have to answer questions from the Mort Cheval Fire Department.

"What if he comes back?" Acetylene asked, fingering Frankie's—now her—ring.

"We'll be here," I said. "Midnight Man and Acetylene."

Outside, I saw no sign of Triple Tombstone's body. Only blood in the grass. He'd lied about how many lives he had in the bank. No surprise there. I turned to Acetylene. "We have another fire to put out. Ready to join the Fight?"

Breath of the Caldera

Wendy Nikel

"DRAGONS, HUH?"

Years ago, when she'd first started fighting fires, Trish Banzier's father had warned her that most crews had their own hazing traditions, but even after the two-hour video presentation, complete with "photographic evidence," she still couldn't believe anyone would actually fall for such a ridiculous story.

The video ended and, as the lights went on, Banzier stared down the base manager for the West Yellowstone Smokejumpers, waiting for him to break into laughter and tell her it was all a joke so she could re-join her team. She hadn't worked for five years on a hotshot crew and all spring on Yellowstone's gruelling training regimen just to lose her nerve on the first real day at her dream job. Nothing—not even dragons—was going to take that from her.

"You're telling me, sir," she said, looking around for a hidden camera or two-way mirror from which her new teammates might be watching and laughing at her initiation, "there are dragons living underground in the caldera, and that nearly half of the Yellowstone forest fires are caused by them wandering to the surface and . . . breathing fire? That the supervolcano is all just a cover for the existence of dragons?"

"Afraid so, Banzier," the manager said grimly. "They tend to emerge from their dens in the summertime, when it's hot and dry. The rangers put up roadblocks and try to guide them back through the hydrothermal vents if they catch 'em quick enough, but you know how dragons are."

"Can't say I do, sir." Banzier crossed her arms.

"They're temperamental. Dangerous." He leaned across the desk. "We couldn't tell you until you were officially in, but the important thing for you smokejumpers is to treat it like any other fire. Parachute in, assess the situation, contain the blaze, and—most importantly—keep these valuable members of the park's natural ecosystem secure and secret."

Banzier set her jaw. How long were they going to keep this prank going? No matter; she'd outlast them, just like she'd outlasted all the other recruits during training camp. They'd have to do a lot better than this if they wanted to psych her out. She touched the piece of half-melted metal in her pocket.

"I won't let you down," she said.

"Good." The manager leaned back in his chair, unaware that the comment wasn't for him. "Glad to see you're taking this so well. Most folks wouldn't, you know. No telling what might happen if word got out."

The siren went off, and the manager nodded grimly. "Time to get your first look at the park's most endangered species."

BANZIER REFUSED TO mention the D-word.

Not when she joined the seven other jumpers aboard the Dornier 228 and the pilot leaned over with a wink and shouted, "First real fire, eh?"

Not when one of her teammates leaned in and asked if she'd gotten "the whole story" yet.

And certainly not when the team leader, Coolidge, passed her a flat plate of silver like you might find on someone's wedding registry.

"What's this for?"

"They like shiny things," Coolidge said. "It's in case you need a distraction."

"Uh-huh." She set it on the seat beside her and, to calm her nerves, triple-checked her chute. She wished they'd drop the stupid dragon gag—she had enough to worry about. She'd been fighting fires since she was eighteen and had jumped dozens of times, but that was just training. Now, she was an official smokejumper. She couldn't afford to mess up.

"Stay close this first jump." Coolidge patted her shoulder. "We'll show you how it's done."

Unable to find her voice, Banzier nodded and ran her thumb over the melted badge, feeling the sharpness of its edge through her thick gloves.

"What've you got there, Rookie?"

Banzier tucked the badge into her pocket. "It was my dad's."

Before Coolidge could respond, the spotters called for Banzier to jump, and she grabbed her gear—over one hundred pounds, wedged tightly into a pack she'd stitched herself—and took a deep breath. The spotter slapped her shoulder, and she jumped.

Air whipped past her, already hazy and thick with smoke. This was her favourite part: the freefall, with the forest all around her, nothing man-made as far as the eye could see, save for the jet droning above. Just her and the clouds and miles and miles of vast, green wilderness.

Her chute deployed flawlessly and she assessed the scene as she navigated the currents, keeping an eye on her teammates' chutes. It was important to stay close, yet not so close that they'd risk becoming entangled. Red-orange flames licked the trunks of lodgepole pines, but the fire hadn't spread far yet. There was still time to contain it.

The ground approached, but as she prepared for the landing something moving near the fire's head caught her eye.

A gust of wind caught her chute and, distracted as she was, she didn't pull it back under control in time. It veered sharply away from her teammates. She landed roughly in her tuck-and-roll, then tumbled down a small escarpment, closer to the fire than she ought to be, with not a single one of her teammates in sight.

There was no time to chide herself for the error. On the ground, in the midst of the fire, every second counted. She struggled to her feet and, as she unclipped her chute, she reached into her suit to ensure her father's badge was still there.

A shadow fell upon her. Something massive towered over her, blocking the wind. She turned and let out a low curse.

A dragon.

An honest-to-goodness dragon that looked just like she'd seen in picture books as a child: scaly and long-necked and vicious. It had teeth that glowed like hot steel and claws that were each the size of a shovel. Smoke rose from its nostrils, and it stared at Banzier with milky eyes.

No, not at her, she realized. At the badge.

She tried to shove it back into her suit, but it was too late. The dragon roared and lunged toward her.

Banzier ran. The team's warnings hadn't prepared her for this. Why hadn't she listened? And what was she supposed to do now with this thing lumbering through the forest behind her? Where was her team?

She stumbled, falling to the ground, and braced herself. Her suit would withstand two thousand degrees for four seconds, but how hot was the dragon's breath?

It can't end like this. Her heart sank with each rumble of the earth as the beast moved in closer, and she gripped the badge. It'd been foolish, she knew, to think it'd protect her when it hadn't protected her father.

Then she remembered: the hydrothermal vents.

She rolled just in time. The dragon bellowed as its claws slashed the air where she'd just been. Banzier held the badge over her head and raced toward the nearest vent. She'd had to learn all the vents' locations during training; now she knew why. Panting, she waved the badge in the smoke-tinged air. It glinted in the sunlight, and—when she was sure the monster was looking—she took careful aim, and then tossed it into the steaming crevice in the earth.

The dragon dove after it, squeezing its massive body through the tiny crack like a mouse slipping beneath a door.

Banzier fell to her knees.

Her crew raced up behind her, whooping and hollering and offering to buy her beers.

"Nice work, Rookie!"

"Nerves of steel!"

"Thought you'd be barbeque for sure!"

"All right, folks," Coolidge yelled, clapping her hands. "The rookie's dealt with the source for us. Now, let's take care of this fire before the wind picks up."

As the rest of the crew gathered their supplies and jogged off toward the fire line, Coolidge reached down to help Banzier to her feet. "Nice recovery, Rookie. You'd have made him proud."

Cilantro

Annie Neugebauer

"Come on. A little poison never hurt anyone." My elbow bites into my husband's ribs. We've realized I forgot to rinse the cilantro before adding it.

The kitchen smells like fresh, meaty garlic and watery tomato blood—sweet and earthy beneath our warm fluorescents. A tiny moth flutters and bumps along their plastic casing.

"Ha. Ha." Moments later, his comeback: "Except all the insects killed by it." A real zinger, my man.

"Well, yeah. If they didn't use *pest*icide on their *pests,* we wouldn't have anything to make our picante with."

It's a low blow. A small dose of salt in an old wound already going green around the edges. Jason is a freelance consultant to farmers and gardeners who want to make their practices more organic and environmentally buzz-word-able. He tells already-struggling growers, like my dad, that to sell their produce for twice as much they need to invest in four times the labour to yield half the product, and that unless they can switch to all indoor production there aren't any guarantees their entire crops won't be wiped out on a bad year. It's how we met—when my dad told Jason to fuck off and I felt bad for him, asking him to come inside for a decidedly non-organic cup of coffee.

It's also why most of the farmers who usually give us free food are fresh out of cilantro this year. I bought this oversized bunch at the big chain store Jason calls Volde-Mart. His cause strikes me as perfectly noble; it's his use of it to further his own personal gain at the expense of others that has worn me down over the years.

He stares into the bowl of red salsa tinged with green and white, his nose wrinkling. He knows exactly what chemical concoctions I've forgotten to rinse off.

"What kind of bugs eat cilantro anyway?" I ask. My family never grew it, and like many girls raised on a farm, I learned as little as possible about the family business and got the hell out of there when I turned eighteen. I pluck our biggest wooden spoon from the canister and stir.

"Cutworms, mostly. Other things too."

My eyes are still watery from the onion. I sniff, nudging Jason out of my way. When we were first married he'd rave over the meals I made for him. He overlooked my hodunk roots as I overlooked his hoity-toity ideals, like a farm-crossed Romeo and Juliet. Now he whines about his clients seeing me at the store, complains that I don't cook enough, and never thanks me even when I do.

What I want to say is, "If you're going to be a little bitch you can make your own dinner." What I actually say is, "If you're that worried about it, you don't have to eat it."

But he will, I know. Jason's nothing if he's not an opportunist. Animals like us can never resist a free meal.

I'VE ALWAYS QUIETLY resented that Jason convinced me to quit my job in advertising to help him build his business. In retrospect I wonder if that's actually why he married me—not love, but utility. I had connections with farmers all across the state thanks to my dad, and I knew how to market.

But today it's actually lucky that I work from home, because Jason is so sick he didn't go to work. Maybe not rinsing the cilantro really was a mistake. We did put a lot in this time—too much. It's made our picante taste sweet with that soapy tang, so I add an extra jalapeño to balance the flavours, making it spicy enough to make our noses run. Could he really be that sensitive to residual pesticides? Maybe it's all in his head. But as I peek into the bedroom to check on him, it doesn't seem like it's in his head.

Our blackout curtains are closed tight against the noon sun that infuses the rest of the house with summer glow. He's stacked extra pillows over the seam to seal out that fine ray down the middle. In the forced twilight of the room all I can see of him is a pale, pupal lump under our down comforter. It's pulled all the way up over his head, probably because the room's so cold.

I hover in the doorway, leaning in while holding onto the frame, peering through the dimness, listening for breathing. I pad across the carpet and sit on the edge of the bed, picking out the dark cave of his face under the edge of the blankets. He's facing me, eyes squeezed shut with a fierceness that conveys pain. I put my hand on his forehead to feel his skin, expecting a fever.

His eyes flash open, wide and almost panicked.

"It's okay," I whisper. His skin feels cool and clammy. I raise my voice to a low murmur. "How do you feel?"

"Like shit." His voice comes out hoarse and wet at the same time. "Why is it so bright in here?"

I look at the tiny strip of light coming in over the top of the curtain rod. "Do you have a headache?"

He shakes his head.

"Maybe you're working on a migraine." He's probably about to have his first aura. I stand, wiping my hand on my sweats, and toss an extra blanket over the curtain rod. "Can I get you something? Tea? Water?"

"I'd love some more picante," he slurs.

"I don't think that's a good idea. What if it's what made you sick?"

"Then it's your fault, isn't it? God damn, you're not my mom. Besides, *you're* not sick."

My face slips blank at his words, chest twisting. It actually makes him more mad if I don't act hurt, so in a pleasant voice I ask, "What else sounds good?"

He sighs in annoyed defeat. "A salad is fine."

"Sure."

I almost skip washing the lettuce, but then I wash it twice out of guilt.

He eats the whole bowl in five minutes, huddled under the

blankets, not bothering with the dressing, and goes back to sleep, pulling the bedding over his head.

The first seed of real unease blooms in my chest.

WHETHER OUT OF guilt, vindictiveness, or simple curiosity, I eat two more big bowls of the picante. It's soapy-spiced but still delicious. I don't get sick. Whatever Jason has, it's not from that.

AT BEDTIME I look in on him again. He's snoring so softly I can barely hear it, his body exposed to the cool air. I almost climb into bed next to him, but I pause. He looks . . . bloated. A tiny shiver fights its way up my spine, and I try to stifle it. I tell myself it is absolutely not from revulsion.

But his skin does look soft and doughy, almost creased into puffy rolls at each joint. It wouldn't hurt for him to start sleeping with a shirt on.

Jesus, I'm terrible. So he hasn't been hitting the gym as much as he used to. Neither have I. Plus, he's sick. Everyone looks terrible when they're sick.

Maybe I shouldn't disturb him. He needs the sleep.

I quietly refill the glass of water on his nightstand and leave. I'll sleep on the sofa tonight. If he's not feeling better in the morning, I'll call a doctor.

A SOFT SOUND wakes me. The box under the TV says 2:23 a.m. The house is dark and still and silent. I wait, listening.

Something indiscernible. The faintest shuffling, followed by a muted thump.

"Jason," I breathe, folding back the throw and hurrying down the hall. I round the corner and stop in the bedroom doorway. The blankets cover him in a lumpy mass. Has he added more?

"Jason?"

He doesn't move.

I edge into the room. "Are you okay? I thought I heard something."

When he still doesn't answer, I sit on the corner of the bed. "Babe?"

I pull the top of the comforter down. Empty. He's not in the bed.

"Jason?" I stand and pace down the hall, checking the

bathroom and office. He's not there. I go back through the living room and peer into the kitchen and dining room. Those, too, are empty. A strangeness slinks through me, as if I know something my mind hasn't acknowledged yet.

I ease down the hallway and into our bedroom, flicking on the lamp that sits on the small wooden desk near the door. It casts an orange glow across the tan carpet.

"Jason?"

My abs tighten involuntarily. It's the feeling I get when I know someone's about to scare me, but Jason's way too sick to jump out at me for laughs. Still, I say too loudly, "If you're in here, answer me."

There's no answer, but I know he's here.

I hem forward and toss the blankets back into place, as if he could be tucked under the fold. Then I circle the foot of the bed and look in the corner, behind the small recliner we've wedged there. With a slimy swallow, I sink to my knees and lift the bed skirt, peering into the darkness beneath. The emptiness startles me.

A sigh of relief slips through my lips at the same time as a thump emanates from the closet. I twitch, a restrained jump. Too tense to take it, I stand, march to the closet, and shove open the bi-fold doors.

Jason doesn't leap out at me. At first, I don't even see him—just the junk we have piled under the row of crammed hanging clothes.

Then the pile shifts, and I see a swollen heel sticking out from under an old cat bed. A board game slides from the pile and clatters to the floor.

Trembling, I kneel. "Jason? What are you doing in here?"

I move aside a fallen blouse to reveal his face. It's large and round and pale, jowly in a way that it never has been before, and only his wide, terrified eyes seem familiar to me. His lips are so puffed it looks like he can barely move them, but he doesn't try. He just whimpers softly, eyes roving.

I start to move some of the things off him, but he snatches at them with hands that are slow and soft, piling things back onto himself even as he tries to push his head back under the rubbish.

"Jason," I gasp, stepping back. "What the hell is going on?"

My husband tunnels further into our closet, slipping even his foot back under the pile, so that no part of him shows among our neglected possessions in the shadowed dark.

I FEEL AS though I've had my feet knocked out from under me. I don't call anyone. An ugly part of me works hard to make excuses. What on earth would I say? Besides, I'm "not his god damn mom."

I shut the bedroom door, have a panic attack, and take some pills. My last emotion as I slip under sleep's blanket is small and hard, strangely anticipatory, almost starved, like an animal fed too long on spoiled feed, but still I vow to check on him in the morning.

THE REST OF the house is bright and chastising enough that I almost laugh at myself—until I open the door. The first thing that hits me is the darkness. He must have piled even more coverings over the cracks around the curtains; I can't see more than two feet in. I flip on the lamp, then notice an unusual odour. Woodsy, fibrous, dank, and almost fishy. Weak with nerves and hazy with medicine remnants, I take one step inside. I don't know how to explain why I don't call out his name this time. The silence seems waiting.

The sole of my foot lands on something rough and damp, like bark. I look down, raising my foot, and grasp some of it between my fingers. It feels like mushy pencil shavings. My eyes catch a pale ring around the leg of the desk, then jump to the next leg, and the next. All four of them have grooves carved out of the bottom, the wood shreds piled around them on the floor.

My pulse begins to thump harder. I glance at the bed, the covers heaped high in a strange lump, but my gut tells me they're empty. I don't know what possesses me to look up, but I do, scanning the corners near the ceiling. Empty. Finally, my gaze settles on the open closet and the chaotic pile within. "Jason?" I mouth, but no sound escapes.

Slowly, oh so slowly, I walk toward it. The carpet brushes the remains of the wood shavings off my foot, leaving a tiny trail. My eyes never leave the open closet. The edges of the bi-fold doors, too, have grooves and gouges along the bottoms. I skim the edge of the bed as I slow, not wanting to get too close to that pile. Is it still? Can I see it moving, or is that my imagination?

Breath held, I take another step forward, squinting into the shadows.

Something grabs my ankle. I scream, jerking. Something wet and hard scrapes along my skin over the anklebone as I drag my foot away, toppling backwards into the desk. The lamp falls, the shade bouncing hard, then the metal base rolls off the edge and crashes to the carpet. The light is thrown askew, lighting the empty ceiling, but my eyes stare wildly at the bed skirt. It moves.

"Jason?" I gasp between pants.

The skirt moves again. Backing up against the desk chair, I pull my feet tightly to my legs. I grasp the lamp and shine it under the bed.

"Jason," I say flatly, but my intended command comes out a plea. "Come out of there."

The bed skirt wavers but doesn't lift.

I edge forward, gripping the lamp like a bludgeon. I peer at the small, dark crack between the carpet and cotton skirting. Finally, mouth open in a silent yawn of fear, I lift the bottom hem of the skirt and shove it under the mattress before snagging my hand away.

Something large and pale takes up the space beneath the bed. I scream, shoving myself beneath the desk. My hands brush the wood shavings and I scream again, brushing them off as if they're alive.

The thing under the bed writhes, but no hands reach for me. It's long, swollen sluggish and slimy like a pile of animal fat. I trace its creased body up from its most tapered end until I see the face. Oh, how I wish it didn't have a face. Not distinguished from its body in any way except for the gaping, gnawing mouth full of tiny, sharp teeth that gnash the air—the thing that grasped my ankle—and those eyes. Those too-small, human eyes that look painfully familiar. Those eyes that are far too aware and terrified to belong to anything that looks like that. They rove until they lock on mine, both hungry and fearful. I see regret there, but also a demand—a type of survival instinct that begs no forgiveness. A pile of wet wood chips sit on the carpet beneath that ever-moving jaw.

"Jason," I cry. "Oh, Jason."

Then I leave the room, slamming the door behind me, to go throw up.

THE NEXT TIME I check the bedroom I'm hollow. I remember the me who used to be in love with my husband, the me broken down by his use of me, angry at his gradual neglect, the me who found him ill and felt guilty for not caring—but I don't feel like any of them.

It's with steady hands that I open the door and walk back into the room. It smells of fetid saliva and exposed stomach acid.

The desk legs have been chewed through. The desk itself lies toppled on its side, some of the writing surface also gauged around the corners. It takes a few moments of staring to realize that the bed is about a foot and half lower than usual. The legs on it, too, have been gnawed off. The frame was metal.

I know without looking that the closet pile is unoccupied, because the only place left in the room big enough to hold him is the large, ovular mound on the bed. It's full and glossy, the colour of an old penny and creased in plump segments. The mattress beneath lies bare of sheets and blankets. The closet is stripped mostly empty. The recliner sits burst open in the middle, stuffing pulled out in long, fluffy strips.

The lamp still lies askew on the carpet, light shining in a crooked pool, but this time I flip on the overheads.

Under the yellow glow, the brown surface becomes shimmery and orange. When I step closer and lean forward, I make out some letters under a hard veneer. A familiar font. "MIDIFI." Part of the box to our humidifier. Then more items become clear. The print of Jason's favourite tie. A spiral notebook. Our quilt. All buried and mixed into mush, sealed beneath the hardened exterior.

I tell myself my initial hesitation already made my decision. Too late.

Heart pounding, I back out of the room and close the door yet again.

TWO DAYS LATER, I stand outside it with my ear pressed to the wood door. From inside I hear shuffling and rustling, like the shifting of large, limp leaves. I picture cilantro, can almost taste our picante, now gone.

The sounds are so soft—a susurrus of feathers. The noise of wet things drying. A large, gentle, subtle, quiet hefting of wings.

I WAIT UNTIL nightfall to open the bedroom window from the outside. I slide it up with shaking arms. Then I part the thick curtains with a jerk, stacked pillows falling noiselessly inward. The bedroom gapes dark and silent, but as soon as the opening is cleared I run away. The night is overcast and thick with heat. Nothing comes.

In the open part of our backyard, I stack twigs. I think of how I used to love Jason for how different he was, and how he used to love me too—or at least how I thought so. Around the twigs I prop three larger logs in a triangular frame. I think of how my dad hated him for his ungrounded ideals, and how Jason secretly never thought I was good enough, coming from such stock, until he bent me to his cause as well. On top of the twigs I cross small sticks. I think of how cilantro tastes the same organic or protected by pesticides, and how the only way to ruin it is to use too much. Above the small sticks I add a layer of larger ones and finally some thick enough that I can't quite break them over my knee. I've begun to sweat.

My eyes travel to the open window and the waiting darkness.

I pull a packet of matches from my pocket and light the pile with one strike.

The growing flame draws my eyes. It's bright enough to reach inside. I think of my home farm, my family, and how I never quite believed that insects deserve to be saved.

The Midwife and the Phoenix

J.G. Formato

THE MOUNTAIN TREMBLED with the force of its contractions. Shuddering beneath a blanket of ash, it expelled dark plumes of smoke with violent, irregular thrusts. They rose, feeding the clouds that eclipsed the sun. Rolling waves of heat blurred the line between summit and sky, and a steady quake rumbled down the mountain to my door. It was preparing for the Rebirth.

The week before Ashton was born, I felt as the mountain feels now. But the hopeful hardening in my belly was a bit less patient. Every day for a week I visited the midwife, certain that my girl was coming. She laughed at my inexperience, my panic at false labour. Told me to trust my body and let it get ready in peace. I would know when it was time, and then she would come to me. She was right, of course.

"It's time," Ashton announced, turning from the window.

"Not yet."

"The smoke is getting thicker. The mountain's shaking. It's coming." Sixteen knows everything.

"I'll know when it's time. And then I will go."

"Then *we'll* go." She ran a hand over the leather sheath at her hip, tossing her tangled mess of black hair. She can barely wield a comb—I don't know what she thinks she's going to do with that knife. But it was her Daddy's, and I don't have the heart to take it from her.

"Yes, but you are only there to watch. You'll need to explain the process to your daughter, just as I have begun to explain it to you. Except you will learn firsthand, so that you may breathe new life into the old teachings. You'll resurrect the ancient knowledge." I hate that part. I want her to stay home, where it's safe. But if she doesn't go, home can't stay safe.

"That's just it." Her golden eyes narrowed. "It's ancient knowledge. The Phoenix hasn't been reborn in almost a thousand years. How do you even know that you're going to do it right?"

"I have a millennium of wisdom at my fingertips, passed down from the women of our family. I will 'do it right.' You just be ready to do your part."

Doubt crossed her face, summoning the spectre of her father.

I WAS STILL in bed when the pounding started. I yawned and stretched, listening as it progressed from agitated to furious to downright wrathful. When it passed the point of knocking and escalated to total house assault, Ashton poked me.

"Are you going to get that?"

"I suppose." I dressed, since one must be respectable for gentleman callers. I made a pot of tea, since one must be hospitable to guests. I tidied up a bit, since one must be neat for company. All social rules thusly observed, I opened the door.

Bradley, my nearest and sweatiest neighbour, stood with his fist raised, perilously close to knocking on my nose. He stopped just in time, dropping an ungraceful hand to his side.

"Bradley." I smiled. "Do come in and have some tea. Knocking is such thirsty work. You must be exhausted."

He followed me into the house and attempted to dominate my poor kitchen, chest puffed out and legs spread wide. Ready to lay down the law.

"Bryn," he growled. "It's high time you did your job."

"Really?"

"Yes, really. You Rebirthers have lived off the work of our people for hundreds of years. You are taken care of, with no other expectation than that you do your job when it's time. So do your job. Bring back the Phoenix."

"When it is time, the Phoenix will be reborn. She's not ready yet."

"You better get her ready then." He stepped forward, crowding me with affected menace. More sad than intimidating. More smelly than daunting. He can't do anything to me, he needs me too much. So he rants, "In case you haven't noticed, the dragonlings are encroaching on our lands. They decimated my cattle last night. You need to bring back the Phoenix, so that she can rid us of these monsters."

"In time, Bradley. They haven't even come into their fire yet. Is that all?"

"No, it's not. Look!" he shouted, pointing to the window.

With unfortunate timing, a dragonling descended upon my last remaining sheep. I could only watch as its glossy black body subdued the bit of white fluff. The creature rolled her to her back, ripping her belly open with jagged talons. The entrails were torn from her body in time to the plaintive death bleats. A red rain splattered the window.

"Oh." Ashton swayed on her feet behind me. "Is that what happens?" She turned white and crumpled into her chair. I swung her away from the window and pushed her head between her knees.

"Breathe, Ashton," I whispered, rubbing her temples.

I wanted to kick Bradley out. But I couldn't very well do that with the beast outside, so we waited in silence for it to move on. Well, Ashton and I waited in silence, our guest spent his stay alternating between mumbled grievances and prayers.

Once the shadow kissed the treetops goodbye and the yard was empty save a few red drops on the grass, I kicked Bradley out. It took a while, as he had many admonishments and directives for me, as well as some terribly misguided advice on how to attend the Rebirth of a Phoenix. Eventually, with the help of a scalding hot tea pot and a frying pan, he was persuaded to go. Ashton and I needed to talk.

"That's what happened to Daddy?" she asked, after the tears had dried from her eyes and settled in her throat.

"More or less. Bigger dragon, bigger prey. But, yes, that's what happened." My tears stayed inside, calcifying within my heart. They were still hard, angry tears.

"He shouldn't have gone."

"No, he shouldn't have."

"Why did he? Why didn't he just let the Phoenix take care of it?"

"Because he didn't listen to me, Ashton. He let his feelings get in the way of what had to be. It was a mistake. Learn from it. When we go, there will be things that will be hard for you. There will be things that you will want to do out of love—sweet, noble, selfless things. But *you must not*. The noblest thing you can do for me and for our people is to put those feelings aside and do what must be done. And for you, that is to keep your eyes open and stay alive."

She nodded, or at least dropped her jaw enough for me to take it as a nod. I hugged her tightly, crushing her against my chest until I could feel her heart knocking against mine.

"Pack some clothes and comb your hair. We leave tomorrow morning." Over her head, through the red tinted window, the mountain convulsed and thundered its approval.

I'D PUT OFF packing until about midnight. I knew I wouldn't be able to sleep, and I figured it would give me something to do. Ashton had packed her bags hastily and turned in early, to be fresh for the morning. For the past few hours, our house had been filled with the rhythmic banging of her headboard against the wall as she wrestled her sheets. I've learned not to fight the insomnia and just tell myself I'm too busy to lay down.

I'd never admit it out loud, but Randal's absence makes it easier. There's no way I could have prepared myself under his watch. He would never have let me leave— he would have let the whole country burn first. Maybe this is how it had to be.

He wanted so badly to keep me from danger that he sacrificed himself on a fool's errand. That last Dragoness was a monster, the likes of which had not been seen for centuries. She was fire incarnate as she flew. Her golden scales captured the sun's light and hurled it like a weapon towards earth, blinding those below with the scattered rays. The true dragonflame followed, blackening those in her path to the bone before they were devoured.

She could be feline in her killing as well. Even when her hunger had been sated, she hunted, playing with the villagers like a cat in a field of frightened mice. We stayed holed up in our homes until farming ceased and the crops failed.

The Phoenix had always protected us in the past, easily destroying any Dragon that dared cross the sea into our land. This one was too much for her. Too cunning and too strong. She evaded the Phoenix at every turn—her glaring scales and razor sharp talons could counter any attack made by our champion. Our days rang with the shrill, frustrated cries of the Phoenix and the amused, rumbling growls of the dragon.

Randal knew what was coming. As our situation became more desperate, so did the Phoenix. The Release was imminent. He dreaded the loss of the Phoenix, that death that led to Rebirth when I would be called to serve as midwife to a birth of fire, flame, and overpowering magic. We'd never thought that day would come, there'd been Rebirthers in my family for hundreds of years, a ceremonial position respected and pampered by the people of the town. They'd never been called to attend, there'd never been any need.

I'd explained it all to him, before we were married. No one outside the family knows what would happen or why. He never quite believed me, or else he didn't want to. The big softie never could bear to see me in danger or pain—he fainted when Ashton was born. There was so much blood, he was certain I had haemorrhaged and died. My midwife tried to tell him it was all part of the process. He didn't listen to her at first either.

So my brave, romantic, ridiculous husband confronted the beast that even the Phoenix couldn't fell armed with nothing but passion and a spear. I locked Ashton in her room, as I watched from our window, unable to step outside my door and aid him. I am the only midwife to the Phoenix. Without me she could never be Reborn, leaving generations to come vulnerable to attack. I had to live, no matter how my love died. I'll never tell Ashton, but that sheep had it easy.

The Phoenix came then, Randal's sacrifice shaming and spurring her to action. We locked eyes through the glass, the burnished obsidian of hers glimmering with apology. Then came the Release. She curled her blazing wings to her chest and threw them wide in one fluid, powerful motion. With a deafening shriek, she ignited earth and sky. The eruption of flames and energy filled the air, as my land and all it held was reduced to ashes. Including the Dragon and the remains of my husband.

Memories are an insomniac's dreams.

"THEY'RE FOLLOWING US, Mom."

"I know, Ashton. Why on earth do you think I'm carrying this bag of steaks?"

She wrinkled her pointed little nose in confusion. "I thought it was for us. You know, provisions."

"You thought I crammed fifteen pounds of raw, bleeding meat into a burlap sack for us? On a day trip up the mountain? I must not be feeding you enough, child. Are you hungry?"

"No, of course not." She rolled her eyes. "I thought maybe you needed the protein, or the Phoenix would." She looked genuinely baffled, and I realized that I had omitted an important part of her education. She was just so sensitive about dragons, I didn't really want to bring this part up before.

"In a way, you're right." I smiled at her. I hoped it was a smile anyway, it felt awkward and wolfish on this end. "The Phoenix will need protein. She'll be starving when she resurrects."

"And she'll eat the steaks?"

"She'll eat the dragonlings. The steaks are to draw them in."

"Oh." She bit her lip and glared at the shadows in the trees. "Good."

We hiked in silence. Human silence, anyway. The air was filled with the startled cries of birds and horrified chitters of squirrels, punctuated by the scraping thump of dragonling steps behind us. They were still young enough to keep their distance from us, young enough to be lured by the mere scent of blood, but still menacing enough to terrify the entire forest.

Ashton broke our silence. "What if there weren't any dragonlings here?"

"We got lucky on that score—the Dragoness laid her eggs before she died. Which would explain her fierceness."

"What would we have done?"

"We would have gone across the sea to capture one. Tried to get it home in time." She looked alarmed at the prospect, and rightly so. I'm not sure that I would have been able to carry that out.

"Rebirther's a terrible job. When I was little, I thought it was the best. Because everyone has to be nice to you and give you things, and you didn't actually have to do anything. But really, it's the worst,"

"It won't be for you. All you have to do is watch, learn, and teach. And let things unfold as they must."

"You really believe that? That things unfold as they must?"

"Well, we're not trekking across the sea to capture dragonlings are we? Mother Dragonesses are the only ones strong enough to warrant the Release of the Phoenix. They are the only ones that can bring about her death—but they are also ones that can provide what is needed to nourish her Rebirth. It's about balance."

"I don't know." She shook her dark head doubtfully.

"That's all right, because I do." She didn't look convinced. I'm not surprised. This was the toddler that never accepted "because I said so" as a reason.

WE REACHED THE summit just as the sun slunk away. Smoke emanated from the cinders at our feet, mingling with the orange fire in the sky. It smelled of pine and juniper, and although it burned our lungs, there was something clean about it. The peak itself was a wasteland. Fallen, burnt trees smouldered on the fallow ground. Blades of grass had long since given way to grains of ash and curls of smoke.

Under the cold, reptilian gaze of Dragon offspring, we built a great pile of fallen boughs and kindling. We pulled the moss from the broken trees and wrapped it around the twisted limbs of our unlit pyre. The Phoenix's ancestral nest would be ablaze with dragonflame soon enough.

I was proud of Ashton. She worked steadily, burying her fear and attending to the task at hand. "Thank you." I hugged her tightly, combing my fingers though her wild mane. "You have been so strong, and I am so proud."

Liquid half-moons from her eyes wet my shoulder as she nodded against me. She hid her face in my blouse, making it easier to hand out reminders. "It will get worse before it gets better. Don't forget your job. To witness and remember. To keep your eyes open and stay alive. There are things I have yet to teach you, and they will come as a surprise. But these are things you need to see, things that you will need to share, for the good of our people in generations beyond your own."

"We'll teach—" Ashton began.

"In a way. But remember, no misguided sacrifices, no noble foolishness. You do as I have taught you." I hugged her fiercely. "I love you, Ashton. Now sit here, and do not move." I shoved her to the ground, bookended by jagged boulders. With a rare bit of sentimentality, I pulled the knife from the sheath at her waist. I ran my hand over the iron hilt, my thumb resting in the groove where Randal's had been. It was a bit like holding his hand. Ashton sad-smiled and nodded at me. She always understands, even before I do.

The dragonlings, hungry from their long hike and wait, approached. I poured the meat onto the ground and stepped forward to greet them. They were still young, barely a year old and only waist-high. There were three, identical in their scales and markings, a deep black that hid them in the night and made them more demonic in the day. Their eyes held the difference—green, blue, and gold.

I shouted. Nothing intelligible—just a pained, barbaric roar as I brandished Randal's knife. Green and Blue recoiled slightly, Gold simply narrowed her eyes. She was the most like her mother. She reared back her head and spewed forth a wretched inferno. I flung myself to the side, rolling across the soft, warm ashes of the mountain.

The bonfire was lit. Ablaze with the glow and magic of dragonflame, the incubator was ready. The mountain rumbled beneath me, heaving as its contractions grew. It was time. The Phoenix was ready.

The green and blue-eyed dragonlings circled me warily as the golden-eyed stared on. Still a child, she was exhausted from the exertion of her first flames. She shrieked an order to her sisters, spurring them to attack. I reached the blue-eyed one first, jamming Randal's knife up beneath her ribs into her heart. Her scales had not yet hardened, and the delicate, overlapping flecks tickled my hand. Blood flowed like lava down my arm, singeing my flesh with a sticky heat. Ignoring the pain, I whirled on the green-eyed dragon.

Ashton had her pinned. My brave, silly girl had left the safety of her rocks and subdued the dragonling. She straddled the creature's back, pinioning her throat against the smoky ground. I ran up behind them and Ashton grabbed the bloody, steaming knife from my hand and jammed it though the dragonling's skull.

The remaining sister screamed, flapping her dark wings in grief and fury. She turned towards the sea and made a running start. Ashton chased her, cursing and wielding her father's knife.

"Let her go!" I shouted.

"What?"

"Let her go. We can't take them all. That's not balance." I turned to the last dragonling. "Go home. Go home across the sea and find your father. Do not come back here or the Phoenix will kill you, I promise you that. Tell all your kind."

The dragonling, with eyes that recalled the scales of her mother, nodded slightly. Or at least dropped her jaw enough for me to take it as a nod, then caught the next wind current and soared from the mountain across the sea.

Once she had disappeared in the horizon, Ashton and I pulled the carcasses of her sisters towards the fire. The Phoenix would feed on them soon.

The mountain quaked beneath us, labouring with an intensity that brought us to our knees. "Go back by the rocks, Ashton. And do not come out again until it is over. Stay back from the flames, no matter what. I appreciate what you did with the dragonling. You were brave and strong. But now I need you to be smart and forward-thinking." I smoothed that crazy hair back behind her ears. "I love you, and I'll always watch over you. You watch over our girls to come."

"I love you." She bit her lip, steadying the quiver in her voice. Her eyes narrowed in determination. "I can do it."

I believed her. Sixteen can do anything.

The heat intensified behind me as the fire roared and licked the awakening stars. The mountain groaned and trembled beneath us as Ashton staggered away, struggling to keep her balance.

In the flames rose the image of the Phoenix. Her apparition, born of the labouring Mother Earth, sought anchor in this mortal land. We locked eyes—hers were still filled with apology, but this time mingled with hope and longing. And connection. I was so thankful for those eyes, the intensity which pulled me in and kept me from looking back towards the rocks.

I stepped towards the flames, my toes brushing the wooden outskirts. Ashton screamed. Before she could even think of running for me, I threw myself into the conflagration of Rebirth. I expected it to hurt, to blister and torture like an amplified kitchen burn scouring my body. But it didn't. It felt like home. Like a warmth I'd been missing. Like the sanctity of the womb.

Flesh melted from bone in one fluid motion and was replaced by feathers and flame. I gave Ashton, my shocked yet stoic Witness, a final forced smile of goodbye before my lips distorted and elongated into a fiery beak. The mountain gave one last push, a quake that rocked the kingdom, and the Phoenix consumed me.

In that instant, my world became a raging inferno of watchfulness, defence, and love. It was not so unfamiliar. I had felt it once for that beautiful dark-haired girl watching from behind the rocks. Now I felt it for the nation, and I could protect them all.

Biographies

Rhonda Parrish
Editor

Rhonda Parrish is driven by a desire to do All The Things. She founded and ran Niteblade Magazine, is an Assistant Editor at World Weaver Press and is the editor of several anthologies including, most recently, *Equus, Tesseracts Twenty-one* and *Fire: Demons, Dragons and Djinns.*

In addition, Rhonda is a writer whose work has been in publications such as *Tesseracts 17: Speculating Canada from Coast to Coast* and *Imaginarium: The Best Canadian Speculative Writing* (2012 & 2015). She also co-wrote a paranormal non-fiction title, *Haunted Hospitals*, with Mark Leslie.

Her website, updated weekly, is at http://www.rhondaparrish.com

Blake Jessop
She Alone

Blake Jessop is a Canadian author of science fiction, fantasy and horror stories with a masters degree in creative writing from the University of Adelaide. You can read more of his speculative fiction in *Glass and Gardens: Solarpunk Summers* from World Weaver Press, or follow him on Twitter @everydayjisei.

Kevin Cockle
Strange Attractor

Kevin Cockle is an author and screenwriter with over thirty short stories appearing in a variety of anthologies and magazines. His novel *Spawning Ground* is narrowly believed to have invented the sub-genre of "dark game-theory", and was published by Tyche Books in 2016. *Knuckleball*, a feature film co-written with Michael Peterson, had its Canadian premiere at the 2018 Calgary Underground Film Festival, and has been accepted into the Cannes film festival among other international markets. Kevin's literary bucket list is now almost complete, with only the boxes for "sell a poem" and "sell a country-and-western song" left unchecked.

Lizbeth Ashton
Magnesium Bright

Lizbeth Ashton works in a museum in southern England. In Magnesium Bright, her first published story, she combines her passion for history and fantasy.

Dusty Thorne
Permanence

Dusty Thorne has a penchant for urban fantasy and character-driven stories, particularly ones leaning towards the liminal side of life. When not writing, Dusty can often be found with her head in a beehive, or treasure-hunting her way through a second-hand store.

V.F. LeSann

Old Flames

V.F. LeSann is a dynamic co-writing duo comprised of Leslie Van Zwol and Megan Fennell, who enjoy adding a touch of grit to their fantastical worlds. Since travelling to Iceland, they've just been waiting for the chance to set a story there, especially as all of their efforts to observe local cryptids at the time were sadly in vain.

K.T. Ivanrest

The Hatchling

K.T. Ivanrest wanted to be a cat or horse when she grew up, but after failing to metamorphose into either, she began writing stories about them instead. Soon the horses became unicorns and the cats sprouted wings, and once the dragons and their riders arrived, there was no turning back. When not writing, she can be found sewing, editing, and drinking decaf coffee. She has a PhD in Classical Studies, which will come in handy when aliens finally make contact and it turns out they speak Latin.

Hal J. Friesen

The Djinni and the Accountant

Hal J. Friesen writes science fiction and fantasy in an attempt to see the stars a few kilometres closer. He's also tried putting a "*Have Space Suit: Will Travel*" ad on Kijiji, wearing a space suit for over 100 days, and shooting things with giant lasers. He graduated from the Odyssey Writing Workshop in 2016 and makes a mean campfire. Find him at www.halfriesen.com.

Laura VanArendonk Baugh

The Second Great Fire

Laura VanArendonk Baugh writes speculative fiction and less speculative non-fiction. She lives in an unfashionable sector of Indianapolis, drives a fast electric car, eats a lot of dark chocolate, and is always in the middle of too many projects. Find her at www.LauraVAB.com.

Krista D. Ball

Bait

Krista D. Ball is a Canadian science fiction and fantasy author. She was born and raised in Newfoundland, Canada where she learned how to use a chainsaw, chop wood, and make raspberry jam. After obtaining a B.A. in British History from Mount Allison University, Krista moved to Alberta, Canada where she currently lives.

Like any good writer, Krista has had an eclectic array of jobs throughout her life, including strawberry picker, pub bathroom cleaner, oil spill cleaner upper, and soup kitchen coordinator. These days, Krista writes full time in her messy office surrounded by corgis, spaniels, and a lot of cats.

Mara Malins

Double or Nothing

An avid gamer, Mara Malins battles spreadsheets by day and romantic fiction by night. She lives in Manchester, England with her menagerie of three cats, two turtles, a social media loving partner, and a disobedient garden. If you want to know when her next fiction is released, or see thousands of pictures of her cats sleeping in a variety of different poses, find her on Twitter at @maramalins or Goodreads on Mara_Malins

Claude Lalumière

A Girl, Ablaze with Life

Claude Lalumière (claudepages.info) is the author of five books and more than a hundred stories. His work has been translated into multiple languages and adapted for stage, screen, audio, and comics. Originally from Montreal, he now lives in Ottawa.

Susan Macgregor

Light My Fire

Susan MacGregor is the author of *The Tattooed Witch* trilogy published through Five Rivers Publishing, the first book of which was short-listed for a Canadian Science Fiction and Fantasy Association Aurora Award. As historical fantasy is one of her favourite sub-genres, she is currently co-editing the next anthology in the *Tesseracts* series: *Tesseracts 22: Alchemy and*

Artifacts (forthcoming in 2019) through Edge Books. Her short fiction has been featured in *On Spec Magazine* (she was also an editor with *On Spec* for 20+years), as well as other anthologies, the most recent being in *Equus* through World Weaver Press. Her story "Light My Fire", is a near-historical fantasy based on the music, life, and death of Jim Morrison. The late '60s and early '70s were times of darkness and hope, loss and love. Who better to epitomize those than Jim and The Doors?

JB Riley

Ring of Fire

JB Riley writes and edits technical healthcare proposals for a major US-based corporation, but has loved reading and writing speculative fiction ever since discovering The Chronicles of Narnia at Age 8. When not trawling the shelves at the local bookstore, she enjoys travel, hockey, beer and cooking. JB lives in Chicago with her family; which currently includes a 90-pound dog, a 15-pound cat, and a 5-pound cat that scares the hell out of everyone. Available on Twitter at @JBRiley8.

Damascus Mincemeyer

Aladdin's Laugh

Having been exposed to the weird worlds of science fiction, fantasy and horror as a young boy, Damascus Mincemeyer was pretty much ruined for ever having a real job and now spends his time creating comics that have seen print in *Heavy Metal* magazine while wandering the countryside around his home near St. Louis, Missouri, daydreaming of strange, far off realms filled with dragons, demons and even a Djinn or two.

Heather M. O'Connor

Phoenix Rising

Heather M. O'Connor is a freelance writer and author, which means she sees stories everywhere. While happiest plotting in fantasy, wild horses have dragged stories from her. So has the guest book in an Oshawa auto baron's mansion. And an unlikely news item about match-fixing in Ontario soccer. And several deep, dark forests. As you can see, she's easily distracted.

Heather's short fiction has appeared in *Geist* and the Prix Aurora Prize-nominated *Urban Green Man Anthology*. Her young adult novel *Betting Game* was published by Orca in 2015. She lives in Whitby, Ontario.

Gabrielle Harbowy

Cold Comfort

Gabrielle Harbowy got her start in the publishing industry as a Pricing Analyst at Scholastic. Since leaving the corporate side of publishing in 2006, she has edited for publishers including Pyr, Lambda Literary, and Circlet Press, and spent a decade as the managing editor at Dragon Moon Press. She copyedits professionally and is a submissions editor at the Hugo-nominated Apex Magazine. With Ed Greenwood, she co-edited the award-nominated *When The Hero Comes Home* anthology series; their latest anthology endeavour is *Women in Practical Armour*, from Evil Girlfriend Media. Her short fiction can be found in several anthologies, including *Carbide Tipped Pens* from Tor. She's also the author of two novels: *Hellmaw: Of the Essence* (TEGG), and *Gears of Faith* (Paizo). For more information, visit her online at @gabrielle_h or gabrielleharbowy.com.

R.W. Hodgson

Aitvaras

R. W. Hodgson lives with her husband and two children in Ottawa, Ontario. As a child in Nova Scotia, she got some cute baby chicks for pets, two of whom turned out to be roosters, who then one day tried to kill each other in a bloodbath battle-royale. Her story "A Walk in the Woods" appeared in *Tesseracts Twenty-One: Nevertheless*.

Chadwick Ginther

Midnight Man versus Frankie Flame

Chadwick Ginther is the Prix Aurora Award nominated author of the *Thunder Road Trilogy* (Ravenstone Books) and *Graveyard Mind* (ChiZine Publications). His short fiction has appeared recently in *Abyss & Apex Magazine, Equus*, and *Fire: Demons, Dragons and Djinn*. He lives and writes in Winnipeg, Canada, spinning sagas set in the wild spaces of Canada's western wilderness where surely monsters must exist.

Wendy Nikel

Breath of the Caldera

Wendy Nikel is a speculative fiction author with a degree in elementary education, a fondness for road trips, and a terrible habit of forgetting where she's left her cup of tea. Her short fiction has been published in *Fantastic Stories of the Imagination*, *Daily Science Fiction*, *Nature: Futures*, and elsewhere. Her time travel novella *The Continuum* and its sequel *The Grandmother Paradox* were published by World Weaver Press in 2018. For more info, visit wendynikel.com

Annie Neugebaur

Cilantro

Annie Neugebauer is a Bram Stoker Award-nominated author with work appearing and forthcoming in more than a hundred publications, including magazines such as *Cemetery Dance*, *Apex*, and *Black Static*, as well as anthologies such as *Year's Best Hardcore Horror Volume 3* and #1 Amazon bestseller *Killing It Softly*. She's a member of the Horror Writers Association and a columnist for Writer Unboxed and LitReactor. She lives in Texas with two crazy cute cats and a husband who's exceptionally well-prepared for the zombie apocalypse. You can visit her at www.AnnieNeugebauer.com for news, poems, organizational tools for writers, and more.

J.G. Formato

The Midwife and the Phoenix

J.G. Formato is a writer and elementary school teacher from North Florida. Her short fiction can be read in *Bracken*, *Allegory*, *Equus* from World Weaver Press, and elsewhere. You can listen to her stories at The Centropic Oracle and Manawaker Studio's Flash Fiction Podcast.

CPSIA information can be obtained
at www.ICGtesting.com
Printed in the USA
LVHW08s1840200718
584283LV00002B/2/P

9 781928 025917